WATER TO MY SOUL

Piñata Publishing
626 Old Plantation Road
Jekyll Island, GA 31527
912-635-9402
www.pinatapub.com

E-ISBN 978-0-9809163-2-4

LIBRARY OF CONGRESS CATALOGING-IN-PUBLICATION DATA

Bauer Mueller, Pamela.
   Water to my soul : the story of Eliza Lucas Pinckney / Pamela Bauer Mueller.
     p. cm.
   Summary: While managing three plantations, sixteen-year-old Eliza Lucas changes agriculture in colonial South Carolina when she develops indigo as an important cash crop.
   Includes bibliographical references.
   ISBN 978-0-9809163-1-7 (pbk.)

   1. Pinckney, Eliza Lucas, 1723-1793--Juvenile fiction. [1. Pinckney, Eliza Lucas, 1723-1793--Fiction. 2. Agriculture--Fiction. 3. Plantations--Fiction. 4. South Carolina--History--Colonial period, ca. 1600-1775--Fiction.] I. Title.
   PZ7.B32628wat 2012
   [Fic]--dc23
                   2011039729

LIBRARY AND ARCHIVES CANADA CATALOGUING IN PUBLICATION

Bauer Mueller, Pamela
   Water to my soul : Eliza Lucas Pinckney / Pamela Bauer Mueller.

Includes bibliographical references.
Issued also in electronic format.

ISBN 978-0-9809163-1-7

   1. Pinckney, Eliza Lucas, 1723-1793—Fiction. I. Title.

PS3552.A8365W38 2012   813'.54   C2011-903140-X

Includes bibliographical references.

Cover art by Gini Steele
Typeset by Vancouver Desktop Publishing Centre
Printed and bound in the United States by Cushing Malloy, Inc.

Water To My Soul

The Story of
Eliza Lucas Pinckney

Pamela Bauer Mueller

Piñata Publishing

*For my beloved daughters, Cassandra Coveney and Ticiana
Gordillo, who helped me find Eliza's blind spot and keep her real.*

You are always in my heart.

"*A man can no more diminish God's glory by refusing to worship Him than a lunatic can put out the sun by scribbling the word, 'darkness' on the walls of his cell.*"

— C.S. LEWIS

author's note

South Carolina has a colorful, captivating history. In 1663, King Charles II issued a royal charter to eight British nobles to settle the area south of Virginia. They created *Carolina* and included the previous settlement. In 1670, a group of two hundred colonists from English Barbados founded Charles Town and named it for their king.

The city of Charles Town became the center of culture and wealth of the colony. However, because of internal problems, the Crown chose to divide it. After another royal charter was written, North and South Carolina were founded in 1729.

South Carolina was blessed with resources, and rice planting predominated in the lowlands. Tobacco, corn and cotton were also grown, but by 1740 England was anxious for the colony to produce indigo as a money maker—thus bypassing the French West Indies to obtain its valuable dye. It required the ingenuity of a young girl to make this happen.

Through the efforts of animated, indomitable Eliza Lucas, South Carolina was provided with the dye of the indigo plant. This single act brought wealth to the south shortly before the American Revolution. Eliza Lucas Pinckney was a child prodigy turned celebrity. Her remarkable success in the eighteenth-century colonial world is a noteworthy achievement that required skill, luck and a strong personality. The fact that she did this while working within the enormous social constraints faced by women make her even more remarkable.

As a girl, Eliza managed to run three plantations, supervise a household of servants and care for her invalid mother and younger sister. Yet by age seventeen she had already achieved what others deemed impossible—successfully cultivating indigo and producing its blue dye.

During my research I discovered that many details of Eliza Lucas Pinckney's life were available in her letters and journals, which had been saved from burning by her great-granddaughter, Eliza Lucas Rutledge. Sadly, any likeness or portrait of her most probably had been destroyed, either in the pillaging of her Belmont Plantation house or in the 1861 fire that destroyed the Pinckney's Charleston *Mansion House.*

Harriott Horry Ravenel's 1896 book *Eliza Pinckney* reproduced many of Eliza's letters and journals. These became the guidelines to better understand the essence of my protagonist. Some of them are quoted directly in my story, with a few alterations in the selection of words and spelling to make them better suited for modern readers.

I have attempted to use "British spelling and colloquialisms" when possible. I also extracted dialogue from my remarkable research resources. Most of the dialogue throughout the story was of course invented. I have also referenced scholarly journals, books, magazines, newspapers and historical documents in my effort to capture this articulate, observant and highly-intelligent woman's life.

I attempt to write into the emotional center of my work—to always be available, vulnerable and truthful. Because my genre is *historical novel*, I owe the reader forthrightness and honesty. In full disclosure, I want to point out the fictional characters in the book. *Cameron Schiller* was invented to represent the many suitors Eliza must have had whose names have not been recorded. The Charles Town factor was an important character in her story, but I was unable to discover his real name, so in the story he became *Mr. Dawson. Tabitha and Gelasius,* her childhood servants from the West Indies, are fictional characters, as are her Antiguan friends, *Nelly, Patty* and *Benjamin.* All the other characters, central and marginal, including the scoundrel Nicholas Cromwell, were real people in Eliza's life. The events are factual, including the journeys, battles and historical happenings.

As with my Mary Musgrove novel, *An Angry Drum Echoed*, I came to understand Eliza so well from immersing myself in her story that I became one with her. Obviously, there is a great portion of myself in Eliza's nature. She was also sculpted from attributes and traits of my two daughters, Cassandra Coveney and Ticiana Gordillo, as were her daughter Harriott and her sister Polly. Hopefully, my girls will see features of themselves throughout Eliza's story.

Eliza Lucas Pinckney knew when to assert herself and when to be properly submissive. Like Mary Musgrove, her story is a legend that has left a vivid imprint on colonial southern history.

Her life story is my offering to you. In honoring the commitment to write it, I have been blessed and gifted by my Creator.

prologue

1741

E LIZA ROSE SLOWLY TO HER FEET, AWARE OF THE TOTAL
fatigue surging through her body. Closing her eyes and
breathing deeply to clear her head, she heard heavy footsteps
and turned as Nicholas Cromwell sauntered through the doorway and stopped abruptly to stand face to face with her.

Eliza stepped forward, a surprising anger filling her—like
acid poured into an empty jug. "Do you call yourself an indigo
maker?" she asked, her voice raw, green eyes shimmering dangerously.

His face turned crimson and his eyes darted back and
forth to scrutinize the others. Facing Eliza, he shrugged and
answered belligerently. "One of the best on Montserrat," he
said in a splintered voice, blinking irritatingly.

"Then why did you ruin my indigo crop?" she shot back, her
face knotted in anguish. "You purposely poured too much limewater into the solution to change the shade." Eliza's eyes burned with
outraged tears. Surprised at the intensity of her anger, she suppressed it before it spiraled out of control. All colour had drained
from Mr. Cromwell's face.

He stood stiff and silent.

She glared at the man, hating every inch of him. She loathed his florid face, glistening mouth, and the cold, dead look in his eyes. The way he stood there, legs spread apart and fat hands clasped behind his back.

"WHY, I ask you, Mr. Cromwell? Why did you harm our crop and attempt to destroy my family? We trusted you!"

She advanced toward him so forcefully he took a quick step backwards, visibly terrified by her intensity. His hard swallow was audible.

"Don't strike me, please. I feared I would ruin trade for Montserrat if your dye succeeded," he sniveled.

Eliza's brilliant eyes burned with disgust. Pressing her lips together to stop their trembling, she turned from him and stormed out the door. Polly ran after her, eyes brimming.

Mr. Dawson's face registered shock and then fury. Turning slowly to Nicholas Cromwell, he couldn't remember a time when he wanted to hit someone more. He wanted to grind his fist against Cromwell's lips until they were bruised and bleeding. Curbing the impulse, he lowered his voice and moved his face close to Cromwell's. "Pack your things. You will be gone by nightfall."

He turned to follow Eliza out the door.

Facing Eliza, he reached for her small hands and held them between his own. "Eliza, you should be very proud. You have succeeded in producing indigo in South Carolina, even with that cad deliberately ruining the dye. Your suspicions about Mr. Cromwell were correct." He searched her red-rimmed eyes, now swimming in tears.

"However, next year you will produce only the finest grade. Congratulations, my friend. This is a brilliant accomplishment!" His smile glowed with affection.

As she tried to speak, a sob split her voice—now softer, with more rounded corners than sharp edges. Swallowing hard, her voice cracking with mounting emotion, she nodded. "Thank you, Factor Dawson. Now could you please take me to my mother?"

Antigua, West Indies

1738

chapter one

A WARM WIND WHISTLED SOFTLY BEHIND HER AS A WAVE
of tropical perfume roused her from her daydreams. She
stretched leisurely, reaching for a scarlet hibiscus to tuck behind
her ear as she scratched her perspiring scalp covered by her bonnet.
It was late afternoon, yet the hot sun of the West Indies streamed
down over her garden, offering little relief.

Eliza rose to her feet, feeling slightly overwhelmed by the heavy
aroma of tropical blooms surrounding her. She laughed lightly as
she extended her fingers toward the delicate blue and black but-
terflies dancing through the jasmine like slow sunlight. Her large
green eyes caught a distant movement under the mango trees.

"Polly, is that you?" she called out to the child in the orchard
beyond, stretched belly-down studying a lizard or toad.

Her little sister looked up and waved. After a long moment
she pushed herself to her feet.

"Papa says it's time to wash up for supper," she called out,
walking lazily in Eliza's direction. Two hummingbirds hov-
ered agilely over blooms of white stephanotis.

Eliza's eyes swept over the expansive garden she treasured.
Sparrows splashed in the shallow bowl of a birdbath. Hydran-
gea bushes were loaded with blue and pink blossoms. Fig vines

and lichen clung to the brick wall enclosure. The serenity of it was inviting.

One of her greatest pleasures was gathering up colourful bouquets for her mother, or arranging them on their dining table. She was selecting a handful when her sister reached her.

"Hmm, I rather fancy a flower under my bonnet as well," she announced, instantly noticing Eliza's accessory.

Eliza pulled down an exotic crimson trumpet from a nearby hibiscus.

"There now, little sister," she grinned, acknowledging her request cheerfully as she tucked the flower into Polly's bonnet. "You look quite stunning, but oh my…your legs and elbows could use a good cleaning." Polly ignored the comment as she re-arranged the hibiscus from her bonnet to behind her ear.

Eliza looked up at the sun surrounded by puffs of white clouds. "Why are we having supper so early today?" she wondered aloud.

Polly shrugged. "Mama's feeling better and wants to join us tonight," she called back to Eliza as she scurried down the path to their home.

Eliza followed Polly into the walled courtyard that encircled a freshly-painted white house with tall elegant windows. As she trailed her sister over the cobblestones through the long double lane of crepe myrtle trees, she thought about Polly's words. Their mother had not felt well enough to eat supper with them for a fortnight, but possibly she had recovered from her ailment. This last episode had lasted longer than the others.

Lost in her thoughts, she did not hear her father approaching. Taking hold of her elbow from behind, he gently turned her around to face him.

"And just where were you off wandering in thought, my child?" he asked, amusement showing clearly on his face.

"Oh Papa, I didn't hear you," she said, with a half laugh. She reached up to untie her bonnet, shaking her head and releasing her silky auburn hair to slide freely down her narrow back.

"Will Mama be joining us tonight at supper?" she asked affectionately.

Major Lucas looped her slender arm through his. Eliza searched his eyes, noticing again how handsome and *soldiery* he looked in his army uniform, serving as Major in the Army of His Majesty, George II of England. She knew that earlier in the day he worked in the sugar cane fields. Why had he changed into his uniform?

Her father opened his mouth and then closed it, clearing his throat.

"I've asked her to join us because I want to discuss a new opportunity I've just learned about. She's agreed to sit with us at the table 'tho I doubt she'll eat much. Go on now and get ready; we'll talk more at the table." He paused a moment, then turned, but not before Eliza noticed a peculiar expression on his face.

Eliza regarded him with unease as he walked away. Then it occurred to her that he had not asked about her garden or details of her afternoon. Her Papa was always interested in how she spent her days.

It was a sweltering afternoon; nevertheless she felt a quick cool breeze bite into her skin.

chapter two

"HOW LOVELY YOU LOOK THIS AFTERNOON, MY DEAR Ann." Major Lucas's voice was full of surprise and delight. He stood up as his wife came into the room to escort her to the solid mahogany chair at the far end of the table. He often paid tribute to her loveliness in words. Searching her face, he celebrated the warmth in the genuine smile she awarded him. "I trust you have had a restful afternoon?"

"Yes indeed, George," replied Ann Lucas. "Tabitha made sure my room was cool and dark, and I napped for several hours."

Eliza observed her parents, sitting at either end of the massive dining table. She often wondered why they weren't seated closer together, especially since both of her brothers were away in England and the table was so long.

She watched as Polly tucked earnestly into her stew the moment Gelasius had set it down before her. She supposed this would bring about a frown from her mother. A glance toward Mrs. Lucas confirmed her theory.

"Polly, have we asked the Lord to bless our meal?" Mrs. Lucas inquired gently.

"Sorry Mama. I was simply quite hungry after playing so

hard today," replied her precocious seven-year-old child, a smile tugging at her mouth.

"Indeed. Well then, please set your spoon down beside your bowl and ask the blessing for us all," suggested her father. "Kindly remember that we owe all these bounties to Him."

"Yes Papa, I will." Polly looked around the table and grinned at the affection she saw in her family's eyes. She completely appreciated her desirable position as the youngest child.

After the dishes were cleared away, Major Lucas sipped his steaming tea and inclined his head toward Eliza.

"I am in receipt of excellent news for our family," he began, turning to his wife for support. She nodded and he continued.

"Ann and I have decided to take advantage of my recent inheritance from your Grandfather John Lucas. You may remember that when he passed he left me three plantations in South Carolina, and I thought we might go there and work them."

"What is South Carolina, Pa?" asked Polly, fidgeting with her serviette.

"It is a place in the new colonies not far from here," he answered vaguely, looking down the table at his older daughter, who was staring at him in disbelief.

Panic ticked at the back of her throat. She swallowed and finally found her voice. "Papa, are you saying we would live in the Carolinas?" she asked, choking on the words.

Ann Lucas looked over at her daughter. "Your father believes the change to a cooler climate might improve my health. He is convinced that the West Indies' heat has destroyed my endurance and sapped my strength," she offered, meeting Eliza's eyes.

Eliza squeezed her eyes shut. Her heart was knocking against her ribs; her hand was curled into a tight fist. After a long pause, she opened her eyes. Her face was so bleak her father's heart went out to her.

"But why, Papa? You have two excellent occupations here and we are well established in our lives and education. Why, even Mama is getting better and soon the cooler autumn will be upon us."

Major Lucas stood and walked over to Eliza's chair. "Dear one, I will be able to continue my services to His Majesty's Army in the Carolinas, and you and I will both be busy planting new fields and gardens. Your studies will continue, as will young Polly's. My main…"

"Papa, STOP!" Eliza's head snapped up as her rage burst out from her. "You are set on destroying my life and I am just fifteen!" She stood and drew back from the table, eyes wide and red and glaring as she stared miserably at him.

The room froze in silence. Eliza's small face turned white; her eyes shone dark with emotion. She turned to face them, eyes welling with tears. A sob split her voice.

"This is our home, Papa. During all those years studying in England I yearned to return to Antigua. I've missed it so much! Mama's health is improving, and what she needs now is rest, not travel. My friends are here and…" she choked. She turned her face to the window, her heart sinking.

"Hush, my child. We'll make this work out," sighed Major Lucas, reaching out to draw his trembling daughter into his embrace.

Eliza stiffened, pushed him away and ran from the room, tears streaming down her pale cheeks. Bolting down the lane, she ran all the way to her garden and threw herself on the soft rich earth, closing her eyes, burning with tears and anger. Her cries dissolved into sobs—mighty rolling sobs that came from some place deep inside. The pain racked her whole body.

How could she possibly keep alive all those beautiful scenes of her childhood if she were wrenched away from them? Eliza was achingly aware that her life would soon be torn asunder.

chapter three

ELIZA DIDN'T KNOW HOW LONG SHE STAYED OUTSIDE. IT was dusk and cooling down when she eased to her side and pushed herself up with her elbow. She could hear herself mewing like a kitten. Tears stung her eyes as she struggled to her feet.

Looking around her, she was drawn to the canopy of droopy arched branches that veiled the flower bed. *There is something heartbreakingly sad about weeping willows,* she thought. *They seem to be mourning with their long branches sweeping the ground like a widow's gown and sighing when the breezes disturb their peace.*

Eliza walked to her house, willing the lump in her throat to go away. Her anger had quieted now; her stomach unknotted and her limbs no longer shook. But she could still feel it inside her, contained and waiting—a new part of her. Weariness overpowered her as she reached the parlour. And her waiting father.

"Hello Eliza." He spoke softly. "I was about to come out and bring you in."

She stared at him, her look of exhaustion switching to bewilderment. She dropped into a chair. Her father watched as she defensively folded her arms in front.

"I was thinking of how you remind me of a rainbow," he began, his eyes quiet on her face. "You have so many shades, each one more beautiful than the last."

Eliza closed her eyes. She felt so tired.

"Besides loving you as my daughter, I love you because you make me laugh. I believe I might even say you're my best friend."

She swiped at the tears coursing down her face; anger once again had found its place deep inside her.

"Therefore, it means ever so much to me that you come willingly to the Carolinas." He ached to put his arms around her shoulders and draw her close, but chose not to.

"Eliza, could we look at this new experience as an adventure that we'll embark on together?" he asked. "I feel certain you will fancy Charles Town, because it is much busier and more elegant than St. John's, and there will be much for you to do."

A tentative smile started across her lips; then her face crumbled. Looking at his drawn face, she felt a fleeting pang of guilt. She yearned to tell him so many things but couldn't find the strength. Her heart ached for her Papa, but even more for herself.

"Knowing how much you love the vegetable and flower worlds, I have arranged for local gardeners to meet with us and help set up all the plants you love here, plus many new ones we've never seen. Won't that be lovely? Why, there is even a botanist who will visit our plantations and teach us what to plant."

Eliza slowly raised her eyes to meet her father's gaze and saw his broken, helpless pain. It was more than she could bear. She took a deep breath to settle herself.

"Yes Papa. I will try to find my way in the new colonies. I believe as you do that this will be better for Mama and Polly." She wiped her cheeks with her fingertips and went on. "Just promise me we will return one day to Antigua. Would you do that?"

A smile broke slowly across Major Lucas' face. He nodded, then stood up and walked over to her, bending down to brush away her walnut-coloured hair from her cheeks. Very gently, he tucked a few strands behind her ears.

"Thank you Eliza. Your faith in my judgment means everything to me. I do not believe I could have endured it if you had fought our decision." He exhaled deeply.

Weeping softly, she gave him her hand and together they walked down the silent hall. Eliza breathed in the sweet night air, heavy with the scent of jasmine.

Eliza wondered if she would find any jasmine in her new home.

chapter four

"WE SHALL SIMPLY HAVE TO CELEBRATE YOUR birthday before you leave next month," declared her best friend Nelly. "Or better yet, you can return to Antigua for your sixteenth ball."

Eliza laughed and hugged her. "Perhaps you and Patty can come to Charles Town and we will celebrate all our birthdays together. Will that not be grand?" She smiled fondly at her good friends, honoured that they had worn their best party frocks.

Walking through the cleared pathways near the harbour, she entered the sparkling shadows of magnolias growing haphazardly among the wildflowers. Here her world was green and rich and alive. She must try to fill her memory with all the sounds and sights and flavours of her beloved Antigua.

Had it been only a year since her return from the finishing school in England? It seemed so much longer. She had been separated then from Nelly and Patty, but upon her return they picked up where they had left off. She had enjoyed the lessons in French, music and literature, and living with the Boddicotts was a lovely adventure, but she missed her family and friends. Polly was just a toddler when she left but had become a vivacious little girl. Her brothers George and Tommy had grown from small lads to young men. And then, not long after her return, her parents sent them to England to live with their friends, the Boddicotts. Papa and Mama believed it was very important to educate their children in Europe. Still, she missed them very much and wondered when she would see them again.

George and Tommy had helped her establish her independent spirit. She believed that any success that lay before her would be partially theirs to share. Her friends, like her parents, were teaching her to be open to life.

Patty's father, Charles Dunbar, was Antigua's Controller of Customs. He and Major Lucas had known each other for years. Their children had grown up together and were close friends. Nelly Brambly's father was a prominent St. John's merchant who met George Lucas when they trained for the military. The three families socialized and worked together. That made this upcoming separation even more difficult for everyone. Nonetheless, Eliza's' friends were determined to make it easier on her. They kept up their light banter throughout the beautiful autumn afternoon.

"Well now Eliza, and what of young Benjamin?" teased Nelly. "He seems fairly smitten with you, and your departure will surely break his heart. However, I should be delighted to step in and help him mend it," she added, winking deliberately at Patty.

Eliza tilted her pointed chin into the air. Her light laugh rang out in the warm air. "Humph! Then I shall endeavor to meet another exciting young ensign in the Carolinas. Papa tells me there is an abundance of them in Charles Town. Besides, if he falls so quickly for you, he certainly wasn't meant for me."

They giggled contentedly and changed the topic. This would be one of their last afternoons together and they wanted it to be pleasant and memorable.

The time for their departure was drawing near. Eliza had finished the majority of the packing, with the help of Tabitha and Gelasius. Her mother had helped by sorting the clothing and household goods when she felt strong enough. As the weeks unfolded, Eliza noticed that Ann Lucas seemed stronger—less pale and more energetic. She would take an extra moment to straighten a cushion on the sofa or wrap her precious crystal pieces with great care.

Perhaps this move is just what Mama needs for a complete recovery, thought Eliza. *Yet as no one has determined her ailment, how would we know?* She pursed her lips in annoyance. *I only wish she had more resolve to fall back upon.*

Polly was extremely excited about the move but then she had always thrived on everything new and different. Her enthusiasm lifted the family's spirits, and soon Eliza found herself consumed with curiosity as to what life in the colonies would be like. Major Lucas noticed the change in all of them and beamed with pleasure. The heavy burden of responsibility seemed to have lifted from his shoulders.

One afternoon Eliza and Tabitha were packing trunks and Polly was playing with her homespun cloth and straw dolls on the floor. Their mother was resting in her room after wrapping pieces of crystal and china earlier that morning.

"Miss Polly, 'pon my soul you near trip me up runnin' undah my skirt like dat," scolded Tabitha, as Polly surfaced from under her dress.

"I'm sorry, Tabitha. I lost one of my dolly's eyes, and I thought it went under your skirt." Realizing that she was tired of being cooped inside the house, Eliza put aside her work to search for a distraction with her sister.

"Polly, do you know that none of the family has stayed on the plantations in Carolina since Grandpa Lucas bought them twenty-five years ago! Won't it be fun exploring them and building forts and secret hiding places?"

"Oh yes sister, and then we can show them to Tommy and..." Her small face clouded over as she peered up at Eliza from under her perfectly straight eyebrows.

"I know, Polly. I also wish our brothers were going with us, but they shall come to join us one day, and then we can show them everything we have made." A deep longing for George and Tommy swept over Eliza like a cold wave, and she struggled to prevail over her sadness.

"How many more days 'til we ride on *Betsey*?" Polly knew they were sailing on a big sloop called the *Pretty Betsey* and brought it up whenever she thought about it.

"One more week—seven more days," Eliza told her. "Now remember that, because I'll ask you again at suppertime."

That evening, Polly surprised everyone by announcing that in one week they would be riding on the *Pretty Betsey*, as if she were proud to have come up with this daring plan on her own. Her mother smiled indulgently. Her father's eyes shone with amusement. Even Eliza's lips curved into a generous smile.

chapter five

GELASIUS WRAPPED HIS LONG ARMS AROUND POLLY'S round body, enveloping her in an enormous hug. The smoky smell of his barrel chest and faded pattern in his party shirt were as familiar to the young girl as the road home. His warm brown eyes filled with tears that he stubbornly blinked away. He wasn't going to the Carolinas with them so Polly needed his reassurance that it would be tolerable for her to be without him.

"Miss Polly, it be alright. I come on by the Carolinas one day and see you. And you be comin' back home befo' you know it," he promised the bewildered child.

"Then why are you crying, Gelasius?" she worried, looking to her sister for comfort.

"Gelasius is right, Polly. And he is sending Tabitha with us to care for Mama. So we shall be fine. Come on now. The carriages are ready and Mama is going in now." Eliza turned to comfort her sister with an ache in her heart.

The long awaited day had arrived and Eliza no longer felt excited or curious. She was miserable yet tried to harden her heart against the pain. Her friends and Benjamin would be waiting to say goodbye at the wharf. She fervently wished to avoid the entire scene, but knew she had to be brave for her family. *There are too many things in life shaded with uncertainty*, she thought.

Eliza threw her arms around Gelasius and gently wiped away a tear trailing down his cheek.

"We will be back, my dear friend. Thank you for sending your only daughter with us to care for our mother. That sacrifice will grant you a huge crown in the Heavenlies."

His smile rewarded her generous words. She felt deep sadness as she held his dark weathered hands in her own.

"Go now, ladies. Be off, and fare thee well." He turned and disappeared stoically into the house.

As they approached the harbour they saw the one-hundred ton sloop that would be their vessel, riding at anchor. Polly squealed with delight.

"Isn't she beautiful? We can fit the whole village of St. John's in there, can't we Papa?"

Bursting into laughter, Major Lucas embraced his youngest. "Just about, sweet child. But it is just us and our household goods, and of course our sugar to sell in Charles Town."

Eliza gazed out over the turquoise water and noticed a flight of pelicans flapping in a solemn procession. They uniformly dove into the water, as if their dances were choreographed.

"Mama, did you see that?" she asked her mother, bundled up and protected in her favourite blue shawl, even in the still warm air inside the carriage. Eliza worried that her mother was not strong enough for the voyage.

Their friends were gathered around the wharf. As expected, a large group had congregated to see them off and wish them a safe journey. Eliza felt a pinch in her heart as she realized that so many of her classmates from over the years were standing on the wharf. A few of them thrust bouquets at her and her family.

Her school friends clustered around her, begging her to write them. Nodding in agreement, she was finally able to excuse herself and move to stand with her best friends, hugging each other and weeping.

"We cannot bear this terrible day," Nelly told her, between loud sobs. "We have no other friend as fun and imaginative as you. Whatever will we do without you?"

"You shall get on just fine," Eliza answered, catching a glimpse of Benjamin standing off to one side, looking somber and forlorn. She motioned for him to join them, but he remained there as if anchored to the wharf.

Eliza tore herself away from the others and walked over.

"Thank you for coming, Benjamin. I shall miss you and the others."

He handed her a small box, his face folded around his small wistful smile. "Eliza, please open this when you embark. May it remind you of me, and entice you to return one day."

"Oh Benjamin, we're not going forever, you know. Once Mama is healed we shall probably come back." Even she did not believe her words.

At last the difficult and awkward moments were over and the Lucas family boarded the *Pretty Betsey*. Eliza breathed a deep sigh of relief as she waved goodbye to her friends. Tabitha and Major Lucas had taken her mother down to her cabin. *Thank you God for Tabitha, and for dear Gelasius who allowed her to make the journey with us*, prayed Eliza, as she watched the seamen raise the sails.

Winds snapped the canvas taut. They were underway— their departure formally announced by loud bells pealing somewhere in the sloop.

Eliza's father came to stand between his daughters. "Girls, take a long look at Antigua. Look at how she stands proud and beautiful against the horizon." He wrapped his arms around his girls, holding them lovingly. "Until we meet again," he offered in a solemn voice, raising one hand in a farewell wave.

They leaned on the rail and watched the island gradually disappear from sight. The ocean turned from its turquoise color to a deep violet as they entered the deeper waters. The dying sun glinted like polished metal on the flying fish shooting out from the water. Their ship departed the warm Caribbean waters and headed for the rough Atlantic Ocean. Major Lucas offered up a quick prayer for Ann Lucas's comfort and health and travel mercies for his family.

chapter six

TWO DAYS INTO THE VOYAGE MRS. LUCAS AND POLLY were so seasick they could not leave their cabin. Polly cried that she was desperately hungry but was unable to keep anything down. Tabitha looked after them as well as she could, but she also suffered from the rough weather. Major Lucas and Eliza took turns staying with them and assuring all three that the heavy winds would soon subside.

The sun rose over the Atlantic water as Major Lucas and Eliza stretched their legs on the bow of the ship, grateful to breathe in the deep mineral aroma of the Atlantic Ocean.

"Look yonder, Eliza," said Major Lucas as he pointed landward with a spyglass in hand. "We're nearing Florida, and in a moment a very large fortification will come into view. 'Tis the St. Augustine Fort, built and manned by Spanish soldiers."

Eliza looked through her father's spyglass until she saw the edge of the fortified walls in the distance. "Oh Papa, it is immense, is it not? Do you think we are in any danger sailing so closely to it?"

"It is indeed immense. Notice how it juts out of the water against the bright November sky," he explained. "But we shan't be in any danger. As long as we keep our distance we will not be bothered." Pausing for a long moment he turned to her. "Have you noticed how the ocean calmed a bit since we've entered the Floridian waters?"

"Oh yes, thank the Lord. Let's go below and see how Mama and the others are doing. Perhaps they'll be able to eat something today," offered Eliza as she descended to their cabin.

The women and little Polly recovered slowly from their bouts of seasickness. Polly was the first to regain her appetite. Fortunately, the ocean remained calm for the rest of the journey. Everyone was now impatient to arrive. As they neared the Carolinas, Major Lucas explained that a medical doctor would examine everybody for diseases before they would be allowed to disembark in South Carolina.

"But Papa, what if he sees that we were all seasick?" worried Polly. "Then are we left on the ship?"

"You will be fine, my child. He is looking for contagious diseases, like distemper or guinea fever. He doesn't mind that you were seasick."

Eliza was most impatient and far too excited to stay down below. She grabbed Polly's chubby hand and led her to the aft of the ship. Sunshine spilled rich and golden onto their faces, warming their cheeks and streaking Eliza's curls a deep copper. Polly's light blue eyes danced when she looked across the water and saw land.

The ocean shimmered in the sunlight as a band of seagulls circled overhead. Tiny dark birds flew swiftly, together in a pattern, suddenly scattering and then effortlessly coming together once again.

"Just look at how they break flight and direction in the same instant," Eliza pointed out.

Their father joined them with the wonderful news that their mother and Tabitha were ready to meet them on deck.

Approaching the shore of Fort Johnson, where the doctor would board the ship, Eliza observed the flat sandy land and wondered if their home would be nearby. She asked her father about planting in that type of soil.

"We will be living on Wappoo Creek, off the mighty Ashley River, and we'll plant our crops in richer soil. What you see around you now is the coastal sandy soil."

"Is Wappoo our largest plantation, Papa?"

"No Eliza. I've chosen to live on the smallest one because of its proximity to Charles Town. The other two are located in less settled territories, and I believe you and your mother will be happier living closer to the city of Charles Town. And that's where our friends live as well," he smiled.

Polly was soon caught up in the excitement. "Eliza, look at all those ships," she exclaimed. "Don't their sails look like huge wings?"

It seemed like hours as they waited for the doctor. But eventually everyone passed the medical inspection, and their ship proceeded into the harbour of Charles Town. A great number of ships were crossing the waters to and from Charles Town. Eliza and Major Lucas explained to Polly that some were so large they could transport cattle, horses and all the food she could imagine.

"Some of those large ones have staterooms larger than our home in St. John's," Major Lucas remarked.

"How can that be, Papa? How can they possibly float?" Polly's eyes widened, filled with wonder at the new world unfolding before her eyes.

Major Lucas left them standing on the deck as their ship entered the arrival area. He wanted to accompany his wife and share with her the first view of their new homeland.

"Oh, George, this is beautiful," she enthused. "'Tis ever more lovely than I imagined. Just look at those beautiful buildings and stately homes," she beamed, a familiar but almost forgotten glint in her remarkable eyes. She turned to embrace her husband.

"Yes lovey, those homes you see are made of the wood of the huge live oak trees. The wood is so hard that they even use it to build ships, like that one over there," he pointed out.

Eliza's smoky green eyes swept the horizon, taking in everything. She watched mesmerized as crew members of the ships roughly unloaded crates and burlap bags onto the wharf. Heavy crates and trunks were dragged up cobblestone paths, looming over frightened horses and squealing children. Even Polly was struck quiet for a change, absorbing the scenes before her.

The anchor finally dropped and they were taken to shore in a small boat. The scent of sea salt was pungent in the air. When Polly's feet touched solid ground, she staggered and shouted out, "The ground is moving!"

Her family laughed.

"It will soon pass, Polly," her mother assured her. "You've been on the water so long your body thinks you're still sailing."

Their small group made its way through a bustling crowd of colourful characters to the customs house. Major Lucas left them seated comfortably while he went in search of his business factor. Polly and Eliza yearned to wander around the dock, booming with activity, but Mrs. Lucas kept them close by. Polly had to be content to catch a glimpse of the dockside through the frosted glass of a small window. Tabitha stood speechless just inside the door, observing the unloading of merchandise from all over the world.

Major Lucas finally returned, accompanied by a handsome well-dressed gentleman, who tipped his hat and extended his hand to Ann Lucas as her husband made the introductions.

"My family, I would like to introduce our factor, Mr. William Dawson. Sir, please meet my wife Ann and my daughters Mistress Eliza and Miss Polly. Our sons, Thomas and George, are away studying in London."

"Delighted to meet each of you," he pronounced, shaking their hands with a smile. Polly had never shaken hands with anyone before and was thrilled with the attention. She curtsied and nodded her head earnestly. "Delighted to meet you, sir." Eliza looked over and saw the smile tugging at her mother's lips.

"I have engaged a quiet place for you to pass the next few days, until you feel ready to take the short trip to your plantation at Wappoo Creek. You may stay here in Charles Town as long as you wish."

"Thank you kindly, Mr. Dawson. I should like to get Ann and the girls comfortable, and then you and I can meet later and begin our business discussions."

"Excellent. Allow me to accompany you to your inn."

Eliza and Polly exchanged eager glances. Suddenly brimming with wide-eyed energy, they wanted to explore the city. Polly whispered to Eliza that she had never seen so many tall buildings or heard so many foreign languages before. She urged Eliza to convince their father to take them along when he met with Mr. Dawson that afternoon. Eliza chuckled and said she would try, but was more entranced by the cheerful sounds of birds in the surrounding trees.

Wappoo Plantation

SOUTH CAROLINA
1738-1744

chapter seven

DAWN WAS FORMING THIN, BRIGHT PINK STREAKS around the closed shutters. Eliza opened her eyes and smiled sleepily. She loved early mornings. She dressed in her favourite checked poplin smock and quietly made her way through the garden into the nearby forests, where a few birds wheeled and turned against the puff-ball clouds. Eliza pulled her journal from her apron pocket and scribbled that they were *exulting their praise of the morn*.

She had discovered her grandfather's leather-bound journal in the library just a few days after their arrival. She read only a few of his entries and knew he would appreciate her claiming it for herself and using it to record this incredible adventure. Her first inscriptions were lyrical prose about the splendour of their plantation.

Beyond the house are the smiling fields dressed in vivid green. My favourite mockingbird, that little darling–sweet harmonist, greeted me as usual as I began my walk. The swirling tree swallows swarmed over my head in total chaos, joining me on my walk through the marshlands. This morning I shall carry my shrimp net and fish awhile at the creek. Soon the household will awaken and I must return to my new home to begin the day.

Had it already been a fortnight since they'd arrived? They were now moved into their plantation house on Wappoo Creek, near Stono River. The plantation was located six miles down the Ashley River from Charles Town. It was not a mansion but was large and clean and built entirely of wood. The house was set among a grove of live oaks—those majestic trees veiled in Spanish moss—unlike any oak trees the Lucas family had ever seen. Their gentle shadows wrapped the house in movement, changing the colour and appearance in an enthralling way.

"Why George, I believe these lovely gnarled trees have formed a frame around our home," exclaimed Ann as they approached it the first time. "Isn't that unusual?" He smiled at her obvious pleasure.

She was even more pleased when she saw what the neighbours and Mr. Dawson had done with the furniture they had shipped here before their departure from Antigua. Several of the neighbourhood women had come by to place the larger pieces in the various rooms, arranged very tastefully. Mrs. Dawson brought over linens and made up the beds. A fire blazed in the hearth and candles scented the air. Mrs. Lucas laughed lightly when she discovered tall vases of gold and russet chrysanthemums mixed with yellow roses on the dining table. Fires burned in every room, offering a warm and inviting ambience.

Ann Lucas was eager to examine the grounds with the others, but her husband requested that Tabitha take her to her chambers, knowing she was extremely tired. He promised he would take her on a tour once she had rested.

Eliza and Polly followed the men outdoors to inspect the stable, the barns and the servants' quarters. Each building had hard-packed earthen floors and looked tidy but in need of some repairs.

"You presently have twenty able-bodied slaves and one indentured Irish servant here at Wappoo," said Mr. Dawson. "Of course you have around two hundred workers total, counting the children, living on the three plantations. If you decide to do more planting here, we can bring some of the others over here to assist you."

"Thank you sir. For now, let's keep the status quo," answered Major Lucas. "We've just arrived and haven't yet decided how we shall proceed."

Tabitha and Ann Lucas were pleased to discover a well-stocked pantry with several hampers of food, delivered by the neighbouring families. They had sent along several bottles of fine Madeira wine, as well as a baked ham, venison, cheddar cheese, several cooked ducks, four or five loaves of bread and some fruit tarts and other delicacies for afternoon tea.

"Why, it look like de general store back home!" Tabitha exclaimed, half to herself.

After their inspection of the property, the family returned to find the gracious gifts of their neighbours. Polly clapped her hands together and broke into giggles.

"Who are these people who have sent us food, drink and even notes of welcome?" asked Major Lucas incredulously.

"Oh, you have a strong body of neighbours in the nearby plantations," his factor replied. "Let me see. There are the Bulls, the Bakers, the Draytons, the Fenwickes, the Godfreys, the Linings, the Middletons, the Rose family, the Savages and the Woodwards. I hope I've not missed anyone," he laughed, then held up a finger. "Oh yes, the Frenchman: Mr. Deveaux of Westpenny Plantation. He lives on the other side of Tiger Swamp."

"From what meets the eye, every one of them sent something and left us a kind welcoming note." Major Lucas was touched by their generosity. Of all the neighbours, he knew only Mr. Woodward, who had been a good friend to his late father, John Lucas.

"Papa, look at all this food!" shouted Polly, who dearly

loved to eat. "Mama will be so pleased that we don't have to work too much for the next few days."

"We? Thank you for volunteering to help out!" laughed her sister. "Tabitha and I are quite relieved since we will be doing most of the work around here."

"Papa, come along. Let us tuck into to these sweeties. I am so very hungry after the journey," proclaimed Polly, her deep blue eyes flitting from his face back to the laden baskets. She scrambled up onto one of the straight back wooden chairs and dove into a cucumber sandwich, savouring its moist crispness.

Their father watched his daughters with amusement, wondering what impression they caused. He was pleased that both his girls were so strong and confident. Yet physically, they hardly appeared to be sisters.

Small, thin, gentle Eliza was completely feminine, whereas Polly was outspoken, chubby and very often boisterous. Eliza, fragile of bone, had delicate features. Her hair was the colour of walnuts with curled tips lightened by the sun. Ann still insisted on brushing her glossy tresses every evening, giving them one hundred strokes with the soft-bristled, silver-backed brush. Yet Eliza's small face was thin, and she had been slightly scarred by smallpox as a child. Her beauty, however, was clear to everyone. She had the same innocence and pureness that he saw in his beloved wife Ann. Her mouth, large and sweet-lipped, was expressive, as were her eyes—large, solemn, smoky green in some lights and cloudy gray in others, fringed with thick black lashes.

He turned to observe Polly, now prancing through the pantry with a plate of raspberry tarts lifted high over her head. The laughing dimpled child with her raven-black curls and cheeky blue eyes was enchanting. Her plump arms peeked out through the short sleeves of her shirt. Unlike Eliza, whose wardrobe was almost austere, Polly preferred colourful dresses with bright checks or tiny flowers.

"Is it time for tea yet?" she inquired, with that determined look on her round face insisting that it certainly must be. Her abundant curls bounced in glorious disarray and her shining blue eyes glowed with vitality. Polly's spontaneous laughter filled the room as the others agreed that teatime was nigh.

Eliza and Polly served their first tea in the plantation home, and for this special occasion they brought out their finest china, imported from London. They served petits fours, open-faced sandwiches, scones, fruit and tarts. There was even clotted cream and homemade strawberry jam, which they ate with coin silverware so soft it was easily bent. The men enjoyed a glass of Madeira wine, preceded by a toast proposed by Major Lucas.

"First to the King! Long may he live! Then to Mr. Dawson, who has shown us such kindness."

"And to the Lucases! May Providence provide prosperity, happiness and good health to each of you," added Mr. Dawson.

"And to our Mama, who really needs the health prayer," chimed in Polly. Her words were met with laughter and light-hearted applause.

Eliza gazed a moment at her mother, whose face appeared out of the shadows as the sun pushed through the window behind her. A sense of sadness, tinged with annoyance, prevailed over her.

chapter eight

ELIZA TOOK OVER THE DUTIES OF THE MISTRESS OF THE plantation and quickly became the woman of the house. Her superior schooling in London, enhanced by Mrs. Boddicott's mentorship, had paid off well. Mrs. Lucas occasionally felt well enough to bake pastries or direct household activities, but Eliza quietly supervised the staff. She also learned as much as she could from her father and regularly suggested improvements to the property, inside and out.

"Papa, the slave quarters are extremely dirty and drafty," she complained one morning as they were finishing breakfast. They agreed to see what could be done, and a little later that cool December morning they met at the quarters. "The Negroes require heavier clothing, and their cabins desperately need to be scrubbed and whitewashed." Her solemn face was drawn with concern for the people who depended on them.

After a brief tour, Major Lucas gave her a free hand to accomplish this enormous task. He needed to devote all his efforts to repairing the fields and stables. This work would require transporting more workers to the main plantation. He asked Juno, the plantation patron who manned the boat, to fetch Pompey the carpenter, Dick the blacksmith and Sogo the cooper from his Garden Hill Plantation.

Then he gathered the slaves and their families together. "My daughter, Mistress Eliza, has told me this plantation needs renovations. I have great faith in her leadership and would ask that you carry out her wishes, which will improve your lives. If you have concerns or questions, you may express them to her. Or, if that makes you uncomfortable, please come to me."

They worked well together and finished the first tasks under Eliza's guidance. In the meantime, she purchased warm clothing for the twenty adult Negroes and thirty-two children. Next she decided to build a nursery, which she felt would benefit everyone. Mothers could leave their children under the care of one woman, freeing the other female employees to work more efficiently.

Polly trailed after her older sister for the first few hours every day. When she became bored she left to play with the younger Negro children. But the construction of the nursery provided her with plenty of entertainment. She and the other children enjoyed retrieving fallen chips from the ax wielders and helping each other build their own play huts.

"Looky here, Isaiah, we can build our own 'child house' like the big one," she trilled to one of her older slave friends. Isaiah responded by making a noisy rhythm using long finger sticks and then shuffling over the dirt in an impromptu dance. Polly squealed with delight and begged him to teach her how to dance.

Every week Eliza held a meeting with the servants and asked them for suggestions. Normally her words were met with smiles and nods, but one day Isaiah's mother surprised her.

"Mistress Eliza," the stout woman asked in her low voice, "where we gunna put de sick ones now dat we be so many livin' on 'dis here plantation?"

"Oh my, I hadn't thought that far yet," confessed Eliza with a frown. "I must speak with my father about that concern, as it is highly important. Eva, thank you for bringing it to my attention."

She and her father discussed the problem that evening.

"Hmm, there are two cabins at the very end of the row that are not being used as living space. We could repair the roofs and interiors and whitewash them, and then I believe they would make a good home hospital."

"Yes, Papa, and we could put the ailing women in one and the men in another," suggested Eliza.

"That's a great solution, my daughter. Are there any among our people who have nursing skills?" he asked, setting aside the book of accounts he had been working on.

"I believe Eva said there were. She also mentioned that Mr. Deveaux has a 'sick house' on his plantation. Perhaps we can have a look at it and get a better idea."

"Good idea Eliza! I will take you with me on the pettiauger when I visit him at week's end. Together we will devise plans for the infirmary, and ask Mr. Deveaux about planting crops."

Eliza smiled happily. She loved traveling in their large hollowed-out log canoe and was very excited to begin discussing their future crops. Although her father told her he would include her in all decisions, she also had her own ideas about which crops she would like to raise. After all, she had done a great deal of the planting in the West Indies. Through conversations with their neighbours she learned there was one crop considered impossible to grow here: indigo. But because it grew in the West Indies, Eliza believed it could grow here as well.

As tall, broad-shouldered Juno rowed them in the hollowed-out pettiauger along the Ashley River, Eliza peered through the scattered clearings on the riverbanks, searching out their neighbours' homes, tucked in among thickets of cypress trees, oleander, swamp myrtle and palmettos. She inhaled the tangy mud and salty river smells and experienced an unexpected soothing calm. The tough marsh grasses were bent by the gentle breezes and swayed back and forth, *whispering out past remembrances*. Eliza jotted down this and other analogies in her journal as they came to mind.

She lifted her head to study her father. "Papa, may I ask Mr. Deveaux his opinion about cultivating the indigo plant on our plantations?"

His brow lifted quizzically. "Of course, my daughter. Ask him whatever you wish. I am so pleased to know you take such an interest in our crops."

Later, sitting across from Mr. Deveaux in his spacious plantation parlour, they praised both the décor of his home and the beautiful landscaping of his gardens.

"Thank you for your kind words," he acknowledged. "These lands and Westpenny Plantation are an inheritance from my wife's father, Monsieur Le Sade. We have been here about five years now."

"Are you perhaps a French Protestant Huguenot, sir?" asked Major Lucas.

"Rightly so, as you may tell from my accent."

"You have my greatest admiration, Mr. Deveaux. The Huguenots have suffered much for their convictions but continue striving here in the Carolinas." He then paused for a long moment.

"Well now, Mr. Deveaux, we shall need to plant new crops soon and hoped you would have some ideas for us. Tell me sir, can one raise silk cocoons in this climate? I had heard so, and we are interested in trying it out."

The Frenchman frowned, and then raised his hands in a slow, exaggerated shrug. "We have attempted it and given up. It is costly and very time-consuming. Rice is the king of crops here, which you already grow abundantly on your lands."

"And what about indigo?" Eliza saw her opportunity and grabbed it.

"Ah, that one's given us Huguenots a run for our money," grinned Andrew Deveaux. "Nobody can grow it so it is profitable. We've tried our hand, but it's harder to grow than even the cocoons. And the Scots, who can grow most anything, haven't yet figured out how to produce the blue dye that the British Crown so desperately wants."

Eliza's brow furrowed and she bit her lip, thinking hard. "Then it might be profitable if we were the first to make it work," she smiled. "Perhaps we need to study up on the requirements to produce this crop?"

The men nodded and turned to other topics. As they stood up from the table, Major Lucas remembered the other reason for their visit.

"Mr. Deveaux, may we visit your 'sick house'? My daughter has encouraged me to provide one for our workers and our employees tell us that yours works quite well."

Mr. Deveaux nodded, smiling cordially, and walked them over to his "sick house." Eliza was interested in every detail and scribbled notes in her journal to consult later.

They rode home quietly, each one lost in thought. The marsh and river were darkening as Juno's oars cut soundlessly through the dark waters. The red afterglow had turned the marsh grasses bronze. A soft, thick hush over the waters held them voiceless.

Soon after that visit they completed the renovation of the two cabins. Eliza found an old woman with medical skills to help out in the "child house" and the "sick house." She then turned her attention to unpacking crates and with Tabitha's help, finished hanging pictures, lining the kitchen cupboards and organizing her father's small library in the back room. Her smile blossomed into a joyful grin as she discovered several of her favourite books among his growing book collection.

As one day turned into another, Eliza realized she was tired. One afternoon it all caught up with her. She noticed her eyes were dark with exhaustion. She had been so eager to help her father, assist her mother, care for Polly and run the household. Now her mind and body ached for rest, and for some fun. *I yearn for some gaiety,* she thought. *I love parties, and young people, and all I've done since we've arrived is work, work and then more work. I can hardly wait to meet some people my age and dance to splendid tunes. Will this ever happen, or was that just an empty promise to bring me here?* She had lived life with passion; it had seemed almost magical, as necessary as food and shelter.

Closing her eyes, she struggled to claim her childhood once again.

chapter nine

THE FIRST SOCIAL EVENT IN HONOUR OF THE LUCAS family turned out to be a grand oyster roast at the Woodward Plantation. Mrs. Woodward and her young daughter, Mrs. Chardon, had called on them shortly after their arrival at Wappoo and offered to host the gala. Mrs. Lucas was thrilled with the proposal and vowed to maintain her present good health so she could attend.

Eliza was very excited and selected her most elegant flowered gown, sewn for her by a fashionable seamstress in Antigua. Her mother chose a stylish lilac-coloured dress, designed by a London dressmaker. Polly would wear a dainty blue frock her mother had made for her. Sewing was an enjoyable diversion that Ann could pursue in the comfort of her new home.

All the neighbours attended the affair. As this was the official initiation of the Lucas family into their plantation society, no one wanted to miss it. Even the Reverend William Guy, Rector of St. Andrew's Church, was among the company. Their new friends, Mr. and Mrs. Deveaux, were the first to arrive.

At three o'clock they gathered 'round the skilled Negroes who were busily roasting oysters over a huge outdoor fire.

Their lilting voices filled the air, exchanging news and stories as the bright sun warmed the chilly December afternoon. The companionship and fresh air gave everyone a good appetite.

In addition to the oysters, they dined on roasted marsh hens, sliced ham, mounds of steaming vegetables and homemade pickles. Mrs. Woodward's cook served freshly baked rolls and hot chocolate or tea, while the dignified butler passed around hot toddies to the gentlemen.

Eliza weaved through the group, hearing the idle chatter but only joining conversations that involved gardening. She overheard Mrs. Woodward telling her father and others that Mr. Henry Middleton had recently sent two English landscape gardeners to turn Middleton Place into a show garden.

Siding up to her father, she whispered discretely. "Oh Papa, we must work with these gentlemen. Perhaps they can teach us about planting the silk cocoons, and hopefully, even the indigo plant." Major Lucas nodded, amused by her dedication.

Eliza took in the latest Carolinian fashions as she wandered through the garden. She appreciated the gentlemen's polished buckled shoes and beautifully cut suits. The women wore fine dresses similar to what she had worn in the West Indies, reflecting all the newest trends. She was concentrating on the people around her and scarcely felt the soft touch on her shoulder.

"Mistress Eliza, please allow me to introduce you to Mr. Cameron Schiller, my good friend and visitor to Drayton Hall," said Mr. Woodward, watching with barely concealed amusement as the young man bowed and lifted Eliza's gloved hand to his lips.

"Enchanted, I'm sure," smiled Cameron Schiller, gently releasing her fingers. "After conversing briefly with your parents, I believe we may have some common friends in England, where I also studied for many years."

As he spoke of his background in England, Eliza observed him modestly. He wondered if she were paying attention as she seemed to be deep in thought. Soon she was able to maneuver his dialogue to her advantage.

"Oh, Mr. Schiller, I'm so new here that I don't have an idea about what crops to plant for our next season," she purred. "Pray tell, what do you think about the possibility of cultivating indigo?"

Cameron was caught off guard by her businesslike question. "Oh my, Miss Eliza, I would have taken you for a high society lady not a whim interested in crops and men's work!"

She leaned forward and whispered, "Oh, I do love the dances and I dote on the high fashion of beautiful clothes, but I am my father's right hand since my brothers are away studying in London. So he and I are attempting to find a new, undeveloped crop to grow here in the Carolinas."

Cameron studied Eliza in a new light. Nodding, he considered her question in the light of what he was learning about the lovely young woman.

"Very well then, I shall study the crop situation with you and do my best to assist you in developing indigo, if that is your interest." Reaching out for her hand he suggested, "Now then, shall we repair to the house for the musicale? I know Mrs. Chardon sings splendidly and her instructor, Mr. Pelham, will be accompanying her tonight. Have you met him yet?"

The rest of the evening passed pleasantly. Eliza noticed her parents laughing and enjoying themselves. Ann glowed, her lovely face lit with pleasure at the cordiality extended to them. Eliza was contented seeing her mother so relaxed and beautiful.

Cameron Schiller never left her side. At evening's end he turned to Mr. Lucas to request permission to visit them the following week. "I should love to bring over my flute and perhaps play for you and your family," he proposed, smiling broadly, flashing even white teeth.

"Yes, kindly give us notice as my daughter will be occupied entertaining the neighbours who plan to visit us soon," Major Lucas answered with a twinkle in his eye. "My wife enjoys that duty but often becomes quite weary in the afternoons, so Eliza takes her place as official hostess."

"Thank you, Major. I shall send over a notification of my projected visits in advance."

Eliza watched him stealing furtive glances in her direction. He amused her, and was very good looking. She wondered how well he danced. She knew he was an interesting conversationalist who also appreciated music. *Now, if only he is an accomplished dancer,* she thought, *I might discover I could truly enjoy his company.*

chapter ten

THE SUN STREAMED RICH AND GOLDEN ACROSS THE spring afternoon. Eliza felt weary and rose slowly to her feet. After several hours of planting figs, she looked forward to a relaxing cup of tea. She wiped away the perspiration dripping from her forehead and headed unhurriedly toward the house. But after a few steps she turned to wander into the woods.

I still have time to write in my journal before helping Tabitha with dinner, she thought, appreciating the coolness the tall pine trees' shade offered. She basked in the silence, walking lightly to avoid making any noise so she could hear the different bird songs in the surrounding trees. The wind was low and she eavesdropped on a deep-throated wren singing *teakettle-teakettle-teakettle*. The path she chose was lined with moss-laden trees, almost as old as the surf. A doe and her fawn, ears pricked forward, were jolted from their grazing by her scent and bolted over a ditch, disappearing into the tall, golden grass.

The forest broke open and was replaced by a panorama of vast soft acres of salt marsh. Eliza detected the aroma of the salt air over the dominant scent of pines. She found her favourite gnarled oak branch—weary, ground scraping, worn down by sea-air erosion and the passage of time. Digging for her journal in her apron pocket, she eased herself onto the thick tree branch.

There's nothing more beautiful than when the earth turns green and the air smells so fresh your lungs hurt, she wrote. She listened intently to the dim clicking of a marsh fiddler crab. *I'm sitting at the primeval home of the varied tentacle-waving forms of sea and mud life: the magnificent marshlands. This is one of nature's most rare and moist places where life loves to experiment. I believe God made the marshes to always appear fresh and new, as if still wet from creation. That is because they are flushed out twice daily by the saltwater tides, and therefore become the nurseries of the tiny sea creatures, like shrimp, oysters, and shellfish. Oh, how I love the glorious marshes!*

Elongating her arms and legs into a cat-like stretch, she glanced up at the sky and realized it was later than she had thought. She rushed home and into the kitchen, where she was surprised to find her mother standing by the stove, flushed from baking. Ann's face brightened when she saw her daughter, and she wiped her hands contentedly on her apron in anticipation of an embrace.

Tabitha gave Eliza a huge grin. "Looky here, Mistress Eliza. Your mama make 'sum good apple crisp and scones for your tea time today," she announced.

"Mama, you look so well. I am delighted to see you in the kitchen again," Eliza said hopefully, giving her a light hug. It had been several weeks since Ann had felt well enough to bake. Eliza was anxious about her, even though her father assured them that her health was improving in this cooler climate. The coughing spells had indeed decreased considerably since they had left Antigua.

"And fancy this, Eliza," Ann stated, her deep blue eyes shining. "I've made some berry preserves as well. Your Papa will be so pleased, as it's always been a favourite of his."

Eliza walked by her father's library on her way to the parlour and picked up the *South Carolina Gazette* from his desk. An interesting article about horticulture caught her eye, so she carried it with her as she joined her parents.

"What have you read this morning, my dear?" asked Major Lucas, eyeing the *Gazette* from his seat at the table.

She smiled. "Today I read Virgil and his ideas on gardening. The way he describes pastoral gardening reminds me so very much of South Carolina. If only I had his fine soft diction to paint the pictures properly."

"But you are learning it, Eliza. When you allow me to read glimpses of your journal, I am most pleased by your calm and carefully selected words."

Her mother smiled encouragingly. "Eliza, your father and I are happy to see you getting on so well here in South Carolina. How wonderful that you are putting your writing skills to work with the many letters to your friends back in the West Indies, as well as those in England. And, you are receiving many as well." She paused, and asked guardedly, "Do you hear anything from Benjamin?"

Eliza looked over at them and answered carefully. "Yes I do, but I am discouraging him from thinking I am longing for him, because it is simply untrue. I'm much more interested in receiving the newsy letters from my friends, especially Nelly. I miss her a great deal."

"Is that perchance because young Cameron fills your thoughts?" asked her father.

"Certainly not, Papa!" Eliza's eyes clouded and she flushed. "He's a friend and he works with me on my horticulture ideas. But I have no romantic interest in him."

"My dear daughter, he certainly has interest in you. I believe he has invited you to the pre-season ball at the Drayton Plantation. Am I correct?" he asked.

"How do you know about that, Papa?" Her nostrils quivered indignantly. "I haven't even given him my consent."

"Eliza, hear me out. The poor lad is worried that you will not accept his invitation and came to me for advice," he clarified. "Pray do not embarrass him and me by mentioning that I've discussed this with you."

With a half-smile she turned to face her mother. "Oh,

Mama, the ways of men," she chided gently, reaching out for her father's hand. Ann laughed—a light, merry sound that washed over them.

The following Sunday, after church at St. Andrew's, Eliza noticed that Cameron Schiller was conversing with the rector. She enjoyed attending worship and thought Reverend William Guy gave interesting and thought-provoking sermons. The arched church roof, made of cypress wood, gave the dignified brick building the appearance of a cross. She asked Reverend Guy if it had been built with that in mind.

"No, Miss Eliza, the transept was added in 1723. We had outgrown our original rectangular structure by then. I, too, have felt this building resembles a cross." His placid face wrinkled in a smile.

Cameron strode smoothly to her side. Grinning, he lifted her hand to his. She smiled encouragingly and noticed how nice he looked with his dark hair tied back, but not powdered—a fashion many young men were adopting.

"How are you, Cameron?" she asked lightheartedly. "Did you enjoy the sermon this morning?"

"Yes, indeed," he grinned, "And I glanced over at you and noticed you were deep in thought while he spoke. Were you not in agreement?"

She laughed at his presumption. "With most of it, yes. But we do have a few philosophical differences. I should be glad to discuss them with you and also with him at some point." Her brow furrowed in concern, and she took a moment to collect her thoughts. With her eyes fixed on his, she continued. "Cameron, 'twas wrong of me not to have acknowledged your kind invitation before now. I want you to know that I should be delighted to attend the ball with you." Her smile was sincere.

"Splendid!" he declared, clearly pleased. "I'm having a new suit cut for the occasion. In an attempt to match your elegance," he added, gently squeezing her hand.

Eliza was quite taken by his enthusiasm.

"We can go over the details when I call on you Wednesday evening. Oh, and I've heard some novel opinions about raising the silk cocoons that I wish to share with you."

Just then, Polly dashed over to them. "Mama is ready to leave, Eliza," she announced breathlessly. "Oh hello, Mr. Schiller. Are you coming with us?"

"Hello, Miss Polly. Not today, but I shall come by soon. Send my regards to your mama. Is she well?"

Polly nodded and took off. "Slow down, young colt. I'm right behind you," laughed Eliza, turning to wave goodbye as her impatient little sister dragged her by the hand toward their carriage.

chapter eleven

GEORGE LUCAS AND ELIZA WERE ABOUT TO SET OUT ON a much anticipated shopping journey to Charles Town. She wanted a new pair of fashionable slippers for her first dance in the Carolinas, and their plantation workers needed shoes and more medical supplies. Their factor Mr. Dawson had suggested that they spend the night in his family's home— an invitation they eagerly accepted. Eliza was looking forward to two entire days away from chores.

"Papa, we need to buy more medicines for the sick house and the child house. I need brimstone, carthamus, aniseed, and what else…oh yes, laudanum. Mrs. Woodward told me we simply must have some on hand for when the workers injure themselves. She even told me how much to administer to them; just a wee bit when they break an arm or…"

"And you'll have plenty of time to shop while I visit the tailor. My one well-worn suit needs replacing, so I'm ordering two more to be cut."

"Oh, that reminds me, I'll need yards of material, three pounds of sewing thread, Hyson tea, and Toledo almonds. Why, I've an entire list written by Mama and Tabitha that will take me hours to work through," she sighed.

"Very well. And please purchase some Flanders lace for your mother's nightcaps. She spoke to me about that as we were leaving, and I completely forgot to write it down on your list," he mused in a lower voice, watching over his shoulder as Juno manned the pettiauger. The only sound was the light splash of the paddle and swishing water. "How much longer do you think, Juno?"

"'Bout a half hour, Major. We makin' good time wif' dese winds."

The three of them fell into an easy silence, lost in their thoughts and plans, until Charles Town sprang into glorious view, once again overwhelming Eliza with its majesty. The houses sitting on the waterfront appeared to be red-brick castles with their lovely English slate roofs. The harbour was crammed with incoming and outgoing ships, like on their arrival day a few months back.

Mr. Dawson was waiting for them with a small city carriage, eager to drive them to the various shops. As they rounded the corner of St. Philip's Street, he pointed out the provincial library.

"Knowing your love of the written word, I would be remiss in not mentioning where it is located. Do you know that it is the first library to be founded in the new colonies?" he inquired modestly.

"I had no idea, Mr. Dawson." Eliza sat spellbound, taking in the comings and goings of this busy city. People dodged between carriages and bumped into one another rushing about on the earthen walking paths.

"Here we are at your first stop! I shall leave you here to make your purchases. You are very close to my house so please come by whenever you finish. By the way, we have invited the Honorable and Mrs. Charles Pinckney for tea. He is the Speaker of our Commons House of Assembly and a leading lawyer in our province; in fact, he is South Carolina's first native born attorney. And he has been a longtime colonel of the militia as well," he added. "Major Lucas, you will enjoy conversing with him, of that I am certain."

Eliza suggested to her father that she would go down the street toward the centre of town to shop while he visited his tailor to make his purchases. In several hours they would meet back there and walk together to Mr. Dawson's home.

Three hours later, loaded down with packages, they reunited and walked to the Dawson house. Eliza felt a twinge of nostalgia for city life as they were received by the butler. He politely informed them they had less than an hour to rest before the other guests arrived.

ɩɍɩ

The six people sharing tea soon discovered they had a great deal in common. Eliza decided the "guests of honour" were the most enchanting people she had met in South Carolina. Mrs. Elizabeth Pinckney was so gracious and friendly, and immediately put Eliza at ease.

"Dear, are you christened Elizabeth or Eliza?" she asked with a warm smile.

"Elizabeth, Mrs. Pinckney. But my father began calling me Eliza as a babe, and it stuck. I quite prefer it."

"Well then Eliza, that is lovely, because we shall not be confused when someone is asking for us. I believe we shall find that we have a great deal in common, as I was also the daughter of a British army officer. And like you, I spent my formative years in London."

"Do you miss it?" asked Eliza. "I so loved that city and found it a bit difficult returning to the West Indies and then moving so quickly to the Carolinas."

"Ah yes, I do miss it at times. But we go back often, and so shall you." Her voice was full of surprise and delight and she encouraged Eliza with her optimism.

Charles Pinckney smiled easily. There was nothing soft in the sharp bones and high planes of his face. He was handsome the way gods might be handsome, but Eliza noticed that his hands were hard and cracked. He exuded good humor and kindness and his smile instantly reached his deep brown eyes. His face reminded her of a painting, with faint lines, marked by the sun's presence, etched into every corner. She enjoyed looking at him and could see the warmth reflected in his eyes.

Mr. Dawson was speaking, and Eliza had to turn her attention away from Elizabeth Lamb Pinckney and her husband to give him her full attention.

"Before Colonel Pinckney became Speaker of our Assembly in 1736, he was the Attorney General of this province. We all admire his common sense and his knowledge of the law."

Charles Pinckney shook his head and raised his hand in protest. "Such flattery, sir. Please do not alarm the Lucases."

The talk flowed freely for the remainder of the afternoon. At one point Mrs. Pinckney turned to Major Lucas. "Sir, pray consider allowing Miss Eliza to spend time with us for some of the gaieties during the season in Charles Town. She really must be properly introduced to our society, especially to the young people, and my husband and I would clearly enjoy doing that. Would we not, Charles?"

Charles turned to her, his eyes warm and loving. "Indeed we would, my love. Perhaps we could arrange to have a little dance for her first visit."

Major Lucas yielded quickly. "I'm delighted to accept your gracious invitation to introduce my Eliza into society. And I'm sure my lovely wife Ann would agree. As you have noticed, she wasn't able to join us today. Her persistently poor health does not allow fatigue. But you will certainly meet her soon, and she will be as grateful as I at your generosity."

Charles Pinckney steered the conversation to reading and his large library. Eliza's huge eyes sparkled at the mention of so many books.

"Oh, you've mentioned *Gulliver's Travels* and *Robinson Crusoe*. Do you not find Gulliver cleverly entertaining?" she asked him candidly.

"I do, and what a remarkable wit!"

Abruptly, he turned to George Lucas and asked pointedly,

"Have you any news of the developments with Spain, Major Lucas?"

"Only that negotiations are nearly at a standstill. I fear Spain has no leanings to peace and is simply delaying for time."

Eliza's ears perked up. Now her father was speaking about the military—his vocation.

"Well, I would like to believe the King of Spain is inclined to accommodate congenial affairs with Great Britain," commented Charles, "but nobody knows when that will happen."

"'Tis better not to trouble our hearts at this point," proposed Mrs. Dawson, noticing Eliza's apprehensive expression. "Eliza dear, may I serve you more tea?"

The rest of the evening moved along quickly. After accompanying the guests to the door, and with a promise of a future social call, Eliza walked her father to his room.

"Papa, you must know I have questions for you, do you not?" she asked anxiously when they stopped at his doorway.

His eyes searched her serious face. He reached for her hand, holding it tenderly to his cheek. "Do not let your pretty head be bothered, my child. At this point no one knows what Spain will do."

"But if the peace treaty is not signed, will you have to return to your regiment in Antigua?"

Major Lucas answered solemnly. "If war threatens, my duty would be to return. And I cannot risk that strenuous voyage for your mother. That means that you and Polly would stay here with her, and you would have to manage the plantation." The stubbornness in his eyes suddenly turned fragile as he watched her reaction.

Eliza nodded slowly. "Papa, if you must go, we will be fine. I have learned so much from you already, and I know the neighbours and the servants would work with me." She sighed deeply. "And as you say, we must have faith that it will all be sorted out before that becomes necessary."

George Lucas gave her a wavering smile and planted a kiss on her forehead. "That's my girl, Eliza. I know I can depend on you. Now, off to bed. Tomorrow is another big shopping day."

"Good night, Papa," she yawned, quickly covering her mouth. "Just know that I'm having a wonderful time in this city, and your friends are so delightful. The Pinckneys are my favourite people I have met here, and I'm looking forward to visiting them again in their home here or on their plantation." Her eyes shone. Leaving him with a kiss, she opened the door and entered her room.

chapter twelve

ON ANOTHER EVENING, CAMERON GRACIOUSLY OFFERED to escort Eliza to dinner at Drayton Plantation. They arrived by carriage and ascended high stone steps that led to the wide hall overlooking the river. Cameron accompanied Eliza in the carriage, even though he was staying with the Draytons on their plantation.

The men were fashionably attired in elegant square-cut coats over exquisitely tailored long waistcoats, breeches and buckled shoes. Wigs were no longer considered fashionable for young men, who now simply tied their hair back with a ribbon and powdered it. Eliza smiled approvingly at Cameron's elegance and polish.

At the first step Cameron turned to admire the view, and to secretly take in Eliza's delicate beauty and elegance. Her gold brocade gown alluringly accentuated her slim yet curvaceous figure. High-heeled slippers matched the shade of gold in her gown, and her champagne coloured silk cape enhanced the resplendent ensemble. She wore her hair swept up and fastened with a glazed ivory clip; soft copper-red curls cascaded down her neck and shoulders.

Cameron gently placed her arm in his as they made their

way up the staircase along its heavily carved balustrade to the paneled dining room above. Eliza caught her breath at its high carved mantels and deep window-seats. *Such beauty I've not seen since London*, she mused to herself. *This feast will surely be gay and cheery, and I am fortunate to be accompanied by the most handsome gentleman around.* She blushed deeply; what if Cameron might read her mind?

They were soon approached and warmly greeted by small groups of friends and neighbours. The Pinckneys had spotted them within moments and joined their small circle.

"Good evening, Mistress Eliza. Hello, Cameron. So lovely to see you both," beamed Elizabeth Pinckney, embracing each one in a heartfelt hug.

Charles Pinckney greeted them with his easy smile. "We thought you might be here, and are delighted to convene with you again. Please join us at our table for dining," he suggested.

"We would be delighted to do so," Eliza said cheerfully. Turning to her escort, she smiled. "Cameron, I see that you already know these new friends of mine."

Cameron nodded. "Indeed I do, Eliza. The Pinckneys are pillars of this community."

Dinner was an epicurean treat for Eliza—a veritable "groaning board": venison and turkey from the forest, duck from the rice fields, fish from the river; beef pasties and rounds of beef; turtle with saffron dressing. Rice and vegetables were heaped high, as well as terrapins and Carolina hams. Each dish was accompanied by a selection of wines—Madeira, port and claret—and Eliza noted that copious amounts were washed down with the feast.

She gasped when the servers brought out the desserts.

"Can anyone possibly consume another bite?" she wondered aloud, surveying the plates of custards and creams, jellies, truffles, puddings and pastries delivered to each table.

Charles Pinckney laughed gaily at her comment, eyes twinkling in amusement. *He is such an affable gentleman,* thought Eliza. *And quite handsome for an older man.*

When dinner was finally over the ladies withdrew to a

smaller area until the gentlemen finished their "smokes" and the scraping of the fiddlers would call them all back to the dance.

Eliza particularly enjoyed the beauty of the movement of the graceful dances, so similar to the ones she'd learned in London. The minuet, stately and gracious, opened the ball. Then the band played a country dance, where everyone—old and young—joined in.

"Cameron, you dance marvelously," she enthused, catching her breath after a lively turn on the dance floor.

He looked deeply into her sparkling eyes. "What did you imagine, dear Eliza? That I'd learned nothing in all my time in England?"

Eliza drew her breath in sharply. His skin was too warm, too smooth and too tempting.

The music slowed. With his eyes locked on hers, Cameron reached for her hand and lifted it up to rest on his shoulder, placing her other hand on his chest. She closed her eyes and melted into the music. A slow, soft smile of satisfaction spread across his lips as he noticed her enticing expression.

Across the dance floor, Charles Pinckney studied the young couple with a charmed patience that might have embarrassed her. He beheld a young woman with a flushed face and smoky green eyes alive with ripened emotions.

chapter thirteen

M AJOR LUCAS SENT FOR EZRA TO HELP THEM WITH
the planting season. Ezra had been their gardener in
Antigua for over ten years, and George Lucas knew he would
take good care of Eliza and assist her if he were called away
to the West Indies. Ezra was an eager worker and the only
person he knew who could pulverize the soil as if preparing
it for a pudding. Ezra's slight frame and humble demeanor
hid a sharp intuitive intelligence, and a lifelong dedication
to all the plants and flowers he so loved caring for. Now she
would be able to share her new world with him, and she was
anxious to do so.

Eliza, Ezra and George Lucas were digging on their knees,
forming the flower beds into a precise geometric shape dupli-
cated from a sketch that Eliza had drawn.

"Look Papa, here in the center we'll plant the roses. We will
surround them with bell-shaped campanulas, Sweet Williams,
and then pansies around the borders. Oh, and Mrs. Deveaux
promised to send us some lilies. Won't that be splendid?"

Her father agreed with a nod. "While you are finishing this,
Ezra and I will plant fruit trees in the orchard. That land has been
neglected so long it will require Ezra's strong hands with the spade.

Hopefully, we can bring back to life some of the damaged fig trees from years past and get some new ones started."

Eliza stood up and gazed over their plantation. The sunlight caressed the left side of her face and felt warm as she contemplated a small gray bird pecking at freshly planted seeds—eyes bright, tail flicking. *Oh how I adore nature and all her creatures*, she mused.

"Eliza, are your clothes in order for your visit to the Pinckneys's home tomorrow morn?"

"No Papa, but I will do that straightaway," she answered, reluctantly returning to the tasks at hand.

That evening she put together the essentials for her week visit to Charles Town, and took a few minutes to deliberate on the perfect gown for the dance to be given in her honour. As she was sorting through her choices, Polly burst into the room.

"It's not fair that you can leave and I must stay here and do your work," she pouted, prompting a deep laugh from her older sister.

"Silly lamb, what work might that be?" giggled Eliza. "Will you organize the house, prepare meals and visit the servants?"

Polly shook her dark curls and dropped her head. "No, but I'll be quite bored until you return," she admitted. Eliza looked closely at the sorrowful face and realized her little sister would truly miss her.

She gathered Polly into her arms and stroked her hair. "Now Polly, listen to me. You are just eight years old and I am sixteen. You've so many children to play with here, and what about your new kittens? They are just beginning to walk now, and surely will appreciate your attention. Just think: now you'll have even more time to play with them!"

Polly tilted her head to look into Eliza's face, a wily grin spreading across her face. "Yes, I shall. Just bring back one gift from the city and another from the dance," she bargained. "Then I shan't care much that you are leaving me behind."

Major Lucas accompanied Eliza to Charles Pinckney's law office in Charles Town, where she felt a moment of trepidation while saying good-bye to her father. She quickly sensed his calm and felt ashamed. Her host's warmth and cordial manners relieved any lingering anxiety she had felt during their ride to his manse.

"You know, Eliza, my wife has been quite excited about planning your dance. My musician Cephas will play the fiddle and you'll find his music enchanting. We've invited your dear friend Mr. Schiller and many other young people—each very excited to meet you. Some are coming as far away as Goose Creek."

The carriage slowed down and as it turned the corner, Colonel Pinckney's house came into view.

"Oh my goodness! How handsome is your home!" she exclaimed passionately. "Look at all the English brick I so adored in London! What a view you have! And such a fine example of Colonial architecture, with that same regal majesty as those huge homes lining the Charles Town harbour!" Her eyes were bright with pleasure. Charles chuckled at her frankness.

Elizabeth Pinckney welcomed Eliza with open arms, then took her to her room to rest.

"Come down whenever you wish, my dear. Tea will be served when you are ready, so please take your time."

Elizabeth Pinckney had laid out a lavish tea on the sideboard for the three of them. They spoke endlessly on a variety of topics. Once again Eliza felt she had known this couple for years. She was brimming with questions, mostly about the crops they raised. She finally found the proper moment to ask them her burning question.

"Colonel Pinckney, I've been trying so hard to find someone who grows indigo or at least has attempted to grow it. Tell me, please. Have you raised it at Belmont?"

Her host seemed amused by her serious interest in agriculture. Eliza read his reaction but had grown accustomed to that same response. "No, Mistress Eliza, I only raise tried and true crops here and leave the experimenting to others. As far as I know, no one has successfully produced the dye from plants grown here. Why do you ask?"

"'Tis almost certainly a silly idea, but I believe it would be such an amazing crop for the dry Carolina ground, just as rice has been in the low, swampy areas. Papa visited Montserrat last summer and told me how it is raised there and how they make the dye. I am willing to experiment here to see if it can be cultivated," she answered carefully, searching his face for approval. She wanted him to understand her strong feelings about needing to grow the crop.

Charles studied his plate as his eyebrows lifted. Then he turned to his wife, gesturing with his eyes that she amend the topic.

"Well now, Eliza, permit me to tell you a wee bit about the guests who will be coming to your dance," interjected Elizabeth Pinckney. "Don't you feel it is always more enjoyable meeting them if you know a little bit about them beforehand?" she giggled.

༺൦൦ঌ

On the evening of the dance, the Pinckney's graceful Charles Town home glimmered with candlelight. The soft glow reflected on the well-polished silver and highly waxed wood. Each moment seemed more magical than the last. Her dance card was full, and Eliza basked in the opportunity to dance with so many of the young men from the neighbouring plantations. Cameron was attentive, good-naturedly awaiting his turn to accompany her to the dance floor.

She received countless compliments that night and tried earnestly to heed her father's warning not to take all the flattery too seriously.

"You are so lovely, and you dance as lightly as a feather on the wind," Cameron praised her warmly as he escorted her back to her table. "It's no wonder your dance card has been full and I've hardly held you in my arms this evening."

She looked into his face but could not read it. *He certainly does a fine job of masking his feelings this evening. I know he wants me to enjoy my dance, yet I have no hint of what he is thinking.*

Certainly he realizes that I would dance every dance with him if only I could. She watched as he waltzed around the dance floor with other young women, wearing his beautiful smile and nodding in amusement at their comments.

⁓⊙⊚⊙⁓

Eliza had mixed feelings when she left the city after her week's stay. She happily accepted the Pinckney's invitation to return and looked forward to another visit. Yet she had missed her family and even her chores. She also worried that she had inadvertently said or done something to hurt Cameron.

Her father and Polly met her at Factor Dawson's office in Charles Town and promptly began besieging her with questions on the return to Wappoo.

"Sister, did you feel like a grown-up at your party? Was it fun?"

"Oh yes, every minute was delightful! Colonel Pinckney made me feel like a princess. He talked to me about books and government and laws and…"

Polly shook her head and made a face. "Eliza, I want to know if their house is bigger than ours. And if they also have baby kittens, or puppies."

Eliza laughed as she answered their questions. When they pulled up to their home she hurried inside, eager to share every moment and memory with her mother and Tabitha. She was travel weary, but already looking back on those seven days as a beautiful, carefree holiday she would never forget.

chapter fourteen

"THIS IS THE LETTER I HAD HOPED NEVER TO RECEIVE, Eliza," Major Lucas said in a choked voice, rubbing his palms against the tops of his thighs. "Peace negotiations with the Spanish have broken off and I am ordered to return shortly to my post of duty in the West Indies." His hand shook as he reached across the desk to hand her the stiff official letter from Lieutenant Colonel Morris.

Her father rose from the table, pacing the room while she silently read the letter. When she peered up at him, he continued. "I've tried to train you properly as a soldier's daughter to face the gravest situations. I have also encouraged you to study nature and books rather than fritter your time away on embroidery and chats in the parlour." His voice quivered, yet he managed to control the expression on his face. "Now I must place upon your shoulders a burden no other girl could carry."

Eliza threw her arms about her father's neck, choking back her gentle sobs. "Oh, Papa, I know I am small of stature but I am not frail! Certainly I am strong enough, with God's help, to accept any responsibility you wish me to carry."

Major Lucas leaned down to tilt her chin up and look him in the eyes. "I believe you are, my brave daughter."

On that warm spring morning in 1739, Eliza left the house at dawn to begin her morning routine. The morning was clear; the cloudless sky was a dazzling blue and the sun was shining. She strolled through the garden into the nearby forest where the birds, her *airy choristers*, were *exulting* their praise of morn. Breathing in the wild honeysuckle's perfume, her eyes swept over the marsh to the sandy island, alighting on the creek, and then searching beyond to where the flat gray land met the sky. As always, she sat for a moment to record her thoughts and prayers in her journal. That particular morning she had written: *I hate to undertake anything and not see it through.*

Eliza had just finished checking on the medical supplies at the servants' quarters and looked up as her father approached. "Leave off the rest of your rounds until later in the day," he said, in a voice impossible to forget. "I would like you to come to the library for a talk."

She listened to him in disbelief inside his library. Then she asked quietly, "When, Papa?"

"I'm booked on the schooner's return voyage to Antigua. It was damaged on the way to Charles Town and will now lie up for repairs to the sails. Probably three weeks. That gives us a bit of time to make proper preparations."

Her shoulders sagged, leading her body into an avalanche of release; folding her arms in front of her, she laid her head down on his desk. Her father's palm on her shoulder cracked open the fragile hold she'd had on herself. Tears welled up in her smoky eyes as she tried desperately to keep them from cascading down her cheeks. Snuggling against him, her head tucked beneath his chin, she finally allowed herself to weep.

Major Lucas stroked her silky hair helplessly, broken pain palpable across his face. And in that moment, he grasped the essence of his daughter—the gaiety, the strength, the openness, the purity, the warmth and the loving personality. There was no deception, duplicity or guile.

Releasing her, he took a step back, eyes fixed on hers. "Eliza, do you understand how proud I am of you? I have never felt prouder of anyone in my life."

The trembling smile that broke across her face made his heart ache. How had he not recognized just how much she needed to hear his approval?

"You have never, ever said that to me before, Papa," she replied longingly.

"My lassie, pray forgive me. I have been remiss," he smiled. "You have always meant so much to me, and my heart overflows with pride each time I think of you."

Eliza blushed and looked down. "Thank you Papa."

"Tomorrow we shall talk about my plans to keep our plantations running. Now my dear, why not wash your face before the others worry about you? Later this afternoon we will tell your mother and sister about my imminent departure."

Sleep was a long time coming for Eliza that night and she was plagued with nightmares. At dawn she arose, overwhelmed by an enormous desire to write down her thoughts. She set out for the forest.

Can I possibly manage three plantations? What if Mama's health grows worse and Papa is not close by to make decisions? Will the employees indeed accept taking my orders? Where can I find the strength to fulfill my father's wishes? What about Polly? And Papa? He must be so very burdened with dashed hopes and fear. Oh God, please take away my selfishness and protect my father. Pray protect us as well.

Ann Lucas took the news calmly. She knew she could not accompany her husband, and she also understood that Polly was better off here with her and Eliza. There was no resistance on her part; she felt an inner peace knowing that Eliza was well prepared to take charge of their estate.

Two days later George and Eliza Lucas sat in the library

with the heavy ledgers in hand.

"Eliza, it has been essential for our plantations to realize a profit. I've just learned from our factor Mr. Dawson that I have more land than money. Because no one has tended these lands for so long, the crops have been meager and our estates are more of a drain than a profit. Add to that the price of schooling you and your brothers in England, our move here, your mother's medical care, and more. The family finances are strained to the limit."

She absorbed these words with silent gravity as he continued.

"I have had to place a mortgage on the plantation with Charles Dunbar in Antigua. My military pay will not be sufficient to cover the mortgage and our living expenses; regrettably, I'm forced to leave you with the responsibility of developing crops that produce revenues. We are not impoverished, but I do have heavy payments to meet." He avoided searching her eyes and seeing disappointment as he concluded his painful speech.

Eliza stood and went to him. "Oh, Papa, I was so fearful you were going to tell me something terrible about Mama's health," she exhaled in a sigh of relief. "This is not a tragedy. Of course the plantation can make money. I've so many ideas of different crops to try out! We shall work together toward our goal, you from Antigua and me right here, supervising our dreams."

Major Lucas could scarcely believe his daughter's youthful enthusiasm, yet it cheered him somehow. "Well said, my lass. I refuse to yield to gloom as long as you are my right hand."

Hand in hand they walked through the newly planted garden, pleased to grasp a preview of the growing oleander buds, yellow jasmine and white Cherokee roses.

"Eliza, you must report to me by letter about the other plantations as well. You will direct the overseers, Mr. Murray at Garden Hill and Mr. Starrat at the plantation on the Waccamaw River. I do not anticipate any problems with them, but remember that you have Mr. Dawson to assist you. Oh, and naturally our London agent, your good friend Mr. Boddicott, will always be available to offer you advice." He smiled as they strolled.

"Will my brothers stay in London?" she asked. "I miss them very much, Papa."

"Indeed they will stay, and I am sorry you cannot be near them. But, do not forget our new friend Mr. Charles Pinckney, who has offered his counsel to us if needed. I know you hold him in high esteem, and fortunately he lives close by." Taking her hand, he paused to study her face.

A small frown crossed her features. "I won't have to give up trying to grow new plants, will I? Like ginger and cotton, and perhaps indigo?"

He laughed. "Of course not, my daughter. In fact, I shall send you seeds once I arrive: alfalfa, cassada and certainly the indigo. We will be partners, just you wait and see. Do you trust me?"

She grinned broadly. "Papa, I always have. And I love you and Mama so much that there is nothing I would not do for either of you."

The air was sweet with the breath of the fruits in the orchard as they passed through it. The skies were a delicate shade of blue, the light was crystal clear, and Eliza experienced a reassuring surge of peacefulness.

chapter fifteen

"ELIZA, WHEN YOU SHIP OUR ORDERS TO MR. BODDICOTT in England, be certain to include three or four hand-written copies of everything. Each order will need its export permit and the bill for the Custom officials. It would be best to send each one by a different ship to ensure that at least one copy arrives. Oh, and keep a copy for yourself."

Major Lucas and Eliza were studying the ledger where they recorded all business transactions.

"And remember, when you order the scythes, saws, axe heads and other tools from England, you will need to plan six to eight months ahead."

Eliza smiled. "Yes Papa. I will remember to plan ahead."

"Juno will transport you anywhere and at any time," he continued solemnly. "He has given me his word that he will watch out for you, Polly, and your mother."

"I know, Papa. He is quite dependable and we get along well. Do not trouble your head about that," she answered.

"Another thing: to pay for the clothes and medicines, you will need to ship barrels of rice, sesame, turkeys, geese and other game you can find to both Charles Town and England. Mr. Dawson will give us credit against the purchases. And I'll need you to send me lamb, beef, pork, butter, corn and canned fruits, as well as our home grown produce. On the returning ship I'll send you sugar, molasses and rum which will sell well in Charles Town."

Eliza nodded. Her father was even more tired than she. He needed her encouragement, if not her enthusiasm, which was harder for her to muster as the days passed by.

"We will do well, Papa. And remember to send me seeds to plant, such as earth figs and alfalfa and indigo."

"Indeed I will! Once I set foot in Antigua, I will purchase them straightaway. Even before reporting to Lieutenant Colonel Morris," he added with a wry grin.

"And here is the best news of all. I shall leave you my entire library, small as it is. I know you've been wanting to read Cicero and Milton. I believe that at age sixteen you have the age and maturity to appreciate them." His face brightened as he studied her reaction.

"Thank you, Papa! That *is* the best news ever! And I promise not to waste my time on embroidery and idle chatter. Not when I have so many lovely books to read!"

"One more surprise for the day, my lovey," he said cheerfully. "I've arranged for Mr. Carl Pachelbel, the composer and organist at St. Peter's Church in Charles Town, to teach you to play the harpsichord. Mrs. Pinckney tells me he's the best to be found anywhere, and you will begin lessons during your next visit to the city."

Eliza's mouth dropped open as she clapped her slender hands together. "What a jolly delight! I have desired to play harpsichord since my days in England. How kind of Mrs. Pinckney to arrange it for me," she chirped. Then her brow furrowed. "But Pa, when shall I have time to visit the Pinckneys if I am managing three plantations? And, more to the point, how can we possibly pay for the lessons?"

He smiled encouragingly. "You will make it all possible, my dear. Your mother is up and about more often now and can help you with your daily responsibilities. Mr. Dawson and Mr. Pinckney have both agreed to assist you in business transactions, and have convinced me that a week or two away from here will do you a great deal of good."

Eliza wasn't certain about that, and noted that her father did not address her second question at all. She knew she would need to visit Charles Town frequently and perhaps would find a way to extend her stay for brief social calls. To study under Mr. Pachelbel would be an honour. She was baffled to learn that at this difficult time before her father's departure, she had been given some good news as well.

More good news came two days later in the form of a boat trip to Waccamaw Plantation. Major Lucas felt it necessary for Eliza to visit their other two plantations, and Eliza always enjoyed these little expeditions. In a small fishing vessel they sailed down the Santee River past the Huguenot homes, and beyond the new settlement of George Town, until they reached Waccamaw. Their foreman, Mr. Starrat, traveled with them from Wappoo, where he had been working in the fields.

George Lucas stooped down to fill his palms with the rich fertile soil and looked up at his employee. "Mr. Starrat, I cannot understand why these fields do not produce more crops. Just feel how rich the soil is here; it is better even than Wappoo. What is the problem?"

"Sir, we have tried unsuccessfully to get more rice from this land, but I think the ground is plumb tired of rice. We should try another crop, 'way I see it."

Scooping up a handful of earth, Eliza's face lit up with her proposal. "What about growing indigo right here, Papa? On the higher dry ground. I believe we should try it here and at Wappoo."

Mr. Starrat looked puzzled. Her father noticed his confusion and chuckled. "That's my lassie! She is quite determined to grow that crop in the Carolinas, and God willing, she'll be the first one to do so successfully." He smiled in approval.

Back at the Wappoo Plantation, Major Lucas and Eliza rested for nearly a week before heading southward to visit their Garden Hill Plantation on the Combahee River. The overseer Mr. Murray and his wife were proud of their 1,500-acre plantation and readily agreed to send Mistress Eliza regular reports on the crops.

The neighbours were aware of Major Lucas's impending departure for the West Indies. As the travel day drew near, they visited Wappoo Plantation to offer assistance to the family. Charles Pinckney arrived by pettiauger the day of the sailing.

Major Lucas was visibly moved by his visit. "The kindness of you Carolinians has astonished me beyond words. You have taken away the dread of leaving my family, just knowing that you will keep an eye on my ladies. Thank you, thank you." He bowed low.

Major Lucas set off for the West Indies in cheerful spirits. For days before his departure, Ann had given her husband a sense that she was getting stronger. She dressed and participated in the household activities, determined to be her cheerful gay self for his benefit. After waving goodbye with the others, she was driven home and returned to her bed. The effort had taken a great toll on her. Eliza now understood that she would be unquestionably in charge of the household and the planting.

"Bye, bye, Papa," she whispered softly to herself, blinking through a blur of tears. "Fear not, as God will care for all of us. Fare thee well."

Polly looked up at her. "Who are you talking to, Eliza? Papa can no longer hear us."

Eliza smiled at her sister. "But God can, and He shall carry my words to Papa's ears. Will He not?"

Strolling toward the carriage with her sister, Eliza was already rehearsing her plans for the upcoming weeks.

chapter sixteen

I rise at five o'clock in the morning, read 'til seven, (I am presently enjoying Plutarch) then take a walk in the garden or fields; after that I see that the servants are at their respective businesses, and then I enjoy my breakfast. The first hour after breakfast is spent at my music, (and how I am enjoying the harpsichord). The next hour is spent in recollecting something I have learned in case it should be lost for lack of practice, such as French and shorthand. After that I devote the rest of the morning to little Polly and two little black girls who I am teaching to read. Then I must dress for dinner. Dinner is followed by another hour of music.

I have the business of three plantations to transact, and that requires much writing and more business and fatigue than you can imagine. Writing letters also occupies much of my time. Infrequently I am able to visit neighbours, and just recently have begun to help the poorer ones by writing out wills for them. I am learning this new skill by reading Thomas Wood's "Institute of the Laws of England". I am certain my father will not object, and my mother told me she considers it an act of charity.

Attending to the details of housekeeping and supervising the work *of the plantations are daily tasks to be attended to. Mama seems to be weaker and can only help me now and then. I encourage her to rest and eat more.*

I have run into a problem with Solomon, the foreman who worked under both Mr. Dawson and Papa, who finds it disagreeable to accept orders from a young female. This I discovered during the rice planting in the marshland, when he worked far too slowly for my patience. That was his chosen method to defy me, and how he humiliated me by making the other slaves aware of his manipulation. My source of comfort is that I forced myself to hide my annoyance and gave him warm compliments when his work finally sped up. Sadly, I have realized that I must prove my capability to many of the workers.

Kind patient Ezra has been entrusted to the flower and vegetable gardens at this point as I am quite overwhelmed with other matters. Together we did manage to get the Indian corn planted on time!

If anyone should read my journal, pray do not consider these words a complaint or too burdensome to a girl at my early time of life, because I assure you I am happy to be so useful to my mother and father. I am now enjoying plantation life, especially horticulture schemes and the planting of crops. I love the vegetable world very much.

Eliza set down the pen to rest her hand. She had been journaling for almost an hour and needed to get back to the house for breakfast. Suddenly her eyes lit up.

"But of course," she exclaimed out loud. "I will copy my journal pages as letters to Papa, and also to Mrs. Boddicott and my brothers! Then I shall not need to spend extra time thinking up new topics for each letter. After all, the majority of my daily musings can be read with interest by any of them. And of course I shall personalize them so that each one is a wee bit different."

Content with her time-saving decision, Eliza walked briskly back to the house, basking in the delicious perfume of the wild honeysuckle. Reaching the creek, she drew in a breath when she saw the stiff purple petals of the Virgin's-Bower plant.

"Beautiful babies," she called to them, "you've just opened your eyes since I did not see you here yesterday! Welcome to our world!" Her deep green eyes crinkled as she laughed out loud.

Eliza waved as she passed field hands "slashing and boxing" pine trees to catch the turpentine as it dripped from freshly-made cuts. Eliza noticed their surprise that she was up so early. She hid a smile, savouring the awareness that she was gradually earning their respect.

Suddenly she remembered—Cameron was coming to call that evening! Although she enjoyed his company and conversation, it was sometimes difficult to remain cheerful and social while dealing with so many responsibilities. Just recently, she had noticed that his face fell when he knew she was not following his conversation closely, yet he was too kind to mention her slight. Instead, he abruptly changed the subject.

"Eliza, would it be easier for you if I came by to fetch you and Polly on Sundays to take you to St. Andrew's?" he asked.

"Oh Cameron, thank you kindly, but I'll hear of no such thing! 'Tis much too far! Ezra enjoys driving us and relishes the opportunity to serve as our *guardian*, "she giggled. "But I do welcome seeing you after the church service so we might hear all about your week."

Stepping into the kitchen, she watched Polly energetically tucking into her breakfast. Eliza frowned at the heap of food on her sister's plate, but only momentarily. That enticing child had everyone wrapped around her finger, and she knew it. At least her disposition was joyful, for the most part, and she was always eager to learn. Eliza's face clouded at the thought of Polly's classes. She had been forced to reduce them; there were simply not enough hours in the day. She hadn't shared this with her father, but her mother assured her that after the planting was over she would be able to renew her teaching schedule.

"Hello Polly girl. What are your plans for this morning?"

"Hello, sister! Mama says Jethro can take me fishing today! His daughters will go too, and we shall have a splendid time. Remember last time I caught a fish in the creek? And today we're going to Ashley River, aren't we, Tabitha?"

Tabitha set a plate of biscuits before her on the bright calico tablecloth. "Why you be askin' me, chile? I not be goin' fishin' wif you."

"But you know where Patron Jethro is heading because I heard him tell you," she bantered.

"Chile, 'pon my soul, notin' get pass you. I do declare," countered Tabitha, with a huge grin showing her deep affection for the youngster.

Placated, Polly turned to her sister. "Oh Eliza, why don't you come too? You never fish with me," she whined.

"Silly goose. I wish I could, but pray remember I've got my household duties to attend to. Perhaps by the time you return we can gather up the other little girls and work on reading."

Polly's eyes shone at the word *reading*. Like her sister, she loved the written word and was advancing quickly with her lessons.

No, I'm not complaining, Eliza silently reminded herself. *This is the promise I made to Papa, and I will fulfill it. There will be time soon enough for more pleasurable activities, such as fishing and visits to Charles Town and social events. I am like Papa's right hand, and I wouldn't want it any other way.*

chapter seventeen

S ITTING AT HER FATHER'S DESK, HEAD BENT LOW
working on her business accounts, Eliza was startled by
Polly's enthusiastic arrival. She dashed through the doorway,
cheeks flushed and hair tumbling loose from her combs, grinning from ear to ear.

"Eliza, do you know who is in the parlour with Mama?"

"No, I do not. Pray tell me who is visiting," said Eliza, turning back to her accounts.

"'Tis your great friend, Mr. Pinckney. All by himself he
came here. Perhaps he has word from Papa!"

"Polly, let them be. Allow him to speak alone with Mama,
and if they want us there, we'll be summoned." Eliza was eager
to visit with her friend, but more concerned that the numbers
weren't adding up. She was also preoccupied that no letters
had arrived from Major Lucas in almost a month. That in
itself was unusual as schooners were arriving to Charles Town
from the West Indies almost weekly.

Polly left her and returned to the parlour. After a while she
came back to inform her sister that tea would be served and
that their mother had prepared it.

"Come along now, Eliza. Mr. Pinckney wants you there to hear about Charles Town, I figure."

"Has he news of Papa? Does he carry letters from him?"

Polly shook her abundant curls, which had once again been properly arranged by Mama or Tabitha. She had also changed into a clean frock and looked quite presentable.

"Polly, please tell them I shall change and join them in a moment." Eliza looked down at her rumpled frock and felt fatigued.

After tea, Charles Pinckney insisted on accompanying Eliza on a tour of her newly-planted gardens. He was very complimentary about her progress, especially the small grove of new oak trees.

"Mistress Eliza, I must send you some of our sour orange trees. You have not much fruit, and that will be a fine addition to the figs you planted with your father."

"Oh, thank you Mr. Pinckney. I miss fruit so much since we had an abundance of it in Antigua." She quickly changed the topic. "Sir, have you news from my father?"

Colonel Pinckney lowered his voice as he replied. "Not directly, but I've heard from a judge in London who advised me that Admiral Edward Vernon is preparing his fleet for war. He has not as yet left the British waters, but will be ready to do so at a moment's notice." He stared hard at her, gauging her reaction.

"My goodness! Are you saying that war may be looming? My father last wrote of his efforts to exchange his commission as Major of the 38th Regiment of Foot in Antigua with Major Heron, who works on the mainland under General Oglethorpe. Has he mentioned that to you?"

Charles Pinckney shook his head. "What a shame it wasn't negotiated before your father left here! I mentioned to him that he should seek a transfer to duty in Georgia due to your mother's illness. I wonder if he has attempted that endeavor at this time."

A streak of colours whirled toward them from the far end of the garden. It was Polly, charging through the flowers and reaching them just as Mr. Pinckney changed the topic of conversation.

"Tell me, Mistress Eliza, how is your French coming along?" he asked with a smile as he patted Polly's head of raven curls, once again bouncing free from the ribbons as she swept into the courtyard.

"Oh sir, it is always in the back of my mind but my accent is quite dreadful these days due to lack of practice. But I continue to sing aloud in that lovely language," she laughed softly. "I'm certain I drive the mockingbirds crazy with my tone, or should I say, lack of?"

"We must remedy that without delay. I meant to speak with your mother about offering you an invitation to Charles Town for an upcoming concert. The musicians have recently played for the Royal Governor of Virginia at the palace in Williamsburg. I think you would greatly enjoy the voice of the Italian tenor, who comes to us from Covent Garden Theatre in London and shall continue on to New York and Philadelphia."

Eliza let out a gasp. "Oh, such glorious news! I would very much love to attend but sir, I am awaiting the arrival of seeds my father has promised to send. I am especially awaiting the indigo seed! I am so eager to plant it and make a dye from it."

Charles Pinckney looked hard at Eliza, hoping she was not serious. When he saw that she was, he dreaded thinking about the certain disappointment she would encounter. Once again he changed the subject.

"Mistress Eliza, it has come to my attention that you have taken to lawyering to help out your poor neighbours," he commented, conscious of the blush he saw rushing over her face.

A small smile tugged at her mouth. "If you will not laugh immoderately at me, I shall entrust you with a secret." Whispering so only he could hear her, she continued. "I have made two wills already."

"And I trust that you've studied the legal process?" His dark eyes twinkled mischievously.

"Of course, sir. I have taken a book course in will making. I read *The Institute of the Laws of England*—such a difficult tome to understand. After all, what can I do if a poor creature lies dying and their family believes that I can serve them at no cost? At that point I cannot refuse, but when they are well and able to employ a lawyer, I would send them elsewhere."

Colonel Pinckney beamed at her. He was slowly grasping the positive impression she had already made around the Low Country.

Eliza and Polly saw him off at the dock. As he took her hand to bid farewell, she noticed the soft look in his eyes. "Diversion is part of a planter's life. I shall tell Mrs. Pinckney that you have accepted the invitation to be our guest and accompany us to the concert."

Eliza nodded in quiet agreement. Both her parents had insisted that she not bury herself in work. And while in Charles Town, she could conduct business with Mr. Dawson during that time.

"Thank you, Mr. Pinckney. I should be thrilled to visit you and Mrs. Pinckney as your guest at the concert. You are most kind and thoughtful to my family and to me."

"Ah, lassie. That is a promise I made to your father, and I shall fulfill it to the best of my ability," he answered lightly, waving as he moved his boat through the calm water.

chapter eighteen

Honourable Sir:

Dear Papa, you know my constant fear of slave rebellion, even though I understand little of their wishes, seeing as how we give them so much. Yet there are so many of them, and the neighbours constantly talk about their Insurrection of 1720, so we must keep our ears and eyes wide open. They say the enslaved population in South Carolina outnumbers free whites two to one!

You must know by now that just five miles from our Wappoo Plantation a group of slaves, mostly newly arrived soldiers from the Kongo, seized a store of weapons and marched southwards toward Spanish Florida, burning structures and killing whites along the way. Colonel Pinckney tells us that the slaves probably reasoned that Spanish Florida would offer them liberty for rebelling against the English. Before the militia dispersed this group, killing forty, they had grown to more than one hundred slaves. He also relates that some of them escaped and made it to their destination. What do you make of this, Papa dear?

Your most obedient and ever dutiful daughter,
Eliza Lucas

Major Lucas, newly appointed Lieutenant Governor of Antigua, had indeed heard about the Stono Rebellion of late September, 1739.

A literate slave called Jemmy, who lived off the Ashley River and north of the Stono River, had led twenty other enslaved Kongolese—possibly former soldiers—in an armed march south of the Stono River. They recruited nearly sixty other slaves and killed twenty to twenty-five whites before being intercepted by a South Carolina militia near the Edisto River. In that battle, twenty white men and forty-four slaves were killed, and the rebellion was suppressed. A group of slaves escaped and traveled another thirty miles before battling another militia one week later; most of the slaves were executed, but a few survived and were to be sold to the West Indies.

The Major was furious with himself for having left his small family of women unprotected, and was determined to minimize their danger.

He sent word to his family that all was well in Antigua, and to distract Eliza he told her he would soon be sending the indigo seeds that he had promised. Major Lucas felt that she would be preoccupied with planting and cultivating the tiny seeds. A few days later he received her next letter.

I am at a loss as to where to write to my Dear and Honoured Father. Are you still in Antigua or have you been sent elsewhere? How difficult it is for us to be without word of your whereabouts. In these times I very much miss Tommy and George and pray that they could be here with us, mostly to give Mama comfort. She worries more than anyone else and far too much. And now we are dealing with a most unpleasant situation, especially for our servants.

Mulatto Quash, a slave you personally know here at Wappoo, was recently accused by authorities in Charles Town of participating in the Spanish efforts. They maintained that he encouraged slaves to go to St. Augustine, Florida—a vicious accusation and completely untrue. I attended his trial, as plantation manager in your stead, and I proudly stood by as he proved himself innocent. You can only imagine the disgrace he was made to suffer!

This accusation added pressure and tension for Mama, who has kept to her bed ever since. As we have not heard from you for weeks, even now I find it difficult to conceal my perpetual fears and apprehensions. We know not if you are in immediate danger in Antigua. We worry that you will be ordered to a place of high risk, or perhaps are there already. I must employ all my strength to keep up a strong front for both Mama and Polly, yet I lack your aptitudes and talents so necessary to manage the plantations.

Colonel Pinckney comes by to check on us, as does Mr. Dawson and most of the neighbours. They strive to lessen my doubts and encourage me, but I know they feel badly for us. To occupy my time, Mrs. Pinckney and I put together barrels of provisions for you and the inhabitants of Antigua and are sending them out on the next ship. We hear from the others that even in Antigua there is much unrest and a real lack of food. Mr. Starrat at Waccamaw and Mr. Murray at Garden Hill have sent you butter, bacon and salted beef. Mr. Charles Pinckney and I put together (from his plantations and ours) rice, corn, peas, and keys of oyster. We know you will distribute them to the needy, and still have some to sell or barter.

Your Obedient and Loving Daughter,
Eliza Lucas

❧❦❧

Polly seemed to sense the household's anxiety and was no longer interested in playing with her plantation playmates. She stayed close to her mother, Tabitha or Eliza.

"Eliza, tell me a happy story," she begged one night, slipping down under the toasty covers as her older sister tucked her into bed.

"Shall I read you one?" suggested Eliza, smoothing a strand of hair away from Polly's face.

"No, I want a story from your heart," Polly answered quickly. "One that ends happy."

Slowly Eliza began to plot out a story about a magic wizard, who could grant Polly three wishes. Polly listened to her soft mellifluous voice and watched her sister's expressions. Her eyelids were growing heavy, but before she was completely asleep, the story ended. Polly snuggled deeper under her blankets to pray with her sister.

She closed her eyes. "Matthew, Mark, Luke and John, bless this bed I lay upon. Four corners to my bed, four angels 'round my head. One to watch and one to pray and two to keep me safe all day. Amen. Oh God, and bless Mama, Papa, Eliza, Tommy and George, Tabitha, Ezra and all the servants, and also the soldiers everywhere. And if you can, God, please make me a good girl."

Cracking open her eyes, Polly gave Eliza a long look. "Am I a good girl, sister?"

"Of course you are, my darling," Eliza answered. "You are my best girl." Leaning forward, she enfolded her small body in an embrace.

Polly's chubby arms circled her sister's neck and held on for a long moment. Finally, Eliza released Polly and settled the child down against the fluffy goose down pillows.

Eliza kissed her cheek, the tip of her nose, and then whispered, "God bless you. Sweet dreams. I love you, Polly."

"I love you too, Eliza." With a soft laugh, she rolled over onto her side and quickly fell asleep.

chapter nineteen

ELIZA SAT BY HER MOTHER'S BED, SIPPING SHERRY FROM a tiny crystal goblet and re-reading the Pinckney's' invitation to the concert in Charles Town. She slipped on her new rose-coloured sprigged dimity. At Ann's request, she arose and twirled in dainty pirouettes to model it, her mother following the graceful performance lovingly.

"I am so pleased you've decided to attend, dear. I simply cannot allow you to bury yourself in work. You work even harder than the men on the plantation!" Propped up by pillows and warmed by a silk coverlet, Ann smiled at her daughter's fresh beauty and quiet charm.

"How I wish you would attend with me, Mama. You seem so much better now than even when Papa left." Eliza's fingertips stroked her mother's face in a fleeting caress; her touch was whisper-soft.

"Yes, I do feel much better with this cooler temperature. And now that the mosquitoes are gone, I feel confident I will get fewer 'chills' and fever. But I am certainly not up to a trip to Charles Town at this time. Moreover, it will give you an opportunity to spend time with Miss Mary Bartlett, Mr. Pinckney's niece, who will be visiting from England."

Eliza nodded and leaned down to kiss her mother's cheek, noting its cool smoothness. She felt hopeful that the fever would not return.

"Mama, you know we reaped the rice over the past few days. Now I feel secure in leaving you under the care of Tabitha and the others." She grinned broadly and continued. "I wish you had seen those rice fields in the sunshine. Their bowed heads looked like burnished gold. And when the sheaves of dried rice grains were carried to the barnyard to flail, Polly and I simply giggled with pleasure at the sight of it. Our first successful crop has been harvested!"

"Your Papa will be so proud, my dear. I've already written him of your success. Hopefully our letters will reach him soon."

Eliza mentally multiplied several numbers. "It will be a pleasure to do our plantation accounts with Mr. Dawson when I'm in Charles Town. I believe with the rice crop we can settle the bills for tools and other items he supplied for the three plantations, and still have barrels to ship to England!" Her eyes shone like pools of deep green jade.

Ann grinned at her enthusiasm and added, "The Indian corn crop will bring us plenty of hominy for here and for you to ship to your father. Won't you also have enough to grind into the meal for our bread?"

"Mama, you truly know what is going on here, even though you don't ask me about it," laughed Eliza.

"I too have ears to listen," Ann chided gently. "And many little elves who keep me enlightened."

"Mama, in my last letter to Papa, I begged him for the indigo seeds and cuttings of other crops. I explained how we have learned how to handle the staple Carolina plants and now must try our hand at the new ones. And I also wrote him that my harpsichord playing and singing have improved." She chuckled, adding, "Thanks completely to Mr. Pachelbel's lessons and his eternal patience."

Changing the subject, Ann turned to her daughter. "Eliza dear, do you hear from Benjamin these days?"

Eliza looked up under arched eyebrows. "No, Mama. I believe he's found another young woman to court back in Antigua. At least that's what my best friends write me, since he never took the time to tell me himself."

Ann drew in a deep breath. "He is certainly a nice young man, but both of your circumstances have undeniably changed. Personally, I quite like your friend Cameron," she smiled. "Will he be attending the concert as well?"

Eliza smiled at the thought of seeing Cameron. "He will be here tomorrow afternoon to play music with me. I shall inquire then, but I find him distracted and a bit off with me these days."

"Darling, it isn't about you. He is trying to study the law but realizes he may have to set his legal studies aside for the Crown's battle against the Spanish."

Eliza gasped in surprise. "Why Mama, once again you know more than I do about my own friends! Wherever did you get that notion?"

Ann laughed then, a light merry laughter. "The last time he visited I spent a few moments with him in the parlour while you were dressing. He asked about your father's work and mentioned he had heard that Lieutenant Governor Bull received a request from General Oglethorpe to send troops from South Carolina to join Georgia's force. He revealed they were preparing to attack St. Augustine, I believe."

"'Tis a fact Mama, that you are better informed than I of Cameron's plans! Is he going to enlist with the Carolina troops?"

Ann nodded and averted her eyes. "Perhaps he wanted me to discuss it with you. Perchance he feared that you would not approve of his decision."

Eliza was stunned. *That explains why he is keeping his distance each time we meet,* she thought. *And I've been worried that he lost his interest in me. In my selfishness to prattle about my world, I have completely ignored his. Yet he told my mother, and she's broken it to me gently.*

"Thank you Mama. You have made me recognize a very unpleasant trait I have: self-centeredness. Tonight I'll ask Cameron about his news—with a gentle and interested approach, to be sure." She leaned over to kiss her mother's cheek and noticed that an errant ray of sunshine had warmed it.

"Now let me be off. Tomorrow I shall leave for Charles Town, and must put my accounts in order for Factor Dawson." She turned back to smile at her mother. "And yes, I shall be very happy to spend several days with Mary Bartlett, who I find fascinating. She reminds me so much of my English school friends."

Mr. Charles Pinckney's niece Mary and Eliza shared many interests and Eliza was looking forward to lively conversations and music sessions together. With a light heart she smiled widely and waved as she left her mother's room.

chapter twenty

ONE BRISK DECEMBER MORNING FOUND EZRA AND ELIZA mulching the flower borders with pine needles. Ezra had stayed on through the planting season and Eliza wondered if he missed his home in Antigua.

"No, Ma'am, I do not. Dis be were I do good, and de sun be a bit coolah den in St. John's," he grinned.

She smiled, completely aware of and grateful for his loyalty to her family. A squirrel scurried across the path near the garden and scampered halfway up a gum tree, then sat scolding them from a branch, flicking its tail back and forth. They both looked up at the sound of horses' hooves galloping toward them and followed Colonel Charles Pinckney's approach after dismounting from his frothy stallion Chickasaw.

Eliza giggled when he bowed so low his hat nearly brushed the earth.

"Hello, Colonel Pinckney! What a pleasant surprise," she said with enthusiasm.

Dusting off his coat with an ample pocket handkerchief, Charles Pinckney withdrew two rumpled letters from the same pocket and handed them to her.

"Mistress Eliza, I am in receipt of a letter addressed to you and one to your mother. I have come posthaste to deliver them since they arrived just this morning on the incoming schooner."

Eliza's face brightened with pleasure. "Ezra, please take Colonel Pinckney's horse to the stable for water and rub him down. We must take these letters to Mama immediately," she added, scurrying from the garden. Charles Pinckney followed her into the sitting room where her mother was resting. Moments later, Tabitha appeared with a serving of tea.

Eliza's face danced with delight as she read her father's letter by the window. "Oh, fancy this! Papa will soon send us cuttings of the ginger plant from Jamaica. And also cotton and cassava roots to try. Colonel Pinckney, did you know cassava can be used as cattle feed?"

"Yes indeed. Tell me, is he sending anything else?" he asked with interest.

Eliza scanned the letter to the end. "Lucerne seed, so we can grow more grass for the animals." Her expression changed as her face clouded over. "Papa says he is unable to obtain the tiny black indigo seeds. He understands that is what I wanted more than anything else and tells me he is so sorry." She dropped her eyes and stared at the floor.

Ann and Charles exchanged glances. Then Mr. Pinckney announced he would be on his way, since the distance to his plantation was more than seventeen miles by horseback. He bid them farewell and offered his regrets on the disappointing news.

"Mistress Eliza, I shall look into these indigo seeds for you, but I fear if your father has been unsuccessful in finding them, I will have even less luck." He lifted her hand gently. "Mr. Schiller asked me to request a visit with you in five days' time. Will that be convenient for you?"

More bad news, thought Eliza, as her heart plummeted. *He will come here to finally tell me that he's going to fight in the war.*

She forced a tight smile as she released his hand. "Yes. Thank you, Colonel Pinckney. Please send my best to your lovely wife and to Miss Bartlett and tell Cameron that five days from now

I shall await his visit. Oh, and thank you ever so much for riding hard and fast to deliver the letters. I trust Chickasaw will be rested enough by now to make the journey home."

❧⊚❧

Five days came and went. After a fast game of cards, which Eliza easily won, Cameron asked her if she would prefer to ride horses or play music together. She knew he wanted to talk, so she suggested playing the harpsichord while he sang with her.

After their duet, Cameron walked to the window and asked her to sit with him on the carved wooden sofa.

"Eliza, I trust you have now learned from your father and others that General Oglethorpe already conferred with the governor and Assembly. They have agreed to raise a regiment of four hundred men to serve with him for a few months," he told her. "Charles Colleton has been appointed major of this regiment, and has requested me as one of his ensigns."

She watched his face as he spoke. He was brimming with excitement as he spoke of his military prospects.

Eliza managed a smile. "Cameron, 'tis an honor that you have been chosen as an officer. I congratulate you on the distinction you have been given."

"I pledge that I will give you much to be proud of," he spoke solemnly. "I will accompany General Oglethorpe to St. Augustine and do my part to beat the Spanish." He smiled at her and took both her hands in his. His voice softened.

"Yet I shall miss you, Eliza."

"And I you, Cameron. Surely that will make your homecoming so much sweeter," she answered with a cheerful voice.

There were crinkles of laughter at the corners of his eyes, which were almost navy blue. She smiled at him, and then moved next to him, touching his face with the tips of her fingers. His skin was cool and the brief touch gave her an unexpected tingle of pleasure.

Cameron lifted her delicate chin between his fingertips. "Yes, it shall," he finally answered, meeting her lips with a soft kiss, gentle as a benediction. He held her tightly, his mouth against her hair as a tear slipped from his closed eyes.

eↃⓄↄ

Eliza eventually received the packet of tiny black indigo seeds from her father in the first days of March. She rushed to find Ezra and Solomon, her best hands, and spent the afternoon preparing the ground for planting. She crouched down and lovingly tucked the first of the seeds in the soil, praying aloud for their success.

"Dear Lord, You alone know just how great a longing I have for these seeds. Please make my dreams come true by giving us a crop to end our financial worries and also make a patriotic contribution to South Carolina and Great Britain. I entrust in You all my faith and love. Amen."

Every morning and afternoon she and Polly visited the field to see if the seeds had sprouted. One afternoon they scampered back to the house elated with joy.

"Mama, we've done it! Their little heads are popping out of the earth! You must come see them now!"

Ann prepared herself for the short walk, making an effort to accompany her daughters to the fields. Her cheeks glowed rosy as she knelt down by the tiny crops.

"Oh my, Eliza! You've done well! Your father will be thrilled and so excited for you! We must write him about your success straightaway!"

Every night from that day on Eliza thanked God for her indigo plants, and each day she sang to them. Her hopes soared each time she checked on them.

"Come along now, my glorious babies! Together we shall succeed," she laughed, giddy with happiness and hope.

One morning in early April changed everything. A freezing wind had blown in from the northwest during the night, whipping wildly through the moss-covered cypress trees. Eliza dreamed peacefully in her poster bed. She awoke to an unseasonable chill in her bedroom, and nervously dressed in haste to take stock of her baby plants.

When she stepped through the doorway, she saw with a heavy heart that white frost covered the ground. Holding her skirts high she ran toward her indigo fields, feeling physically ill at the sight she knew awaited her. Her tiny plants were slanting toward the ground—black and burned by the unexpected frost. Solomon, who had worked with her on the seed planting, was right behind her, shaking his head sorrowfully and telling her he had never experienced a frost this late in the year. Her hopes were as limp as the plants.

Blinking back tears, Eliza refused to be beaten down. "Solomon, I will get more of the seed. It's not too late to try again this season. There will be no more frost to kill the next planting." She looked up and saw compassion in his eyes.

She hurried back to the manor house and sat down at the desk in her father's study. She took the quill pen from its pewter holder and wrote to her father, begging him for more seeds.

The seeds were sent quickly, and once again she dropped them into the black dirt, just as the evening sun sank behind the horizon. She wrote to her father, telling him that the new indigo seeds were planted in Carolina soil. But this time she was plagued with misgivings as she waited for the seeds to sprout. Was the soil too damp? Would the weather again turn unseasonably cold?

Her answer came surprisingly soon. Early one morning in May Solomon knocked on the kitchen door, eyes big and crestfallen in his kind weathered face. "'Lil Missy, dem worms done ruin yo' indigo. Dey gobbled dem up. I be so sorry 'bout dat," he explained, pain written across his face.

Eliza felt numb as she gripped the door. Lightheaded, she swayed, then drew in a deep breath and ran from the room, tears coursing down her cheeks. Wiping away the wild flow of tears, she raced past Solomon toward her indigo plants. She found complete ruin. All her plants stood naked, their lives eaten away by cutworms.

Eliza dropped down to the dirt, caring nothing about her clean muslin dress. All her work was wasted. How could she handle this second failure? She realized she would have to tell her father and finally acknowledge that indigo was too difficult for a girl to grow.

Sitting upright, she shook her head fiercely. NO, she would not admit it! There were lessons in these failures. If she kept trying, kept learning, one day she would succeed. Breathing in the essence of black earth carpeted with pine needles, Eliza managed a weak smile as she heard the call of a finch near the wooden fence. She dried her tears and turned to her God.

Oh God, what will we do now? We needed the indigo and dye to make our payments and keep the plantations. Now I've raised Papa's hope with my false pride, boasting of my success before the plants were harvested. How foolish I am, and how self-centered. Please bring us peace over this failure and show me what You want me to learn from it.

A farewell ball was held in Charles Town in honour of the Carolina regiment before their departure to Florida with General Oglethorpe. Although Eliza had no desire to dance or be merry, she arrived on Cameron's arm and graced the evening with her warm smile. She went out of respect for Cameron and the other soldiers. In her heart she felt a haunting sadness for these young men, and wondered how many of them would return. And she imagined how much she would miss Cameron, who knew how to entice her to be gay and enjoy life. Another loved one would walk away from her life. Numbly, she added his name to her list of losses.

chapter twenty-one

ELIZA WAS DETERMINED TO PUT ASIDE HER OWN CONCERNS and instead focus on her family's well being. She began with Polly, waking her up early each morning to go riding. The cool morning air made for very pleasant rides.

"Polly, listen closely. Do you hear that song?" She pulled Star to an abrupt stop.

Polly nodded and searched her memory for the name of the bird with that high-pitched persistent sound. She couldn't come up with the answer.

"I don't know which one it is, sister, but 'tis a bit annoying to me."

Eliza laughed. "'Tis your favourite one—your mascot."

Polly's face brightened. "Oh! Yes, the indigo bunting. I do love the dark blue colour of the male. Please, let us ride and find it." She nudged Midnight off the shady trail and into the thick woods.

They rode their horses deeper into the woods in pursuit of the male indigo bird, trotting by glossy blossoms of laurel roaring down the sides of the rocks like pink waterfalls. They chose a path with over-arching strands of gums and oaks and pines; the lower trunks were half-hidden in thick tangles of vine and palmettos. Eliza inhaled deeply, filling her lungs with the pungent scent of jasmine.

The indigo bunting was not to be found that morning, and Polly's focus quickly drifted elsewhere. Eliza was pondering her indigo planting disaster. Her little sister interrupted her.

"It's not right that the male indigo is so beautiful and dark blue but the female isn't pretty with those ugly brown and yellow feathers. Why is God so unfair? He always makes the male animals more colourful than the female ones," she noted.

"What are you nattering on about? Look at women! We are much lovelier than the men, don't you think?"

Polly tossed her raven curls and grinned. "That's mostly because we try harder. Why don't animals have to try as hard as we do?"

Eliza shook her head and turned away to hide her laughing eyes. She had resumed giving classes to Polly and the young slave girls and discovered to her delight that Polly was retaining most of what she read. While that pleased her, unbidden thoughts of her brothers saddened her. She missed them so much, realizing it had been almost three years since she'd seen them. Tonight she would write them and also to the Boddicotts. As much as she missed her brothers, she knew she could never ask Tommy and George to come home. Their education was simply too important.

Her mind wandered to Colonel Pinckney's last visit, when he had brought her a pamphlet about the shorthand technique he acquired during his law studies. She was eager to learn more, believing it would save her time keeping the financial records. He had also brought her his copy of *Plutarch's Lives,* which she was now savouring a little at a time. Her fascination with the book was the discovery that great men had also overcome difficulties to achieve their fame.

"I want to learn to overcome my difficulties gracefully," she announced as they cantered back to the stables, Eliza's black stallion prancing in the lead.

"Eliza, I think you are all done learning. You already know

so much your brain will explode if you try to put any more in there." Eliza turned lovingly to her cheeky sister, appreciating her up-turned nose—freckles flowing across its bridge onto her rosy cheeks. They laughed together.

"Yes, I believe perhaps I do have too much deposited in there already. Now, shall we join Mama for breakfast?"

∽◦◎◦∽

That afternoon Eliza received a letter from Cameron, describing General Oglethorpe's force of two thousand men: Scottish Highlanders, Creek and Cherokee Indians, and the Carolinian troops. He wrote that they were only three miles from the Castillo de San Marcos, the massive fortress in St. Augustine, Florida. The letter ended with the tender words of a man missing his woman. Eliza's face glowed after reading the warm sentiments.

She continued learning everything she could about growing indigo, determined to do better the following year. She understood she could not produce blue dye until she had raised a large quantity of indigo plants, because each one yielded only a few tiny cubes of the dye. Frost and worms had ruined her chances in early 1740, but she was determined to prevail the following year.

After weeks of silence, Eliza received a letter from her father expressing his pleasure at her success with the plant. He told her he would send an experienced but expensive indigo maker from Montserrat to show her how to make the dye. Her head reeled as she digested the news. *There was no crop to process!* How would she explain this to her father, and face this gentleman from Montserrat when he arrived? And why had she waited so long to write him the truth about their indigo disaster?

Dear God, here I am again, troubling you with my tribulations. And just today, I heard in church a sermon about not borrowing tomorrow's troubles. What shall I do? Can you at least give me some peace? I make so many mistakes, but they are all based on good intentions. I ask you to help me win this battle with indigo, so we can save our plantations. Thank you for your patience with me. Amen.

chapter twenty-two

ELIZA SAT IN THE SITTING ROOM OF HER CLOSEST neighbors, Mrs. Woodward and her daughter Mrs. Chardon, sharing the latest letter from Cameron Schiller.

She told them he was weary and dispirited, writing about his troop's loss in St. Augustine, Florida under the command of General Oglethorpe. Not only had they failed to capture the bastion, but they had been forced to retreat. The Spanish had strengthened the fort's walls and driven thousands of stakes into the ground outside to keep the British troops out.

"He shall not return with the rest of the Carolina regiment," she read. "He says General Oglethorpe is a true soldier, with whom he wishes to remain." She set the letter down and offered up a trembling smile. "He is staying on with the Georgia troops." Eliza blinked away the tears pooling in her eyes.

"Dear Eliza, you must be so worried about him." Mrs. Chardon deftly pulled the needle through her embroidery. "I know how much he means to you." She had been widowed at a young age by a Huguenot gentleman with no family in the area. Her mother had urged her to move back home.

Eliza nodded and looked down at her needlework. "Just lately I've come to realize he has probably been my best friend here. I do not have the right to think of him as a future husband, as we are nowhere near that stage, but he makes me laugh and keeps my spirits light. While I try to leave this all in God's hands, of course Cameron and the other soldiers, especially my father, are in my prayers nightly. War is such a terrible experience for us all, is it not?"

Mrs. Woodward nodded and reached across to touch Eliza's hand reassuringly. "I am very happy that you come to us now and again to share tea and conversation. You do entirely too much work for a girl your age. And we dearly love it when you bring young Polly along with you. I declare she is coming along quite well on her sampler."

Their conversation turned to the November 18, 1740 fire in Charles Town. Eliza had been in the city visiting the Dawson family when the bitter stench of smoke reached them just after supper.

The sound of running feet in the street sent Mr. Dawson rushing upstairs to change clothes.

"Fire, Fire—Fire on Broad Street!" came the frantic shouts.

Mrs. Dawson hurried Eliza into her bedroom and found two cambric handkerchiefs. "This is utterly dreadful, Eliza. We have long feared such an event," she lamented, handing her friend one of the cloths.

When Mr. Dawson reappeared, his wife and Eliza were waiting, wrapped in woolen cloaks with hoods, linen sheets in hand, ready to accompany him.

"Ladies, this is no place for you. It will be dangerous and detrimental to your health." He spoke gruffly and turned to leave.

"You need us, dear. We will make bandages and use them to nurse the injured; you and the men will fight the fires—we will nurse the injured," his wife answered firmly.

The three of them hurried through the doorway and joined the crowd of neighbours pouring down the street. A blanket of smoke hung over the entire town, blotting out the vanishing sun. The stench of fire burned their nostrils and choked their throats. The flames, shooting up into the sky, left no doubt of the location of the fire—the naval stores.

"We will have a bloody time fighting the fire with these winds," fumed Mr. Dawson. He turned to the ladies. "Go stay with the other women and give aid only to those not actively fighting the fire."

Looking upward, Eliza saw thunderheads of smoke reaching far into the sky. She had to shout to be heard. Sparks had spread to the wooden buildings and the women watched in dismay as they went up in a tumult of fire.

"Dear Lord," exclaimed Mrs. Dawson, eyes wide and fearful. "The flames are jumping to the mill and the rooming house!"

Church Street collapsed in flames. The women saw landing parties from several of His Majesty's ships of war fighting the fire side by side with the residents. A number of house servants fought next to lawyers and merchants.

"Come Eliza," shouted Mrs. Dawson through her wet handkerchief covering her mouth. "Over there the women are caring for the injured. Let us join them."

Snagged by heat and smoke, the women gasped and moved toward a crowd of injured at the assistance station. A desperate woman, separated from her child cried out, "My baby, my baby," as Mrs. Dawson pulled her sobbing back into the group. Women and children were hysterical in the streets, searching for fathers and brothers as they were driven out of the decimated homes.

The hours passed quickly while the exhausted women nursed the burns, cuts and gashes on the men. One man had a broken leg, and Mrs. Dawson sent for a doctor she knew.

They had to move their station as smoke overcame them. Eliza overheard a young man yelling orders to the others to get powder from the Powder Magazine to blow up several houses.

"Why?" she asked incredulously.

"To halt the flames and keep them from spreading," answered her weary friend.

At some point a fatigued Mr. Dawson returned for them. Together they organized homes to shelter the homeless. The Dawsons and Eliza led two families to their own place as well. Eliza's heart was heavy with grief for the sufferers, yet swelling with pride for their courage.

She looked around and smiled.

"You know, I believe I have truly become a South Carolinian—through the baptism of fire." Her tone was warm and soft.

Her friends smiled at her. "You were very brave, Eliza. And we've heard you've sent food from all three of your plantations to help replace Charles Town's burned food supplies."

"As have you, I am certain. This is a loving community and we understand that Charles Town must be rebuilt. Colonel Pinckney says that nearly three-fourths of the city is destroyed. St. Andrew's Church has raised a tremendous collection for that, and Colonel Pinckney and the others in the Commons House of Assembly have passed a bill to restrain the greed of workmen and dealers in building materials. But all of these acts together won't be enough, I fear," she said glumly.

"Here's some cheering news, ladies," announced Mrs. Woodward. "I've received word that the British Parliament voted to send twenty thousand pounds sterling relief money for Charles Town. Pray do not quote me on the sum, but we shall certainly receive crucial assistance from Mother England."

Eliza clapped her hands together as her face lit up. "That *is* truly wonderful! In fact, the best news I've had in months! And it gives me hope for the future, my personal future and that of the city. Thank you for providing me with such brilliant news to take home to Mama. We are both in need of renewed faith in our lives." Her cheeks were rosy and her deep green eyes sparkled. "I am so happy I came by to visit with you today!"

That evening Eliza wrote a letter to Mrs. Boddicott, asking

her to share it with her brothers. She wrote all the news and ended the letter with these words.

I assure you I consider myself happy that I can be useful to so good a father. To be happy we must have one steady rule for our conduct in life: we must consult reason and follow where that directs.

Your most affectionate and obliged humble servant,
Eliza Lucas

chapter twenty-three

THE WAR WITH THE SPANISH MADE IT DIFFICULT FOR ships to travel from the West Indies to the American colonies. Eliza and her mother were extremely concerned because they had not heard from Major Lucas in months. Without any word, Eliza had no idea when the indigo maker would arrive from Montserrat; she finally decided to proceed without him. She had acquired a small amount of the tiny black seeds and planted them immediately, knowing there were not enough seeds to make the dye, but hoping to receive more to supplement them.

The morning was lovely, as spring mornings tended to be, with a host of feathered choristers singing behind the house with typical abandon. The sun shone through a dazzling blue sky as Eliza and Polly trudged through the woods gathering up purple violets for their mother. A pack of dark birds flew swiftly overhead, scattering apart and effortlessly coming back together.

"Polly, I have ordered the rice planting to begin tomorrow. Solomon and Ezra have already carved the trenches for the seed, but we have so few. I often feel so frightened the crops will fail, but then I remember something Papa told me before he left."

"What did he tell you, Eliza?"

"He said: 'Only a fool knows no fear; only a coward runs from the battle.'"

They considered this silently before Polly spoke again.

"When will he come home, sister? I miss his hugs and his big fat smile," she said softly.

Eliza laughed lightly. "As do I, my pet. But we must be patient and not lose our faith. We need to help Mama feel safe and secure. Please help me by staying happy."

Polly nodded absently. Each night she prayed for her father's return for her ninth birthday, now only a few months away.

Eliza knew she needed to keep a cheerful face for her family, yet she struggled under the heavy load of her responsibilities. She missed the carefree good times in Antigua with her girlhood friends. She missed sharing her music and social activities with Cameron. Her thoughts turned to her brothers in London. They had received news that Tommy was not well, and that worried her. Mrs. Boddicott wrote that George was studying with a military career in mind. George had turned sixteen and Eliza knew she could not influence him; nevertheless, she wrote him urging him to give other careers some serious consideration.

Her new and special English friend Mary Bartlett visited Charles Town often, residing in the home of her aunt and uncle, Elizabeth and Charles Pinckney. Eliza's time was consumed in preparation for the planting season at Wappoo, so she had not seen Mary since her arrival six weeks prior. The girls exchanged frequent letters, and each looked forward to seeing the other. They were about the same age and both had been schooled in England. Eliza was pleased to have found a dear friend with whom she could share intimate details.

ↁੋਁ

At the end of March of 1741, Colonel Pinckney visited Wappoo Plantation by boat.

"Hello Mistress Eliza. I hope you are well," he told her formally as she greeted him at the dock. "I have come to bring you and your mother news of the war."

Eliza felt a moment of anxiety and feared the worst, but accompanied him up the hill to the house. His next words calmed her nerves a bit.

"I also brought you a series of new books—*Virgil's Georgics*. They are about the joy of country life. Mind you, they are a translation of the Latin text, so they may be difficult to absorb at first read."

They walked to the house amiably. Mrs. Lucas met them at the door and embraced him with pleasure. "'Tis always so good to see you Charles," she proclaimed. "Eliza, would you please ask Tabitha to bring some Madeira for Colonel Pinckney and the tea service for us."

After the refreshments were served, Colonel Pinckney shared his news.

"Ladies, I have heartening news to impart. A small sloop arrived from New Providence Island in the Bahamas. Its master reported that Admiral Vernon and his forces have captured Cartagena from the Spanish."

"HURRAH!" shouted Eliza impulsively, jumping to her feet.

"What wonderful news you have brought us," added Mrs. Lucas. "This may mark the beginning of the end of the war with Spain," she affirmed in a cheerful voice.

"How long has it been since you have word from the Major?" asked Charles Pinckney solemnly.

Ann Lucas's eyes filled with tears. She looked away as Eliza answered for her. "Nearly six months, sir."

"I feel certain that will change shortly. Boats should be coming in now with letters," he offered.

One week later, Mr. Dawson's patron brought a message to Wappoo. It was a short and quickly penned note to Eliza containing information about her father.

A fast schooner has anchored in Charles Town. The captain says he overtook Captain Magnus Watson's "Brother's

Endeavor," after a tedious journey from Antigua. The Captain estimates Watson's slower craft will make port tomorrow. Should you care to be on hand for his arrival, doubtless he will bring news and cargo from your father.

Eliza left early in the morning to be on hand for Captain Watson's arrival. She was overjoyed to find that her father had sent them rum, sugar, molasses and a great amount of coffee. Captain Watson reported that her father conveyed instructions that she fill his hold with their plantation products.

"Sir, I shall have plantation boats loaded at once with shingles, lumber, salted meat, rice, corn, peas and a keg of eggs I have preserved in salt. We are indeed indebted to you and your benevolence."

"Very well, Mistress Eliza. I aim to be off at once because the passage was slow. I will await your cargo and set sail," replied Captain Watson. "Oh, and your pa sent a passenger by me as well."

"Whoever could that be?" Eliza contemplated aloud, looking around the docks.

Captain Watson pointed at a figure in the small boat coming from the "Brother's Endeavor." She watched as he lifted himself onto the dock, pulling his canvas bag behind him. He was short, stout and somewhat clumsy. When he turned to face her, Eliza felt an instinctive distrust. His small, beady eyes darted around the dock as she observed him. She noticed his face was pitted with acne, probably from smallpox.

"Mistress Eliza, please meet Mr. Nicholas Cromwell. Your father asked me to pick him up at Montserrat."

Eliza banished her foreboding and welcomed Mr. Cromwell with a smile and extended her hand to him.

When they reached her plantation and Eliza showed Mr. Cromwell her small stand of leggy indigo bushes, he reacted at once. "You brought me all the way to the New World for this?" he asked with a sneer, his eyes snapping with disdain.

"Mr. Cromwell, we shall make it work. I trust you are delivering more indigo seeds, am I correct? We are just now at the end of March and still have plenty of time to plant and harvest them."

"Ay, there are more seeds in my bags. But I can already see and feel from this weather that indigo will not grow here." He turned away and spat on the dark earth.

Eliza held back her temper as she showed him his room and explained to him about meals and working hours. She had been surrounded all her life by people with manners—her family and friends, their Negro workers, and the courteous English servants in London. She was shocked by this man's blatant lack of etiquette.

Yet she was determined to produce indigo in this British colony, and resolved to learn to work with Nicholas Cromwell.

He demanded brick with which to build the vats for the dye making process. Once again she was stunned at his orders.

"Why brick?" she asked dumbfounded.

He scowled at her. "You ever process indigo, Miss?"

Eliza flushed bright red at his audacity. "No sir, I have not. But I have read that using wooden vats will work wonderfully for the indigo, as it does for the fermenting of grapes. We have the wood here on our plantation."

Mr. Cromwell glowered at her insolence and shot back at her. "Mistress Lucas, your father sent me to you as an expert in indigo dye processing. I must work with brick for my vats, and you will respect my wishes."

A red mist of rage nearly blinded her. She willed it away—slowly, carefully choosing her words in response.

"Yes sir. I will order the brick from Charles Town. It will take many days to be made and reach us." Shards of prickling dread shivered down her spine. Deflated, she rode over to confer with her dear friend, Mr. Deveaux.

"What do you think of this twaddle?" she asked him, still simmering. "I suspect his methods will be harmful in the end."

His eyes were kind as he answered. "Your father has gone

to great expense to send him and believes in his skill. I feel you should allow him to do it his way, at least for the time being."

With a heavy heart Eliza sent away for the brick. They waited a considerable time for the bricks to be fired and delivered. In the meantime, she retreated to the cool forest and to her journal writing, fighting her exasperation and contempt for this indigo maker.

I distrust this man, and how I wish it were not so. He is being paid for doing nothing, as he insists on using brick vats which are costly and unavailable, so here we sit, waiting on them. He spends his days talking with the servants and employees, and I have discerned that he is duplicitous in his words and actions. Already he has told Ezra that I know nothing about the crop, and would be better suited finding myself a husband and leaving the decisions to him. What bloody cheek! If only Papa were closer and we could discuss my feelings. I have a very bad suspicion about Mr. Cromwell, and know I must be extremely careful around him.

chapter twenty-four

"MISTRESS ELIZA, MAY I SPEAK WIF' YOU?" ASKED EZRA, bowing slightly in his gentle manner. Eliza looked up in surprise as he stood in the kitchen doorway.

"Of course, Ezra." She wiped her hands on a linen towel and offered him a seat at the table, which he declined.

"I be speakin' for the Negroes workin' wif' Mr. Cromwell to build dah trenches. We all knows Major Lucas's rule 'bout givin' orders clearly expressed and in dah spirit of kindness. We work well dat way. Dat's how Major Lucas learned in de army, and he always use dat wif' his workers."

Eliza's eyes narrowed. "Is Mr. Cromwell not following those instructions, which I clearly and explicitly explained to him when he arrived?"

"No Ma'am. Mistress Eliza, he be 'ornry and mean spirited wif' us, and jus' yesterday he kick a young Negro who dint understand his order. I tink you should know what happnin', jus' in case he tell you sometin' else."

Eliza felt a cold fury seize her. "Thank you, Ezra. I will speak with him about this. Please tell the workers this will be corrected."

Mr. Cromwell had refused to dig the foundations while

awaiting the bricks, and then demanded that slaves belatedly dig the trenches while he put together his vats. At every turn he scolded and rebuked her workers. She had already spoken to him once about this after witnessing his rude behavior.

She found him resting in the shade of a large oak. Sitting down a few feet away, and holding her temper in check, she began in a calm voice.

"Good day, Mr. Cromwell." She waited until he looked up and saw annoyance etched in his features. "I am here to speak about a report of slave injustice."

They locked eyes for a second and Eliza's mouth went dry. She noticed that his eyes were gray, an anti-colour. He gave her a hard stare and mumbled, "They need to pay attention to my orders. They're lazy savages from the jungles of Africa and don't wanna work without me driving 'em hard."

Eliza's smoky green eyes flickered fiercely, boring a hole into his.

"My workers are neither lazy nor savages. They are respected members of my plantation and I must insist that you treat them decently." Her nostrils quivered in indignation. "Otherwise, your work here shall be terminated. I will not tolerate any more abusive treatment of them. Have I made myself perfectly clear?"

She caught an unmistakable glimmer of hatred flash across his eyes. Then he looked down and spat tobacco juice, narrowing his eyes and refusing to answer her. He lifted himself up unhurriedly and sauntered off toward the workers.

"Very well, then. Now that we understand each other, you may carry on with your work." Her voice was low but controlled. She knew he had heard every word.

You will not manipulate us, she whispered to herself.

෴

The reports filtering into Wappoo were far from good. Eliza's grandmother had passed away in Antigua, and her oldest daughter, Ann Lucas, had been unable to be at her side. She was too weak to make the journey for her own mother's burial. Depressed and grieving, she took to her bed for days.

The British expedition against Cartagena had been defeated after encountering a bloody fight, and was driven away. Yellow fever was devastating the British forces.

Nicholas Cromwell had loitered so long constructing his brick vat that the leaves of many of Eliza's indigo plants had darkened and withered off.

What shall I tell Papa? She felt at a loss as how to proceed. *I cannot write him of my suspicions of Mr. Cromwell since I have no proof of his incompetence. It would only upset him after all he's gone through to provide me with Cromwell's help.* Eliza knew her father needed cheerful tidbits after the rash of bad news.

One day Mr. Cromwell announced that the indigo leaves were ready to be cut. Eliza was overcome by a fever of excitement, yet determined not to display it to Mr. Cromwell for fear it would antagonize him.

She worked with good cheer with the men in the field, cutting the indigo plants carefully so the bluish tinge of the leaves would be retained. She stood back and watched them gently lay the plants in the vats with the stalks up. She noticed every step, and a smile broke across her face as she observed the clearness of the water covering them.

Eliza's good nature and upbringing prompted her to share her emotions with Mr. Cromwell. "Oh sir, we are so fortunate to have an excellent dye maker to process our indigo plants," she gushed.

His gray eyes darkened with bitterness. "Yes, and I'm probably selling out my own island by coming here and teaching you the process. I should have listened to my mother. She told me not to come."

Nicholas Cromwell's words cut Eliza like a whip. This process of turning her plants into dye had been her dream for two long, frustrating years, and he was determined to ruin her joy with a few bitter words. She knew it would take years to establish an indigo industry in the Carolinas, and this man had been sent here to give her the necessary tools. He was paid very well to do this. Could her father have been mistaken in his trust?

She forced her negative thoughts away and stood near him, firm in her decision to watch and learn everything she could. Her father had written down the steps of indigo processing from his last visit to Montserrat. She carried this document in her apron pocket and was determined to experience each step firsthand.

The leaves are cut and steeped in water in large vats open to the sun until they ferment and turn the water a greenish colour. This fermentation process takes several days, after which the solution is drawn into a lower vat and beaten with paddles for several hours. The indigo maker takes frequent samples until he perceives a purple trace in the solution. When he decides the process is complete, the solution is strained and poured into a second vat, the battery, with a small amount of limewater—the amount, stirred in gently, will stop all fermentation and precipitate the "bluing." This agitation determines the colour of the dye—the longer the mixture is beaten, the darker the colour. Finally, it is put in the third vat, and the muddy blue dye will settle and sink to the bottom before the clear water is drawn off; leaving sediment that is formed into blue mud cakes. The cakes are strained through a sieve into linen bags, drained and kneaded to press out any remaining moisture. Finally, they are carefully dried in the sun and later the shade, and then are ready for market.

Eliza did not know the chemistry of the process or the proportion of limewater to be added to precipitate the blue dye. She watched Mr. Cromwell closely as he drew the liquid from the steeping vat into the "battery" and realized there didn't seem to be much liquid. She listened as he growled orders at the men to begin beating the liquid. His coarse words were intended to humiliate her and let her know he was in command of the process. She held her tongue and prayed.

At one point she asked him, "Mr. Cromwell, is that how you expose as much of the liquid as possible to the air?"

His reply was haughty, employing words he never would have spoken to a man. "Don't bother your head with facts. It takes too long to learn the method. Girls cannot understand this business." Observing him closely, Eliza caught an unmistakable flicker of cold contempt swell across his face.

Rather than allow her temper to control her speech, Eliza chose to ride to Mr. Deveaux's plantation. Pushing Star into a steady gallop, she reached his home in record time.

"Please come back with me, Mr. Deveaux. I am so worried I cannot think correctly." Her words stumbled over each other in her haste to convince him to accompany her.

"You've done well to come to me, Miss Eliza. His rudeness toward you is appalling." Mr. Deveaux's features clouded as his lips set in an uncompromising line. "I am now beginning to fear that he is capable of working harm to the indigo crop."

They rode together back to Wappoo Plantation. Mr. Cromwell was working at a leisurely pace.

With Polly at their side, they stood directly next to Mr. Cromwell as he added the limewater to the much-paddled mixture. When he walked away and turned his back on them to measure more limewater, Eliza's heart did a double clutch. Her studies and instincts conspired a warning, while her lack of experience gave her doubt.

Her voice was stuck in her throat. "Is he putting in the right amount, do you think?"

Mr. Deveaux's kindly face was stern and hard. He marched over to the dye maker and stood at his side to determine exactly how much limewater Cromwell was measuring out.

Mr. Cromwell snarled at the workers to retrieve their paddles and showed them how to stir the limewater into the juice. Eliza noticed that he omitted his coarse words in the presence of Mr. Deveaux.

Mr. Deveaux took her hand in his and smiled. "Patience, my dear. This must be very difficult for you as you have worked so hard for this." He released her hand and stepped directly in front of Nicholas Cromwell.

"Tell me, sir. What are the proportions of limewater usually administered to the juice?"

Mr. Cromwell's face started to flush. "Could not tell you, sir. A dye maker has that knowledge inside himself, like a chef with his recipes." His eyes pinched together. ""Course if anything goes wrong, 'tis the inferior quality of these plants. I ain't a bit happy 'bout this mess 'o crops I been handed."

Mr. Deveaux eventually suggested they repair to the house to rest. Eliza would not hear of it, but sent him back with Polly to visit her mother. She feared taking her eyes off Mr. Cromwell or the vat lest he throw dirt into the vat to ruin the dye.

Finally, Mr. Cromwell pulled the stop and began draining off the fluid. Eliza raced to the house to bring Mr. Deveaux and her sister back to see the final results.

They watched him scrape the soft blue paste from the bottom of the vat and put it into linen bags. Once he had shaped the remains into cubes, he laid them on clean wooden trays. His workers set them under a shed. Eliza could hardly breathe. Her eyes shone with amazed humility.

Mr. Deveaux chuckled, overcome with emotion as well. "Miss Eliza, I rejoice with you. This is a great moment for you and everyone in this colony and also for the Crown of England. Those few blue cubes have just proven that indigo dye can be made in South Carolina! You have the distinguished honour of being the first colonist to achieve the cultivation of indigo dye! And you've just reached eighteen years of age! Mademoiselle, mes félicitations."

Eliza curtsied to her friend, her eyes welling with joyful tears. Glancing in the direction of her dye maker, she overheard his comment.

"Bah, 'tis such an inferior grade. On Montserrat, we'd be ashamed of such dye and dump it."

Not even his unkind remark could dampen her spirits. She was elated, and knew they would be able to improve the grade of the dye the following year. Her dreams had come true! How happy Papa would be, and this would bring them money. Perhaps even enough to pay off the mortgage on their properties. She sent word to Factor Dawson to come quickly for a visit.

A day after the cubes of indigo had dried, Mr. Dawson arrived at Wappoo, accompanied by a Frenchman.

"Miss Eliza, may I present Captain Amedee. He tells me he sails into Martinique to buy indigo and transport it into France. I've brought him along to judge your indigo and be a consultant for you."

They went immediately to the drying shed, where Captain Amedee and Mr. Dawson picked up cube after cube of the indigo, studying each one warily. The Captain's face grew somber and his brow furrowed in concern. Turning to Eliza and Mr. Dawson, he slowly shook his head.

Eliza's eyes expanded with shock. All colour vanished from her cheeks. She had the peculiar notion that the events swirling around her had nothing to do with her. Darkness seeped into the edges of her sight. She felt herself sway as she sensed her body weightless, boneless, and empty of all its parts. She was traveling backward in time, lost in dark regions of her mind. Her palms went damp just as Mr. Dawson reached for her trembling hands.

"Are you all right, Miss Eliza? You've suddenly turned quite pale." He spoke so softly only she could hear. She blinked swiftly, terrified at her anguish.

Staring speechlessly at him, she rubbed her eyes with the heels of her hands and crumpled to the ground.

chapter twenty-five

"ELIZA, CAN YOU HEAR ME?" THE VOICE SEEMED TO come from far away, as in an echo. Eliza forced her eyes open and realized she was lying in the shed on top of someone's cloak. A thin blanket covered her.

"What happened?" Sitting up gingerly, she peered into the anxious faces of Mr. Dawson and Captain Amedee. Mr. Dawson attempted to assist her to her feet, his hand under her elbow, but she shook her head and remained seated. Polly grasped her hand, squeezing hard as tears streamed from her eyes.

"You fainted, my dear," answered Mr. Dawson. "Only for a few moments."

Eliza blinked, thoughts racing through her mind. *It was the indigo; their faces; Cromwell.*

"Where is he?" she whispered.

"Where is who?" answered Mr. Dawson.

"Nicholas Cromwell—the man who ruined my indigo. Bring him to me straightaway."

The men exchanged apprehensive glances. Ultimately, Mr. Dawson walked out the door to find him, leaving Captain Amedee and Polly standing by. Polly fell down next to her sister.

Portrait of Charles Pinckney. When forty-five-year-old Charles Pinckney married Eliza Lucas in May 1744, he had already served in important positions in the colony: speaker of the Commons House of Assembly and a member of His Majesty's Council. Taken from The Letterbook of Eliza Lucas Pinckney. COURTESY OF THE SOUTH CAROLINA HISTORICAL SOCIETY

The Mansion House of Charles and Eliza Lucas Pinckney, built in 1745, is seen on the extreme right in a line engraving by Samuel Smith—A View of Charles Town—taken from a painting in London by Thomas Leitch. COURTESY OF THE SOUTH CAROLINA HISTORICAL SOCIETY

General Charles Cotesworth
Pinckney (1746-1825)—
eldest son of Eliza Lucas
and Charles Pinckney and a
framer of the Constitution.
Taken from The Letterbook
of Eliza Lucas Pinckney.
COURTESY OF THE SOUTH
CAROLINA HISTORICAL
SOCIETY

Mrs. Daniel Horry
(Harriott Pinckney,
1748-1830), daughter of
Charles and Eliza Lucas
Pinckney. Taken from The
Letterbook of Eliza Lucas
Pinckney. COURTESY OF THE
SOUTH CAROLINA HISTORICAL
SOCIETY

*Thomas Pinckney (1750-1828),
son of Charles and Eliza Lucas
Pinckney, from the miniature
painted by Charles Fraser in
1818. Dressed in the uniform of
a major-general, he commanded
all U.S. troops in the southern
half of the country throughout
the War of 1812. Taken from
The Letterbook of Eliza Lucas
Pinckney.* COURTESY OF THE
SOUTH CAROLINA HISTORICAL
SOCIETY

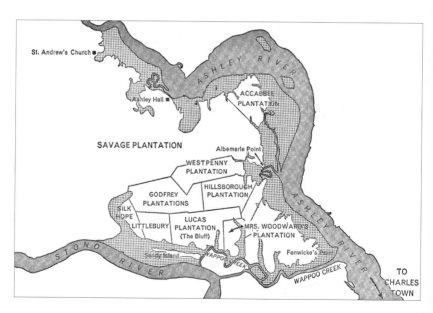

*Map showing the Lucas Plantation on Wappoo Creek and nearby
plantations.* COURTESY OF THE SOUTH CAROLINA HISTORICAL SOCIETY

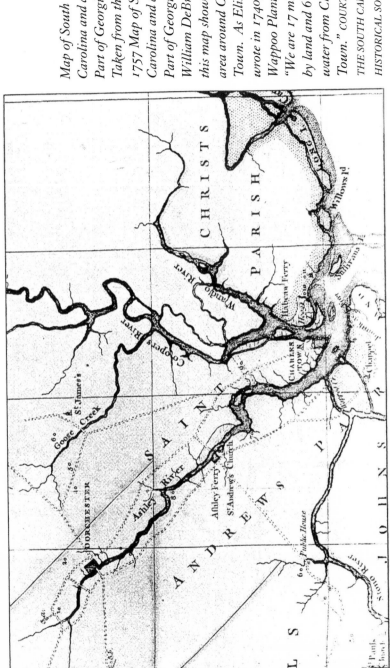

Map of South Carolina and a Part of Georgia. Taken from the 1757 Map of South Carolina and a Part of Georgia by William DeBrahm, this map shows the area around Charles Town. As Eliza wrote in 1740 from Wappoo Plantation, "We are 17 miles by land and 6 by water from Charles Town." COURTESY OF THE SOUTH CAROLINA HISTORICAL SOCIETY

My dear Children Charles and Thomas Pinckney. August 1758.

xx you have met with the greatest two my children you could meet with upon earth! your dear, dear father, the best and most indulgent of parents is no more! (a faint tremulous letter)

To Mr Gerrard

Hampton Plantation, home of Daniel and Harriott Pinckney Horry. Eliza Lucas Pinckney lived here with her daughter after the Revolution. On this portico, she and her daughter welcomed President Washington in 1791. COURTESY OF THE COLLECTION OF RICHARD & GINI STEELE

The Pinckney Mansion after the Charles Town fire of 1861.
COURTESY OF THE LIBRARY OF CONGRESS

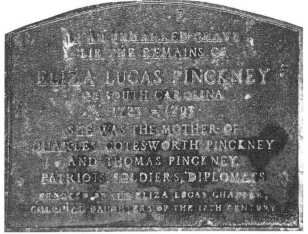

Grave Marker of Eliza Lucas Pinckney. She died on May 26, 1793 in Philadelphia, and was buried in St. Peter's Churchyard. The specific site is not established, but this marker has been placed within that cemetery. COURTESY OF THE SOUTH CAROLINA HISTORICAL SOCIETY

Mrs Washington presents her compliments to Mrs Horry. Mr Trumball has
been so polite as to say he will be happy
to attend Mrs W— at any hour tomorrow morning which she shall find most convenient — if therefore Mrs Horry will
be so good as to name the hour which
will be most agreeable to her, Mrs W.
will call on her at the time. —

Friday — 8 P.M.

*Letter written by Martha Washington to Eliza Lucas Pinckney's
daughter, Harriott Pinckney Horry, announcing President George
Washington's visit to their home, Hampton Plantation, in 1791.*
COURTESY OF THE SOUTH CAROLINA HISTORICAL SOCIETY

"Shush, Polly; stop crying please. I'm fine." Strength flooded back into her arms and legs. She reached over to gather her sister into her arms, kissing the top of her head.

"But sister, you fell on the ground and it frightened me so much. I talked to you and you didn't answer me," Polly whimpered, eyes wide with fear.

"Hush, lovey. I'm well now. Just a wee scare for a moment. Now, be a big girl and help me stand up."

Eliza rose slowly to her feet, aware of the total fatigue surging through her body. Closing her eyes and breathing deeply to clear her head, she heard heavy footsteps and turned as Nicholas Cromwell sauntered through the doorway. He stopped abruptly and found himself face to face with her.

Eliza stepped forward, a surprising anger filling her—like acid poured into an empty jug. "Do you call yourself an indigo maker?" she asked in a low voice, green eyes shimmering dangerously.

His face turned crimson and his eyes darted back and forth to scrutinize the others. Facing Eliza, he shrugged and answered belligerently. "One of the best on Montserrat," he said in a splintered voice, blinking irritatingly.

"Then why did you ruin my indigo crop?" she shot back, her face knotted in anguish. "You purposely poured too much limewater into the solution to change the shade." Eliza's eyes burned with outraged tears. Surprised at the intensity of her anger, she suppressed it before it spiraled out of control.

All colour had drained from Mr. Cromwell's face. He stood stiff and silent.

She glared at the man, hating every inch of him. She loathed his florid face, glistening mouth, and the cold, dead look in his eyes. The way he stood there—legs spread apart with his fat hands clasped behind his back.

"WHY, I ask you, Mr. Cromwell? Why did you harm our crop and attempt to destroy my family? We trusted you!"

She advanced toward him so forcefully he took a quick step backwards, visibly terrified by her intensity. His hard swallow was audible.

"Don't strike me, please. I feared I would ruin trade for Montserrat if your dye succeeded," he sniveled.

Eliza's brilliant eyes burned with disgust. Pressing her lips together to stop their trembling, she turned from him and stormed out the door. Polly ran after her, eyes brimming.

Mr. Dawson's face registered shock and then fury. Turning slowly to Nicholas Cromwell, he couldn't remember a time when he wanted to hit someone more. He wanted to grind his fist against Cromwell's lips until they were bruised and bleeding. Curbing the impulse, he lowered his voice and moved his face close to Cromwell's. "Pack your things. You will be gone by nightfall."

He turned to follow Eliza out the door.

Facing Eliza, he reached for her small hands and held them between his own. "Eliza, you should be very proud. You have succeeded in producing indigo in South Carolina, even with that cad deliberately ruining the dye. Your suspicions about Mr. Cromwell were correct." He searched her red-rimmed eyes, now swimming in tears.

"However, next year you will produce only the finest grade. Congratulations, my friend. This is a brilliant accomplishment!" His smile glowed with affection.

As she tried to speak, a sob split her voice—now softer, with more rounded corners than sharp edges. Swallowing hard, her voice cracking with mounting emotion, she nodded. "Thank you, Factor Dawson. Now could you please take me to my mother?"

chapter twenty-six

NICHOLAS CROMWELL DID NOT DEPART FROM THE Carolinas. Two weeks after his stormy dismissal from Wappoo, Colonel Pinckney came by to see Eliza and her family. He rose to greet her as she entered the sitting room.

"Brilliantly done, my little visionary," he congratulated her with an embrace, his grin blossoming into a joyful smile. "I feel certain you and others have informed Major Lucas of this sensational news. It is without doubt the main topic of conversation in Charles Town."

Eliza blushed. Although this recognition brought her immense comfort, it also embarrassed her when others praised her. Especially Colonel Pinckney. She nodded modestly and lowered her eyes. "Yes, we've written Papa and are awaiting his response as to where to go from here."

"You beat all the odds! Do you know that, Eliza dear? Even I doubted it could be done. And your timing is brilliant! The war with Spain is cutting off access to the established indigo markets, providing the opportunity for indigo to get a foothold here in the Carolinas." Observing her closely, he saw that her emotions were very close to the surface—her inner turmoil clearly visible on her strained face.

He reached into his coat pocket and pulled out a letter from her father's attorney. Eliza took it from him and read it quickly. When she had finished, she glanced up at him in disbelief.

"Is this stating that we must keep Mr. Cromwell under our employment?" she asked, plainly shaken. "After he betrayed me, sabotaged us and took our money to do so? I think not!" Her vivacious green eyes burned with anger.

"I'm afraid so, Miss Eliza. Hear me out. Your father had signed a contractual agreement with him and lawfully must pay him according to the terms, which will end in six months' time. His attorney and I have spoken and we've come up with a solution we believe should be suitable."

Eliza knew that her father was a man of honour and would keep his part of the contract. She and her family had already decided not to make the dye this year but would grow a large crop of indigo and save the seeds to plant next year. By then, her father would send her another indigo maker and they would make very good dye. She fought her anger. Breathing deeply, she could feel it slowly receding.

"Pray enlighten me to your plan," she said after a long moment.

"We might send him to work under Overseer Murray at the Garden Hill Plantation. He would work in the fields and supervise no one."

She smiled. "Yes, I quite like that idea. But will he agree to be a mere worker?"

"Apparently he cares not what he does as long as he retains the large salary your father is paying him."

"Sir, how do you know this? Has he been 'round to see the attorney?" she asked, incredulously.

"Oh yes, the very next day after he was forced to leave your plantation. Mr. Cromwell showed the attorney a copy of his contract and made quite a fuss about your not fulfilling your end of the agreement. So we've been forced to come up with a quick resolution."

"What bloody cheek the man has!" There was a brief flash

of fire in Eliza's arresting eyes. "Very well then, just make certain I shall never have to set eyes upon him again."

Colonel Pinckney nodded and pulled out another letter for Eliza. It was from Cameron, and had just arrived on yesterday's schooner. Her facial features softened into a deep smile; a hopeful nod of thanks transformed her spirit.

"Mary Bartlett sends her love, as does my Elizabeth. Oh, and Mary mentioned to me that you have recently planted a few oak trees to be made available for ship timbers in the future."

Eliza fixed her eyes on him, a faint smile playing on her lips. "Oh yes, Colonel Pinckney. I fell to thinking of the years ahead when ships would be built here in the Carolinas. That will require fine planking and great timbers which we could provide. My Papa approves of this new scheme, but perhaps you…" She watched as a look of pleasure spread across his face. "Pray do not think my projects simply whims, as one day they may be triumphs."

He laughed out loud. "Little visionary, just look at what you've done with the indigo plant! I would never question your intuition and the detailed research you do for your projects. I believe those fig trees you planted last year will also be a money maker for your family." His eyebrows lifted. "I sit in awe of your visions."

Eliza was relieved. If truth be told, she sought his approval in her schemes, certainly more so than anyone else's, with the exception of her father.

As he rose to leave, Charles Pinckney suddenly remembered the package at his side. "Oh my, I'd almost forgotten the package. This arrived from London for your family."

Polly dashed into the room at that moment, most certainly having eavesdropped on the conversation. "Colonel Pinckney, what have you brought us?" she asked ingenuously, as if her sixth sense had alerted her to the arrival of gifts.

"Let's open it together, lovey," interjected her sister with an amused look. "The notation inside indicates that Papa ordered it for us. I wonder what it could be." Curiosity was getting the better of both girls as they ripped open the box and plunged through the contents.

"'Tis material for new gowns! Oh my! Just look at the delicate gauze and the colours of Pompadour silk! Polly, let us hasten to show Mama! I believe there is enough for all three of us!" squealed Eliza. "We can use it to make our gowns for the King's Birthday Ball!"

Polly's face fell. "Humph, you and Mama may be attending, but you know I shan't and that is simply not right," she pouted, still not acknowledging the presence of their guest.

"Polly, you know I'll bring you back the pretty muff I spoke about, so pray do not fret." Eliza managed to console her naughty sister, who looked up mollified and finally broke into a reluctant smile.

As she fingered the lovely material in her room, Ann Lucas praised her husband's selections and professed amazement that he had ordered the fabrics for them sight-unseen. Eliza wondered if Mrs. Boddicott had selected them.

Writing in her journal that evening, Eliza realized it was gradually becoming easier to address her tribulations.

Is it my maturity, or the fact that my achievement with the indigo makes me more self-confident? The problems are still with me, but I seem to accept and contend with them better. The war with Spain goes on; we must still wait for Papa's infrequent letters and worry about his health or his getting wounded. Mama's failure to recover is never far from my thoughts; my daily management of the properties and care of the slaves makes me weary; then I come to realize that Polly has a dire need for friends her own age. The troubles go on and on but somehow, my God is providing me with inner peace about them. At least Cameron's letter assures me he is in good health and happy to be with General Oglethorpe, so that is one less trepidation. My brothers are again well and may be able to visit Charles Town in the near future. Even my own future seems insignificant when one weighs it against true tribulations. I am an extremely fortunate young lady.

chapter twenty-seven

"There is a moment in late autumn when the leaves curling on the trees and those fallen to the ground are in equilibrium: golden dry pools spreading under gold-crested oaks. The forest floor mirrors the treetops, and the trunks almost reflect a painter's palette of red-gold and orange flora. The unblemished autumn sky seems lit from below by these fiery treetops. And then arrives the vibrant magnificence of the sky as it also spins gold, red and orange, before reluctantly accepting its mantle of darkness."

Eliza blushed as she listened to her own words—expressions she had written in her last letter to her friend Mary Bartlett. To her surprise, Charles Pinckney was repeating them verbatim as they sat together in his parlour at Belmont Plantation.

"Did I surprise you, Miss Eliza?" He scanned her face with amusement.

"Why yes. 'Tis only a school girl's random thoughts." Her eyes averted his. "Did you like them?"

"Of course. I found them to be particularly good and so I memorized them."

Eliza was flabbergasted. Her mind seemed to be floating

above her as she listened to him; he spoke as if her writing were exciting and poignant. When she finally replied, it sounded to her ears as if she were speaking in the voice of a passing stranger. "It's just that I am perplexed that Mary would find them interesting enough to share with you."

A broad smile spread across Charles Pinckney's face and his eyes crinkled at the corners. "Did you not know that she shares most of your letters with Elizabeth and me? Naturally, not the personal portions, but she often reads us the vivid descriptions of your plantation and the comments on your family." He was surprised at her bewilderment, fearing he had said too much. His eyebrows lifted in doubt.

"Pray do not fret over it, Mr. Pinckney. I should have asked her to share my missives, but simply did not feel you would find my prose to be of interest." Blushing deeply, Eliza realized that his opinion did indeed matter to her. But why was it so important?

"Very well then, shall we discuss your father's promotion? Mrs. Lucas must be quite proud of Major Lucas, is she not? Or rather, Lieutenant Governor Lucas," he announced, clearing his throat.

Eliza's face lit up. "Oh yes; we all are! Imagine: *Lieutenant Governor of Antigua*! Of course that may dictate it will be even more time until we see him here in the Carolinas. And he will continue his military duties. But Mama and I understand that it is quite a remarkable recognition from England."

"It certainly is!"

"Colonel Pinckney, does that imply that there is little possibility of him exchanging his military post in Antigua for one in Georgia or South Carolina?"

"Only time will tell, Eliza." Changing the subject, he asked gently, "Have you heard recently from Mr. Schiller?"

"Not in a while. I believe he is still in Georgia with General Oglethorpe. It is strange, because I feel a strong dislike for the General since my father was not given his position of Royal Governor of Georgia. General Oglethorpe has even been called a bully by some, yet my friend Cameron thinks quite highly of him."

Charles Pinckney shook his head and grinned. "Tell me, how is bonny Polly enjoying her schooling in Charles Town?" he asked.

"Oh that. So you know that she attends several weeks a month for now and only when I am in Charles Town visiting Mrs. Mary Perrie Cleland and her husband John. Their home on Union Street is quite convenient to the school. Mama will not yet permit her to board full-time at Mrs. Hick's School, as she considers Charles Town a bit dangerous because of the Spanish situation."

She gave him a very direct look. "I don't mind telling you I've written to Papa explaining that Mama's indulgence of Polly has made it necessary for her to board. I really did not want to overrule Mama's decision, but she does not realize what she has done to my younger sister by allowing her to stay home. Fortunately, I have Mrs. Hicks in my corner. We are slowly convincing Mama that it is so much better for Polly to be around girls her own age." She gave him a wide smile. "And Polly simply adores studying there! You know how outgoing and sociable she is!"

"That I do! Allow me to speak with Ann about it on my next visit to Wappoo. I also believe the child should be receiving a formal education. You, my dear friend, have too many other duties to fulfill." A smile spread over his face. "Are you still schooling the Negro girls on Wappoo?"

"Oh yes sir! I fully intend them to be school mistresses for the rest of the Negro children. Both Mama and Papa seem pleased with the idea."

"As am I, my little visionary. You are always thinking of others, which makes it even more remarkable." He rose as his wife entered the room. "Come sit with us, my love. Are you feeling better this afternoon?"

Elizabeth Pinckney had been complaining of severe headaches and an upset stomach for the past two days. Eliza considered

returning to Wappoo, feeling that Elizabeth felt obligated to entertain her during her visit.

"You have both been so gracious to me once again. I feel I
should refer to you as "Auntie and Uncle" since I am so fond
of you. However, I must return to the plantation tomorrow.
There is simply so much for me to carry out there before we
meet again at the King's Birthday Ball."

Elizabeth giggled. "Oh yes, Eliza. I rather fancy that. Please
call me *Auntie*...how charming. And you, Charles, would you
like to be called *Uncle?*"

His face flushed. "If you wish to call me that, Eliza, it would
be fine with me."

Observing him closely, Eliza got the impression that it really
would not be gratifying to him. Perhaps he considered himself more her age, although he was at least twenty years her
senior. Or, when she studied his eyes, she sometimes detected a
warmth and tenderness that intrigued her.

෴

The afternoon was still warm; unusual for early fall. Eliza
spent over an hour reclined under her special oak tree by the
river, writing a long letter to her brothers and the Boddicotts.
She was tired and her hand ached from gripping the pen for
such a long time. She considered leaving just as the mocking
bird began his song. With a quick smile and wave to carry on,
she settled back down and decided to re-read her missive: as
good a reason as any to spend more time outdoors and enjoy
her little warbler.

*No doubt you have heard about the "Battle of the Bloody
Marsh" on St. Simons Island, Georgia in July past. My
friend Cameron fought there under General Oglethorpe, and
they defeated the Spanish. Because of that battle and sub-
sequent reports that the Spanish were regrouping to attack
Georgia and South Carolina, palisades were driven around*

the lower end of the peninsula where Charles Town sits. I've not yet seen this but know this through Cameron's letter, which has just recently arrived, and from reports of others in Charles Town. Cameron was stationed temporarily on a small island in Georgia: Jekyl Island, I believe he called it, where he and others protected Ft. Frederica, the large Georgia military garrison, from the Spanish vessels in the waterways. He told me in his letter that he feels "mentally and emotionally beaten down" (his words) and has taken a leave from military service. He is recovering somewhere in Georgia and does not know if he will return to this part of the country. Sad as that strikes me, somehow I knew in my heart that we were only meant to be friends.

On another topic, Mrs. Boddicott, I am remiss in not thanking you immediately after the large package arrived from London. Those lovely pieces of fabric for Mama and me in addition to the lappets to embroider for our hair are exquisite, and we are all looking forward to getting them made into frocks for the King's Birthday Ball. Along that train of thought, have you received the seventy pounds I sent you for Mama's lovely four wheel post chaise? It too is stunning, and she looks so very lovely when she rides the streets of Charles Town or attends church services in it.

As each of you knows, I cherish reading my Bible. How necessary I find it to lay down a plan for our conduct in life. God in His goodness provided mankind with reason, which is His natural revelation and His written word, revealed and delivered to mankind by His son, Jesus Christ. As Anglicans, we believe in the rational approach to religion, even at the expense of having to reject emotionalism.

I've become rather good friends of George Whitefield during his time in this area. He brought "The Great Awakening" to

Charles Town in January of 1740. In doing so, he thoroughly antagonized Mr. Alex Garden, with whom I also enjoy a friendship. Mr. Garden took Mr. Whitefield before an ecclesiastical court and had him suspended. It was all quite the talk of the town!

Thomas, do you remember when you were so sick I encouraged you to not despair of being cured but to resign yourself to God's will? I praise God that you are now well, yet know in my heart of hearts that He is in control of our lives. I myself continue to suffer agonizing and severe headaches. I do not know the reason for this infirmity, but have discussed it with Charles and Elizabeth (who also suffers from the same) in great detail. We have decided that prayer is the answer, and that it will be lifted in His timing.

To conclude, let me share a short poem I've written inspired by my favourite songster, the mocking bird. The very first time he opened his soft pipes this spring, he motivated me with the spirit of rhyming and caused me to produce the following three lines.

> Sing on thou charming mimic of the feathered kind
> And let the rational a lesson learn from thee
> To mimic, not defects, but harmony.

> Your most obliged humble Servant,
> Eliza Lucas

chapter twenty-eight

HIS MAJESTY'S JAMAICA FLEET HAD SAILED INTO THE Charles Town harbor to protect South Carolina. Seven transports carrying over five hundred of Brigadier General Wentworth's soldiers were on board; just in time to attend the King's Birthday Ball on October 30, 1742.

Eliza and her mother were staying in the city with Mr. and Mrs. Cleland. Ann knew that Captain Broderick, a friend of her husband, would be on one of the ships. She was so excited to receive "fresh news" from George. Eliza pleaded with her to accompany her to the ball, since they both had new gowns sewn for the occasion. But her mother was adamant.

"Eliza dear, I feel fortunate to have made it this far. I have enjoyed riding in the beautiful chaise once again, admiring the lovely houses tucked among the thickets of Cypress trees, oleander and swamp myrtle. From this chaise I am able to inhale the spicy tang of mud and salt: an unexpected balm to my jangled nerves. How I've missed those aromas," she reflected. With a half laugh, she turned to her daughter. "You go and enjoy yourself. Perhaps next year I shall accompany you," she smiled.

Eliza was excited as she prepared herself for the dance. Her thoughts wandered to previous dances, where Cameron was either at her side or not far from her. If only she could see him again! She fought back tears pooling in the corners of her eyes.

I am almost twenty years old, she whispered to herself. *I shall enjoy myself and celebrate my December birthday with friends while we are here.*

When Eliza entered the ballroom, her eyes widened and she squealed with delight. The whole room was luminescent. She surveyed the other ladies dressed in brocade, taffeta, satin and silk, shod in high-heeled matching slippers. Their cloaks were expansive to cover enormous hoops, and made of silk or satin and lined and quilted, set in small yokes. Hoops started at the waist and extended the skirt like a barrel.

She knew she looked as graceful and stylish as the others in her gown of numerous layers of a translucent silver fabric trimmed with bejeweled ribbons. To the observant eye, Eliza appeared to be clothed in a billowing cloud that descended in shimmering waves around her willowy body. Her lips twitched into a delighted smile as she sensed the effect she generated on others.

The women's jewels, as well as the officers' dress swords, epaulets and shiny buttons, caught the light from the hundreds of candles shimmering in the overhead chandeliers. The men, outfitted in square-cut coats, long waistcoats, satin breeches that came just below the knee, and silver-buckled shoes, were absolutely elegant. Most of them, excluding the military officers, powdered their hair and tied it back with a dark ribbon.

The dancers were enthusiastic but a bit tentative. Most had had few opportunities to practice the dance steps they knew were in fashion back in England. These men seemed amusingly concerned about getting the rather complex steps right.

Eliza danced the first minuet with Captain Broderick, who then introduced her to a younger officer, Mr. Small. They waltzed several dances together while Eliza listened to a great deal of flashy nonsense before pleading weariness and asking to be escorted to her table.

Mr. Charles Pinckney stood up at his table near the corner. He approached her and took her hand. "Miss Eliza, my wife has been asking about you. Would you care to sit with us for a spell?"

Her eyes smiled at his quick thinking as they took their seats. "Sir, did you realize that I needed rescue?" she whispered with a charmingly wayward grin.

"Yes, from the expression on your face, it appeared that you did." Brushing his gaze lightly over her luminescent auburn/golden hair and elegant silver-tinged gown he whispered, "You are ever so lovely this evening, Eliza." She felt her face flush.

Elizabeth and Charles filled Eliza in on the local news as they sat together sharing refreshments and enjoying the music. Two young officers from the ships approached their table and asked Eliza to dance, and to each she replied that perhaps later as she was catching up with old friends.

The band struck up a beautiful waltz and Elizabeth spoke up.

"Charles, I think this would be a nice minuet for you and Eliza. She has come to have a good time and I know she loves to dance, don't you dear?"

"Oh, I am quite content just chatting with you both," Eliza answered hastily, taken aback by Elizabeth's proposal.

Charles turned to her with a slight bow, extending his hand. "Will you give me the honour of this next dance, Miss Eliza?"

As they whirled around the dance floor, Eliza could not help basking in the admiring glances. Her smoky green eyes shone under the chandelier's soft glow. When the music changed to a cotillion waltz, Charles and Eliza flawlessly adjusted their steps and tempo in tune with the band.

Eliza realized with a start that this was without doubt the most thrilling, dreamlike experience she had ever felt at a ball—moving slowly, instinctively around the dance floor with his arm guiding her. Charles sensed the abrupt stiffness in her back and spread his fingers wide along the base of her spine, his fingers reaching from her tailbone up to her waist. There was a layer of dress and a layer of corsetry between his hand

and her skin, yet she could feel the heat of his fingers. A warm melting pleasure spread through her body.

Charles's voice sounded husky and Eliza felt herself fluctuating from hot to cold. She nodded slightly to acknowledge his remarks and sank a little closer into his arms, close enough to feel the warmth and pleasant scent of his neck when she inhaled.

"Eliza dear, are you feeling well?" he asked, noting her slight intake of breath.

"Oh yes. I'm simply enjoying the music and the moment," she said, closing her eyes for a long moment. He lowered his chin to her luxurious hair, shining like polished mahogany.

"Your hair smells like spring flowers," he whispered.

After lingering there for a tantalizing few seconds, his hand left her back and he tucked Eliza's arm in his to lead her off the dance floor.

The last thing she remembered before reaching their table were his words, whispered softly and tenderly so only she could hear. "You are like a poem of joy—a pillar of hope."

Her eyes filled unexpectedly with warm tears.

chapter twenty-nine

L ETTERS FROM LIEUTENANT COLONEL LUCAS WERE arriving with greater regularity since his son George had joined him as an ensign in Antigua. Against his mother's and sister's advice, he had chosen to pursue a military career.

Ann Lucas's health had improved simply because her husband and their son George were together again. "Eliza darling, won't it be wonderful when Tommy finishes his school in London and joins us all in Antigua?" Ann's eyes shone with anticipation.

Eliza turned to her mother, stunned by her words. "What did you say, Mama? Are we moving back with Papa?" She tried to throw off the feeling of trepidation that suddenly gripped her. "This is surely news to me."

Her mother smiled pleasantly. "'Tis only a whim of mine, dear. How I'd love to see all of us together again. Perhaps we can sell the three plantations and return to our home in the West Indies."

Eliza's eyes flashed. "No, Mama, we shall not do that! I have finally succeeded in growing a strong crop of indigo and we can actually make a good amount of dye this year. You know that Papa needs the income from it, which requires my running the plantations." She sighed, and her voice softened. "Perhaps you and Polly could go for a long holiday to see them."

Ann lowered her head and turned away. "Most likely we shan't, Eliza. Polly is now studying fulltime at Mrs. Hick's, and Tommy's health is still not good enough for the long journey. We shall do fine right here."

Eliza observed her mother with a twinge of sadness. Ann seldom expressed her wishes and hopes and now that she had, Eliza's self-centeredness had dashed them.

"Oh Mama, I am so sorry. How very selfish of me to only think of my work here. Let us write Papa to see if he might favour your proposal."

She frowned at the memory of her father's recent letter chastising her lack of interest in his "securing" a husband for her. Although Eliza understood that marriages were frequently "arranged" by fathers, she was too strong-willed and independent to accept that interference, especially when he was too far away to personally discuss the issue. She knew she could manage the mortgages by herself if left to cultivate the indigo. She wanted no part of the newest "wealthy prospect" her father had singled out for her.

Papa dear, always mindful of your generosity, I should feel compelled to obey you. But as you've instructed me over the years, I must speak my mind; especially on this subject because it is of the utmost importance to my peace and happiness. Since you have proposed Mr. L to me, you should know I am sorry I cannot have sentiments of him favourable enough to take time to dwell on the subject...and I beg to say to you that even the riches of Peru and Chile, if he had them put together, could not purchase a sufficient esteem to make him my husband. Marriage, being of such consequence, requires the nicest distinction of humour and sentiment.

This proposal was especially annoying to Eliza because two years prior, when she was eighteen years old, her father had chosen another rich prospect for her. She had responded to that proposition with a gentle but firm refusal as well, hoping that her father would allow her judgment to prevail.

I have so slight a knowledge of him I can form no judgment at all. At this point, a single life is my only choice. Believe me, Papa, when I recount that I am enjoying my life immensely at this tender age of eighteen. I do hope you will put aside the thoughts of my marrying for the next two or three years at least.

Seeking to appease him with a cheerful change of topic, Eliza went on to thank him once again for sending the Negro indigo maker from Montserrat, Jasper Boyles, who was everything that Mr. Cromwell was not: well-mannered, kind, considerate and an excellent teacher in the art of dye making.

"You doan' need me here, Mistress Eliza," he teased, "'cuz you knows all 'bout dis' indigo. Jus' looka how strong dese plants you growin' are, and see dere rich deep colah."

"Thank you Jasper. Yet I need you to guide me through the dye process until I no longer feel like a mere novice. You command the nuances of indigo to make the superior dye," she smiled widely. "Every time I see our results my confidence soars."

Jasper was respected by workers and plantation owners alike. Eliza invited men from surrounding plantations to work with him and learn as much as they could. She knew ultimate success would depend on everyone's working together. They all continued to grow rice as well, since the indigo crop was cultivated during the reverse planting season.

⌘

The world was green and rich and alive. Paths had been cleared and azaleas grew along them in staggering, willful bloom. Wildflowers and evergreen spears grew side by side with magnolia and tupelo on the hills. Lilies danced in the wild fields, forming a colourful parade, and the delicate yellow irises were already blooming in the spring shadows like tiny sunbeams. It was late spring and Eliza was absorbed in her world of nature.

She heard the twitter of birds and breathed in the perfume of the dark earth and the ripe flowers. Slivers of sunlight shimmered through the tangled canopy of branches and moss and dappled the forest floor. Their lovely patterns turned the green light into something hinting of gold. She reached the river and stretched out on her stomach, dangling her long arms into the water, appreciating as always her place of great mystery and beauty.

"Most glorious nature, you are water to my soul," she whispered reverently, conscious of the magical moment she was experiencing. The air around her was sweet with the breath of apples, the aroma still clinging to her senses from the orchards she had just walked through. After a while she stretched her long limbs and sat up. Removing her pen from her apron pocket, she began to write.

These musings will never become part of a letter to my friends or family. I come to you, my river friend, and to you, my God, in great need of consolation. My life feels as if it is in shambles, and I am at a loss as to how to handle it. My father wants all of us to return to Antigua, and I do not wish to go. I fear this is a direct result of his regiment's devastating loss to the Spanish at La Guaira and Puerto Cabello, Venezuela, where my father was in command. His troops broke ranks and fled in disobedience. Papa is heartsick over this military defeat, and now longs for us to be close to him. He wants my brother George to escort Mama, Polly and me back to the West Indies. His plan also includes Tommy leaving England to join us. Naturally Mama wants to join him, as does Polly. I, selfishly, want to stay here for the indigo—my indigo, for which I've toiled so incredibly hard. This year I am convinced I can make a top-grade dye! There will be so much seed this year that I can finally plant an enormous crop for next year. And if I am truly honest, I must admit that I do not want to leave Elizabeth Pinckney, who is not well and whom I love. And even more so, I dread leaving Charles Pinckney, whom I have discovered I love in an unusual way—something even I do not understand. He is my mentor, my companion, and my closest friend, but there is something more in my heart, which I dare not attempt to pursue. Only you, Lord, know how I feel, and we shall keep it closely contained between us.

The wind sang strangely in her ears: *see you soon.* She smiled a soft smile.

That afternoon Colonel Pinckney arrived unexpectedly at her house.

"Eliza, the word is going around that your father wishes to send all of you to the West Indies. Is this true?"

She dropped her head, her large eyes expressive. "Yes sir, I fear that it is."

"I have a proposition to make to you and your mother. Elizabeth is not well, as you know, yet she requests a tour of farewell visits. She has asked me to bring you along as her companion, and I cannot deny her any request. She refers to you as her 'tonic.' Such is the esteem she feels for you."

Eliza's face brightened. "Let us discuss this with my mother, but I feel certain she will allow me to accompany you."

Ann encouraged her daughter to travel with the Pinckneys, so it was settled.

They got along well together on the tour, enjoying each place they stopped to explore. The highlight of the trip for Eliza was a week's visit with the William Middletons at Crowfield. She took great pleasure in their beautiful gardens, and was finally able to read Samuel Richardson's romantic novel *Pamela*. She had looked forward to reading it since her friend Mary Bartlett had told her how much she enjoyed it.

The two young women sat side by side as the golden afternoon light deepened to amber, orange and fiery pink.

"I am quite annoyed that Pamela exhibits that disgusting liberty of praising herself and repeating all the compliments others give her. Whatever happened to modesty? Praise should be spoken by others. I personally feel that people say nice things only to encourage me and I take them to help me aspire to higher goals. However, we should not put much stock in those words or allow our heads to swell because of them." Eliza was adamant.

"Eliza, she is only a country girl. She knows nothing of life and therefore, it is natural for her to be pleased with praise. She simply has not enough art to conceal it."

"Mary, I will say this. The author did well in giving her that particular defect, because without it, the character of Pamela would be terribly unnatural." Eliza grinned. How well she understood the internal conflict of pride and modesty.

Eliza was consumed with asking Mary's opinion about a personal matter. "Mary, would you kindly give me your definition of love?"

Her friend faced her, a perplexed expression on her face. "In general, or do you wish my personal definition?" she asked.

Eliza dropped her eyes. "I know nothing of the definition, but I believe I may have experienced it. Yet I am not certain," she added timidly.

Mary took both her hands in hers. "Look at me, dear Eliza. When you fall in love, you will know. But often it fosters inside your heart until it is ready to spawn."

Eliza smiled and hugged her, grateful for a friend's understanding.

⁂

The trip had been a happy experience for the Pinckneys, but did not prove to be as beneficial to Elizabeth's health as they had hoped. Her illness continued and eventually drove her to remain in bed. Eliza sent gifts and delicacies as well as clever notes, and continued to visit Belmont whenever she could.

On one of the visits, Elizabeth asked her husband to leave the room.

"Eliza, I have written your father explaining my reasons why I do not consider it wise for you to go to Antigua. He may choose to share the details with you; I will not. But I want you to know that my reasons are selfish, and primarily in the best interests of my family." Eliza was bewildered and remained silent. She loved both Elizabeth and Charles, and could not bear to see either of them so unhappy. These were extremely difficult times for all of them. Her anxiety mounted when she thought of leaving them and returning to the West Indies.

After Eliza's departure Charles sat at Elizabeth's bedside, wrapping a cool towel around her throbbing, feverish head. Gradually she focused her eyes on his and spoke. "My beloved Charles, I am now willing to step down and let her take my place. You must have your children with this young woman, who already loves you."

"Elizabeth, pray do not speak of that. You must remain with me," he whispered, dread tightening his throat.

Charles monitored her with deeply troubled eyes, unable to answer. His heart stung with sadness. He refused to think about how easily his life could be shattered. If he recognized and accepted this reality, he would surely lose his mind.

chapter thirty

ON DECEMBER 19, 1743, THREE DAYS BEFORE ELIZA LUCAS'S twenty-first birthday, she stood on the wharf in Charles Town awaiting the arrival of the Royal Governor of South Carolina, James Glen. She listened enraptured as the cannons boomed out a welcome to His Excellency, who had finally arrived to take up residency in Charles Town.

Eliza enjoyed the pomp and circumstances of the Governor's arrival. Edward Aitkin, of His Majesty's Council, and Colonel Charles Pinckney stood on either side of her. They were obviously also caught up in the pomp and ceremony. Yet Eliza could not help but notice how downhearted Charles seemed because of his beloved wife's critical illness.

Elizabeth Pinckney's condition continued to deteriorate. Charles soon retired from his duties and kept vigil at her bedside. At last, her body worn down from her long illness, Elizabeth Pinckney slipped away on January 13, 1744 from complications of an enlarged spleen. Her death came as a relief to those who loved her. Even with the deep sense of loss in her heart, Eliza deemed it a reflection of the goodness of God.

One month later, Eliza's brother George landed in Charles

Town, thin and pale from his own extended illness. He brought the bad news that young Tommy's health had not improved; he would remain in England. In spite of this dismal news, having her son back with them renewed Mrs. Lucas's strength and she attempted to participate in their plantation life.

"George, tell me more about your father," she insisted, with rekindled hope. "Will he come himself for us, or has he sent you?"

"Mama, he believes that a British man-of-war will soon be available to sail here and transport all of us back to Antigua."

Eliza's heart dropped. "When, George? Have you any idea of how soon?"

"Papa thinks it will be late spring," he replied, noting her downcast face. "We should be able to get the indigo seeds planted by then, Eliza. If not, I'm certain Mr. Deveaux will help us out."

Over the next few weeks Eliza avoided discussing her feelings with anyone, and was kept occupied packing for the move. She expressed her inner turmoil with the written word instead.

Am I to live out my life moving on...never finding the one person with whom I can build a satisfying life? Will joy elude me forever? These days my thoughts are as dismal as the harsh cawing of the gulls in the winter winds.

❧❧❧

Eliza gazed at the overcast sky, which had turned the colour of old iron—bitter, remote and forbidding. Dusk was slowly descending and the meadows were filling up with shadows. A faint mist rose above the winding Wappoo Creek, thick and vaporous, like a gray veil. Through that veil she dimly caught the glimpse of a pettiauger pulling up to the Wappoo landing.

Who could that be? she wondered. *We are expecting no one. I shall go outside to get a better look.* Walking swiftly through the bitter cold to the bluff's edge, her eyes swept over the landing.

Much to her surprise, the visitor was Charles Pinckney. She could hear the gaiety in his voice as he shouted up to her. "Hello Miss Eliza! What a sight you are to my sore eyes on this gray, wintry day!"

She burst out laughing—a sound so full of life it sounded like the peal of bells. "What brings you here, my friend?"

He did not answer her until he reached her side. She noticed a burning intensity in his dark eyes. "I've come to check on your family, and to gather news about your father. When is he expecting your family to leave for the West Indies?"

"Sir, I beg you not to ask me about our move," she snapped, her face crumbling. "It is simply too upsetting to speak about." Her eyes glistened with disappointment.

Charles Pinckney took her arm to guide her up the hill. He was mindful of how warm and soft she felt. They turned to face the water in tandem, gazing in wonder as extended fingers of tangerine and rose colours suddenly leaped across the dusky blue horizon. Gone were the mist and dark shadows.

"Oh Charles! Did you see that amazing sunset?" She realized with astonishment that she had just called him *Charles*. To cover her embarrassment, she added, "I am sorry I was cross with you. That was certainly no way to receive a guest."

Charles gave her a searching look, uncomfortable with what he was about to ask her. "Miss Eliza, may I speak with your mother and your brother George…privately?"

Eliza's eyes widened at his request. She nodded, muttering that she needed to go to the stables to check on her stallion. She left him standing at the threshold of their home.

Rubbing Star's silky nose, Eliza unveiled her thoughts.

"Star, what are you thinking? Do you wonder if we shall take you with us or leave you behind? I cannot bear the notion of leaving this area, which has become my home, and you are such a part of it. I despise the idea of returning to Antigua, when just a few years ago I rebelled against coming here. And leaving Charles—how can I ever do that? He is my dearest friend and I depend on him in so many ways." Choking back tears, she shook her head and hugged her stallion. "Oh, Star, isn't life so senseless at times?"

Star snorted and tossed his heavy head. Eliza buried her face in his neck, warm tears slipping from her closed eyes.

She must have dozed off for a moment, leaning against her horse. Her eyes flew open when she heard footsteps on the path and Charles Pinckney stood in the small doorway. His face seemed relaxed and hopeful and the intensity of his eyes held her in its dark brown depths. She felt captive to those fathomless eyes.

"Eliza, for some absurd reason, I had not realized how utterly dear you have become to me until I learned that George was booking passage to take you and your family back to Antigua."

Eliza stared at him, transfixed. She studied the long plane of his cheeks, the curve of his forehead, and the shape of his deep brown eyes sloping down slightly on the sides.

He cleared his throat, spellbound and encouraged by Eliza's brilliant gaze. In this light her eyes were almost amber—it was like gazing into a flowing stream and watching the moon bathing them in a pale glow.

"I cannot wait a minute longer to ask you, my darling. I want you to marry me and stay with me always. I cannot bear to think of life without you. You must not leave South Carolina." His words gushed out, searing the back of his throat and taking his breath away.

Eliza stood immobilized; she reached for words but found her voice stuck somewhere. With her wide expressive eyes riveted on Charles, she finally addressed him in a strangled voice.

"It seems nothing short of a miracle that you wish to marry me." Her heart was pounding as if it would burst her ribs. She felt an explosion building up inside her.

Charles had been prepared for an assortment of answers, but certainly not that one.

"My little love, you have brought something into my life that I've never known." Reaching for her hand he smiled warmly.

Eliza glimpsed tenderness in his velvet eyes, now quiet on her face. "Eliza, will you kindly answer my question."

Eliza heard the flutter of night beyond the door: the wings and whines that were the music of the marsh. An owl hooted somewhere, and the note seemed stretched—endless and rich.

"What was the question, Charles?"

"Will you be my wife and stay with me here in South Carolina?"

Her throat closed, and not from fear but from hope. Grasping hold of it, she fell into his arms. With tears streaking her face and mouth, she reached up to touch the side of his face. Sliding her hand around the back of his neck, she kissed him softly on the lips.

He ran his fingers through her hair, stroking her scalp, outlining her ears, then her eyelids, her lips and finally, his warm hands came to rest on either side of her face. He leaned forward and kissed her so hard she thought she would faint with the sudden flood of pleasure surging through her. His warm breath melted her insides and she felt her legs would collapse.

Charles enfolded her in his embrace, cradling her against his chest. She laughed then; a light lyrical sound washed over them.

"Charles, what have you told my mother? And George?" she managed to murmur.

He released her and burst into a smile. "Your mama has given her approval. George also. Yet I must have your father's approval before George and your family leave. That is why this is so sudden, my dearest one. I would have preferred to pay court and woo you, but time is against us."

"Pray do not mention that ever again," she grinned. "We love each other and…oh my, you do love me, do you not?" She blushed a deep pink.

Charles laughed aloud—a deep joyful sound that filled the air. "I love you dearly, my little woman. And always shall."

Eliza held his face between her delicate fingers. "And I love you, dear Charles. I believe I've always loved you. You just gave me the reason to admit it." Her brows raised in amazement. "Is that possible?" she asked.

"Anything is possible, my beauty. Now, let us repair to the house and tell them you have accepted me!"

The wind had quieted and the moon, thin and pale like a shard of glass, escaped through the clouds.

"Charles, can you smell it? The jasmine? I never asked you, but do you love it as well?"

He looked down at her striking face, bathed in golden moonlight.

"Yes, my love. I always have."

They walked hand in hand as the jasmine blew its heavy sweet fragrance into the night.

chapter thirty-one

E LIZA HAD NO TIME TO WORRY AND WAIT AROUND FOR
the letter of approval from Lieutenant Governor Lucas.
She already considered herself engaged and went about her
daily business, giddy with happiness. She oversaw the preparation of her 1744 indigo planting and by April was in the field
with the workers, making certain the little black seeds were
sown correctly. She even helped dig the furrows in the ground,
applying the techniques she had learned from Jasper. This
time she was taking no chances.

"Come, Polly. You must learn this too. Perhaps you'll be
planting your own field in Antigua." A smile broke through,
lighting up her face as she watched her thirteen-year-old sister.

"No Ma'am. I shall be studying French and learning to
dance properly at the balls," replied Polly, with a giggle and a
toss of her bouncy raven curls.

"This will be our banner year, my sweet! Mr. Deveaux
is again raising a crop, and this year Overseer Murray has
planted a large acreage of indigo at Garden Hill." Eliza found
that even though she was extremely busy, she was at peace.
She and Charles knew in their hearts that her father would
approve of their proposed marriage. She fairly floated on air.

Oh Lord, now I realize why I never felt more than a deep friend-ship for Cameron or the other gentlemen I knew. I measured them all by Charles, who possesses every desirable attribute. I revel in his stimulating conversation and enjoy studying his sensitive face light up with tenderness and compassion. I marvel at his modest manner, even though he holds such distinguished posts of leadership. If there is anything that makes me hesitate, it is that the eminent people of the colony will not consider me suitable for him.

In the end, she took this concern to him. "Oh Charles, you hold such high positions in the community, and I am simply a young woman with no particular gifts. Will the Charles Town society accept me into your circle?" she asked with anxiety.

Charles threw back his head in a hearty laugh. "My darling, allow me to be the judge of your gifts, which are abundant." His dark eyes twinkled as he held her to his chest. "You possess the power to love and to enjoy, which charms and refreshes my soul. You have the most questing mind of anyone I know. You are spirited, like a young colt, yet soft and lovely—the most beautiful woman I know." He smiled, "Shall I go on?"

Eliza was holding her breath. She nodded. "Please do."

"Your enthusiasm and admiration for the success of others delights me. You are very generous to everyone you know. I know that in my official life ahead you will be a great asset. Your charm turns strangers into friends. And darling, your loyalty and devotion to old friends, to your family and now to me is what captured my heart. I love you deeply, and I admire you with my all heart and soul."

Eliza let out a small sigh of bliss. He *did* love her for herself; that was all she needed to know to be convinced that her place in the colony was at his side.

⤫⦿⤬

At last Lieutenant Governor Lucas's letter reached Charles Town. He was extremely pleased with the match, and gave them his blessing. He also offered the most generous settlement he could. Because Wappoo Plantation was mortgaged, he could not offer it as Eliza's dowry. However, he and Ann Lucas gave Colonel Pinckney all of the indigo growing at Wappoo. This pleased Eliza enormously as it showed that her experimentation and hard work had become a main segment of her marriage covenant.

Charles's response to this settlement proposal was a quick visit to Mrs. Lucas and George. "No settlement is necessary. I will marry Eliza for herself and the happiness she will bring us. I am content with no dowry, yet I shall be happy to accept what he so kindly offers."

The days ran together, bittersweet for Eliza and her family who were excited to return to their West Indies island. They were already beginning to miss Eliza. Radiant in newfound happiness, she pushed aside any distress she felt about their impending move to Antigua. The separation would be exceedingly hard on all of them. Because of the expense of moving the family back to Antigua, Eliza refused to have an extravagant wedding. She made several trips into Charles Town with her mother and sister to purchase what she would need for her future wardrobe. On one of those visits, Eliza brought up her other concern with her family's friend in Charles Town, Mrs. Cleland.

"I imagine there is much talk about dear Charles marrying so soon after Elizabeth's death," she prompted.

Mrs. Cleland smiled encouragingly and hastened to reassure her. "Naturally my dear, we have heard some discussion. Those who know you also know how Elizabeth esteemed you, and know that she would wholeheartedly approve of your upcoming marriage."

Eliza nodded. "And surely they understand that the wedding is taking place so soon after her death because of my family's imminent departure?"

"Yes, they do. Fear not, dear child. Will you move to Belmont directly after the ceremony?" asked Mrs. Cleland.

"No. We want to spend as much time as possible with Mama, George and Polly before they sail to Antigua. Papa is pleased we will all be living at Wappoo until the merchant ship sails. You know, he was unable to arrange for them to travel by warship, so now they will not leave until July."

ↄらᎶᎧↄ

Eliza Lucas and Charles Pinckney were quietly married on May 27, 1744 in St. Andrew's Parish. The Reverend William Guy presided over the ceremony. She felt a pang of sadness that her brother and father could not attend. Their reception was held at Wappoo in her beloved garden. Eliza was also accompanied by her "airy choristers," singing from the boughs and bushes. Her exquisite green eyes radiated joy.

"This is truly the most glorious day of my life, my beloved Charles. Thank you for choosing me."

Charles was speechless with emotion. When he recovered his voice, he murmured, "Let us thank God, my love. It is He who has put us together for eternity."

Charles Town

SOUTH CAROLINA
1744-1753

chapter thirty-two

IN THE NEXT FEW WEEKS, EVENTS ESCALATED. FACTOR
Dawson left the shipping business after his wife inherited
a large legacy. Charles's mother Mary fell ill and he needed to
care for her in Charles Town. Accommodations were found for
the Lucas family and their servants to sail to the West Indies
on a merchant brig. Charles communicated with Eliza from
Charles Town that he would be happy to handle the business
that Mr. Dawson had managed for them—news that Eliza
conveyed to her father in a hastily scribbled letter the night
before the ship sailed.

The following morning was the most heartbreaking day of
Eliza's young life. She tried so hard to stay strong for her distressed mother and frightened younger sister, to little avail.

"I cannot leave you, sister," sobbed Polly, clinging to her
billowing skirts on the harbour dock before boarding. "I've
changed my mind. I want to stay at Mrs. Hick's School and
have you come 'round for visits. At least I could see you then."
Eliza saw the broken pain spread across Polly's reddened face.

"Darling, you'll continue your studies in the West Indies.
And soon Papa will send you to London, where I attended
school. Won't that be lovely?" Eliza removed Polly's fingers

from her frock and cradled her against her breast, feeling her sister's racing heartbeat beneath her blouse as her tears spilled on Polly's dark tresses. Gently, Eliza reached over to smooth down the raven ringlets.

Ann Lucas stood by, maintaining her dignity as their friends and family bid them farewell. Eliza noticed that her cheeks were crimson too, and that she looked fatigued.

"George, please take her inside. The excitement is too tiring on Mama. Make sure she lies down. I'll follow momentarily."

Charles kept a close watch on his bride. He felt an overwhelming sorrow that circumstances were dividing this loving family and promised he would find a way to unite them again.

Eliza and Charles remained on the dock beside the still-cold sea, until the ship had sailed out of sight. Then they returned to Wappoo to close up the house and find work for the servants who remained behind. Eliza let them choose where they wished to live. Ezra and Solomon stayed on at Wappoo, taking care of the plantation and overseeing the indigo crop.

"Now my love, I shall carry you off to your new home," smiled Charles. "And we will spend a summer of happiness together."

They moved into the handsome Belmont Plantation, five miles from Charles Town on the Neck, on the Cooper River side. Knowing how much Eliza missed her garden, Charles encouraged her to plant oaks, mulberry and magnolias. Each week they returned to Wappoo, keeping up with the progress of her indigo crop. They both believed this would be the year her efforts would be crowned with genuine success.

⁕⁕⁕

Eliza's 1744 crop was harvested. Seventeen pounds of excellent dye were manufactured at Wappoo Plantation, and a good quality of seed was saved. Mr. Deveaux also made some very good dye from his plants, and the successful indigo plants at Garden Hill were allowed to go to seed. Eliza and Charles passed these tiny seeds out to their neighbours so they could begin planting their own indigo crops the following year.

"My darling, you've done it!" exclaimed Charles, lifting Eliza into the air and twirling her lithe body 'round and 'round with a rich joyfulness he hadn't felt since their wedding. "'Tis proof that a fine grade of indigo can be produced in South Carolina! Now we shall send a sample of the dye to our London agent James Crokott for his expert opinion. And a larger sample to Parliament in England to show them what we have done!"

Eliza's eyes stung; grateful tears slid down her face as she wrapped her arms around her husband's neck. Charles held her tightly, his mouth inhaling the sweet scent of her mahogany hair.

"Will they pay us a bounty on our dye?" she asked him after the emotional interlude.

"Of that I am certain," he answered evenly. "And soon our own colonial government should offer us one here at home."

"Charles, how can you be certain? Perhaps England will not have an interest in such a small amount," worried Eliza.

"It will grow to large amounts, my precious one. England needs dye for her large weaving industry. Because of the general war in Europe, she no longer trades with Spain or France. Our timing is perfect!"

Eliza considered his words. "Yes Charles. Papa wrote me that France made an enormous mistake by sending squadrons to the West Indies to support the Spanish. And then they attacked British merchant ships. Hmm, it is all beginning to make some sense to me."

"Splendid! So now you understand that England must look toward her colonies in the New World for the dye. Parliament will grant South Carolina a bounty to encourage a large-scale production of indigo right here. And you are the visionary, dear Eliza! You were the first one to do it!"

"How soon will they grant that bounty, Charles?" she asked uneasily, feeling the tension return.

"Ah, my little love. You must be very patient. Parliament moves very slowly. I cannot answer that question." He kept his tone gentle.

"But I *hate* waiting! All of my life I've had to endure waiting for this and for that!" she snapped, cutting him off.

Charles studied her flashing eyes. She met his gaze, pressing her lips together to keep them from trembling. He reached for her hand and uncurled her fingers. The back of his fingers stroked her cheek.

"You, my darling, have shown more patience than I believed a woman could possess. I am enormously proud of you and your achievement, and I will do everything possible to see that indigo making becomes a major revenue in our colony. Great wealth will be made from indigo, and you are its pioneer. You were the one to persevere when others gave up." He smiled broadly. "Please, Eliza, just give it a little more of that patience. You will not regret it."

Eliza cried in teary relief, her lips twitching into a shy smile. "I shall learn patience, dear husband. But in the meantime, can we import the eggs of silk worms and produce raw silk?"

Charles laughed happily. "Always the visionary, are you not? Yes dear, we shall grow silk worms straightaway." Scooping her into his arms, he gave her the sensation that he was sheltering every inch of her body. His mouth was warm and soft, his arms a safe and gentle haven.

The sun steamed the nearby marsh like a golden shower of light. They stood at the window, watching the falling stars. Heat pressed its damp fingers against the glass. Charles leaned down and kissed her deeply. Eliza felt his large hands on her back; warm, strong, pressing her into him. She loved the warmth of his hand in the curve of her waist. She caught a hint of his scent as he captured her chin in his teeth—a brief nip that shot an ache down the center of her body.

He stroked her hair, and she felt her muscles unclench. His lips lingered on her neck as she leaned back against him, feeling the heat of his body flow into hers like honey. His confident caresses melted Eliza's insides.

"Come, my lady," he whispered in a voice so low it sent shivers dancing through her. Scooping her up and cradling her against his chest, he carried her to their bed. Sealing his mouth over hers, he urged her body into his. Breathless, their eyes burning with desire, they undressed each other without haste.

Their bodies fell at once into a natural rhythm—like waves on the shore. The vibrations rose and fell, gathering intensity, stealing breath, demanding everything. Passion peaked, leaving them flooded with intoxicating sensations. Eliza's mind seemed to lift above it, release it, permitting nothing but feelings. She was slipping backwards—falling into an enchanting empty space. Grabbing his shoulders, she let herself fall and floated back to earth, like a leaf on a breeze.

As the sparks died down and the colours faded, she settled into his embrace. He brought her closer, discovering that in relaxation her face was even more ethereal, her emerald green eyes more arresting. Charles fell asleep with thoughts of her shimmering auburn hair, highlighted in the flickering rays of their bedroom candle.

chapter thirty-three

ELIZA CONTINUED HER CUSTOM OF WRITING COUNTLESS letters to friends and family. She was enchanted with married life and especially with her husband Charles. In each letter she described him as *"this gentleman that I have chosen comes up to my plan in every aspect."* To those who had not yet met him, he was *"the best of husbands; the greatest of friends."* Eliza Pinckney was very much in love.

Charles also wrote them letters. He wrote to Ann and thanked her for *"the great care"* of his wife, and for her efforts in *"framing her tenderness—pointing out to her the road to virtue and happiness; fixing those principles in her that made him the happiest man in the world."*

Across the sea, Polly was pleased to be living with both parents and her brother, but she missed Eliza very much. She also took up letter writing, corresponding with her sister at least once a week. Sometimes several letters arrived on the same ship. Eliza longed to see her as well. In the meantime, she convinced herself she would be content to hear about Polly's life on Antigua, looking forward to every letter from her family.

Mama and Papa are so happy together, when he's not away fighting the war. Tommy is coming here soon because he has recovered from his illness in England. I am tutored by an old English woman; she also teaches a lad about my age who is rather nice. (He is only eleven; I am thirteen!) We are discussing sending me off to school in England next year. I will stay with the Boddicotts, just as you did. The only thing that frightens me is thinking I will never see you again. Sister, please tell me that isn't so.

Eliza smiled, imagining her sweet Polly with the round rosy cheeks and untamed curls. She sometimes worried she might not see any of them again, especially her dear mother. She forced herself to drive those thoughts from her mind and remember to be thankful for her many blessings. Charles assured her they would find a way to reunite with her family.

She continued with her vision of silk production. She wrote to her father about her interest and asked him for advice. He replied that he would send her two weavers to build looms to make the plantations self-sufficient in cloth. She wrote back that she would need the necessary silk worms to get the raw silk. To avoid wasting any time, she and Charles planted mulberry trees at Belmont. This was, at the very least, a first step. She read everything she could find on silk cultivation, enlisting merchants in her quest to import silk worm eggs.

"My darling, I have a wonderful surprise for you," announced Charles one chilly November afternoon, a smile tugging at his lips.

She looked at him, eyes wide and curious. "What is it, dear?"

"I shall tell you at tea," he replied, reaching for the plate of cucumber, tomato and egg sandwiches and the homemade strawberry jam from the counter. Eliza brought the steeped tea, the scones and the clotted cream to the table.

"I wish to build you a handsome home in Charles Town, and I want us to plan it together," he told her, biting into the cucumber sandwich and savouring its moist crispness. "It will be a 'mansion house' built of plum-coloured English brick with stone copings. It will be built in the middle of an entire block of property from Market to Guignard Street, on the western side of East Bay. It must face the water, and the view will be magnificent. I know how much you love to be near the water! And, my darling, most importantly, there will be plenty of room for your garden." She could hear the husky intimacy in his voice.

Her hands flew to her face. She could not believe her ears. Where would this money come from? Was he counting on the indigo?

But Eliza jumped to her feet and went to her husband, throwing her arms around his neck and hugging him fervently. "Thank you, darling. You are too good to me," she murmured.

True to his word, construction on the mansion began immediately. She visited the building site whenever she could, yet found herself occupied with her duties as the mistress of Belmont and her husband's other plantation on the Ashepoo River—Auckland Plantation. This had been his father's home and Charles had inherited it upon his mother Mary's death. Eliza continued to supervise the three Lucas plantations, often bringing to mind her mother's advice: *remember that your husband has the final decision in all business manners.*

Eliza's reflections were repeatedly on her family; now and again she broached the subject of a visit to Antigua. This idea was abandoned once she knew she was going to have a baby.

"A baby?" exclaimed Charles, flabbergasted. He framed her face with his hands, tenderness radiated in his gaze. "We're having a baby! This is splendid news! Just wonderful, my beloved! Shall we name him Charles Cotesworth, my mother's maiden name, in her honour?"

Eliza burst out laughing. "How do you know we'll have a son?" she teased.

On February 25, 1746, Eliza Lucas Pinckney presented Charles with their first son, Charles Cotesworth Pinckney, in their new home they called *The Mansion*. Their baby was healthy, Eliza was joyous and Charles was ecstatic. For the first time, Charles and Eliza spent over thirty days together in one spot—their new home—enjoying parenthood and doting on their baby.

The Mansion stood on a large lot facing the water and was constructed on a basement containing kitchens and offices. It had two additional stories covered by a high slated roof, where they stored wine and lumber. There was a wide-flagged hall from the front to the back door. Four large rooms opened into the hall: the dining room and a bedroom to the south and a library and housekeeper's room to the north. The staircase spiraled down into a side hall and contained a beautiful window of three arches with heavily carved frames. This remarkable feature was designed by Eliza. She also designed a deep window seat below this window, extending the entire length of the landing place.

There were five rooms on the second story, which is where the family slept. Charles and Eliza's drawing room connected to their bedroom and was more than thirty feet long, with high coved ceilings and a heavy well-proportioned cornice. The entire house was wainscoted in the strongest paneling; the windows and doors with deep projecting pediments and mouldings in the style of Chamberlayne. Their home was said to be one of the loveliest in the city.

Eliza stood beside the river, her hand shading her eyes as she followed the flight of a flock of white herons winging the way over her home from the Ashley marshes toward the bays at the head of the Cooper. *How blessed I am,* she whispered to the birds as they passed overhead. *I am truly home.*

Eliza took great pleasure in motherhood and totally enjoyed her baby son. After a month she brought one of the Negro women into her house as a nanny, and reluctantly allowed Mariah to care for baby Charles when she was working the plantation. Yet every moment away from her son was difficult. She jealously guarded her time with her baby and missed him whenever they had to be apart. *Do all mothers feel this way?* she wondered. *Is my love for baby Charles so fierce because he depends on me, or because he is a product of Charles's and my love?*

Lieutenant Governor George Lucas sent seeds of hemp and flax. The three of them decided that they could augment their income with flax so Eliza's father sent two Irish indentured servants: a weaver and a spinner from the West Indies. Their local carpenter Pompey worked with them to build a loom.

Toward the end of the growing season they unwillingly accepted the reality that the flax crop failed to materialize. She and Charles asked the spinner and weaver to work with wool and cotton instead, and trained several Negro women as spinners. Charles ordered spinning wheels to be built for them. By the end of the season, the new weavers had produced enough wool cloth to supply the winter needs of the workers on the Lucas and Pinckney plantations.

In the meantime, the Pinckneys continued to supply their neighbour planters with indigo seeds. Eliza came up with the idea to start a "convivial club" to meet once a month at the Old Tavern on Bay Street. There they shared English topics and news, normally over a month old, and the future prosperity of the indigo they were producing. Then they drank to their success.

"Say there, Charles," asked a visiting planter, "are you aware of the three shades of the indigo plant?"

Charles nodded. "We're just now experimenting with that, sir. We've already used the *Fine Copper* to dye the wool. We've heard that the *Fine Purple* is excellent for dying linen and soon, we hope to experiment with the *Fine Flora*. You see, we're also trying to produce silk here, and we hope to utilize the *Fine Flora* in the silk industry."

Charles, Eliza and her father were convinced that the indigo crop would be the "money-maker" that would eliminate the Lucas's mortgage on Wappoo. To their great pleasure and relief, the indigo produced from their fields and their neighbours' plantations allowed them to export 134,000 pounds of indigo dye in late summer of 1747. And the British Parliament at long last voted in the bounty that Charles Pinckney had requested.

"Oh my dear Eliza, do you realize what we've accomplished? Our indigo is already valued at more than two hundred twenty-five English pounds! " Charles could scarcely believe their blessings.

"I know we've now lifted the mortgage on Wappoo! My father will be delirious with joy," she replied, an enormous smile spreading across her delicate features. Then her eyes clouded over. No one in the family had heard from her father in months. He was away fighting the Imperial Wars, but should have sent some news to them by now.

"And we've opened the way for indigo raisers in South Carolina to hopefully double their capital every three years, at least by my estimation. Long live the *Indigofera Tinctoria*!" Charles's tone was exuberant.

"Charles dear, I have more good news for you," she murmured softly, slipping her arm around his waist. "I feel this is the perfect time to tell you that we are going to have another child. Perhaps a daughter this time?" She smiled cautiously, hoping her excitement would overcome the nagging symptoms she had been experiencing during the first three months of this pregnancy.

Charles looked at his wife, eyes brimming with surprise and delight. Turning her around in his arms, he removed the wayward hairs from her face. "Oh, my sweet Eliza. I am truly thrilled with your news. Now Charles will have a baby sister to adore, just as I adore their mother," he smiled.

They held each other, sharing their celebration, holding fast to the moment.

chapter thirty-four

SEVERAL MONTHS BACK CHARLES WAS ABLE TO OBTAIN, through a family friend in France, the seed eggs of the silkworms. The mulberry trees were planted, and Eliza was teaching the slave children how to feed the leaves of mulberry trees to the tiny worms. She mobilized all the elderly women on the plantation and a few of the servants at Belmont to make up her work team.

Advanced in her pregnancy, Eliza felt particularly bothered by the hot sun beating down on the fields. Her eyes filled unexpectedly with tears as a sliver of pain slammed into her belly. Protecting her stomach, she doubled over and dropped to her knees, suddenly chilled to the bone.

"You all right, Mistress Eliza?" asked one of the women, rushing to her side.

Eliza's hands circled her stomach and she squeezed her eyes shut, shaking her head. The woman ran to notify Charles.

A bright sun streamed rich and gold as Charles carried her into the house. Shutters were open in their bedroom and the sunlight washed over her face as he laid her down on the bed.

"Please, no light Charles. It makes me queasy," she pleaded

softly. Tentacles of pain slithered inside her, tangled with a fear so fierce she wondered if it would burst out. *Oh Lord, please let nothing happen to my baby.*

"I'm sending for the doctor, my love. You have not felt well for a while and I want him to examine you."

The pain subsided but was shadowed by severe headaches and vomiting. The doctor seemed puzzled and ordered bed rest for a minimum of one week. Eliza felt overwhelming fear.

Sitting next to her on their bed, Charles passed the hours away reading to her from Plutarch. Their small son slept in his cradle by the window. Eliza observed her husband as he read, noting the mixture of concern and distress that washed over his face when he looked into her eyes. Eliza's unsettling expectations threatened even these peaceful moments together.

Thunderheads rolled in across the sky, darkening the hue from pale blue to leaden gray in an instant. There was a loud rumble of thunder in the distance. Eliza looked up into her husband's dark eyes, filled with love, warmth and tenderness mixed with a deep sadness.

"What is it, Charles dear? Have you something on your mind; something you need to share with me?"

His eyes held hers for a long moment. "I want you well, my little visionary. I want you up and beside me at all times. And then I want you to deliver a happy, healthy little girl baby and give her the name you have selected. Oh, but if he is a boy, I want to name him for your father, George Lucas." He smiled bravely and then looked away, his brow furrowed in concern.

Eliza understood. Charles must be very anxious about her father, as she was. There had been absolutely no news of him: none since the beginning of the year. If only she could speak to someone and learn of his whereabouts.

"Charles, please leave my side now and go down to the wharf. I feel certain you can learn something from one of the ship captains, or the merchants. Everyone knows my Papa and someone will have fresh tidings."

"I will go in a while, Eliza. It is storming outside and no one will be on the dock." He lifted the covers over her and kissed her forehead. "Sleep now, while our son sleeps. I will be back in a matter of hours. Sweet dreams, my love."

Outside the storm raged; lightning streaked through the darkening sky; thunderbolts rattled the windows. Eliza and her small son slept through it. Charles tiptoed in to check on them, and then left the room with a heartbroken expression. How would he possibly tell her? *Oh God, this has been the most grueling mission You have ever given me.*

⋅⊙⊙⊙⋅

Eliza was feeling better and decided to bring the plantation accounts up to date. Searching through the ledgers in the library, she came across a letter written by her mother and addressed to her, tucked carefully inside an adjacent book. She opened it up and felt the blood rushing to her face. This letter was received in March of 1747, and it was now almost November. Her husband had concealed this letter from her. Reading on, she understood why.

> *My darling, your beloved father was captured in 1746 by the French military from an Antigua ship. He was taken to France as a prisoner and died in Brest in January of 1747. I am inconsolable; the pain is more than I can bear. Yet I have my family with me. I know this loss will be unbearable to you, and I am begging you to stay strong. When you can, please come to us and let me hold you in my arms once again.*

Dense grief filled the air and came down to sit beside her, ripping her heart apart and covering her fine-boned features like a veil. Her father was dead. She would never see him again. The profoundness of the moment wrapped itself around her. They had always been so close. She was grieving him and also her mother's loss. Why hadn't she been told so she could have written to her mother and siblings?

Charles found her collapsed on their bed, tears streaming down her face. She felt broken; paralyzed; incapable of getting up. There was anger spreading through her now, circulating to its own rhythm. When her husband walked through the doorway, that anger burst out through her mouth.

"How dare you keep this from me?" she sobbed, tears running down her neck and spotting the front of her gown. "You, Charles, of all people, knowing how close I am to my family?" She took a deep breath. "You know bloody-well this is unconscionable!" she screamed at him.

Charles embraced her and held her tightly to his chest, brushing her cheek with his lips. She felt his cheeks wet with his own tears and drew back to look into his eyes.

"Forgive me, Eliza. I did what I thought was best for you and our baby you are carrying."

She studied him—his strained face, his eyes bleak with pain—and saw in him a mirrored image of her heartache.

"Oh Charles, I know you did what you thought was best for me. But my mother? She needed me." She turned from him to hide the rush of tears streaking her face and his arms.

"She is managing, Eliza. I have been in contact with her and with your siblings. They know you are expecting and agreed with me that you should not be told until after the birth. Please forgive me for misleading you."

He held her away from him, his hands firm on her shoulders, and looked deeply into her eyes. Those exquisite green eyes—now red and puffy—reflecting the rawness of her soul.

"Let me take you down to the water, my beloved. There we will sit together and celebrate your father. We will pray for your family and for ours."

He helped her to her feet and placed a heavy wrap around her shoulders. They walked from the house toward the river. The marsh and the river were darkening; a red afterglow turned the grasses bronze. A soft, thick hush held them both silent, leaving the small noises to the sleepy marsh hens at the water's edge.

"Here I can mourn him, near the water. I've always needed to go to the marshes and the rivers during times of deep pain. You knew that, didn't you?" She glanced up at him with respect.

Charles ran his hands through her thick auburn hair, catching her curls and wrapping his fingers around them. He brought his face down to hers and grazed her soft lips with his mouth.

Eliza responded, embracing him tighter than ever. It almost felt right, as if they were two pieces of broken ceramic bonding back together. She needed to believe they could meld so tightly together that the raw wound would somehow fade away.

chapter thirty-five

"MAKE HASTE! SEND EZRA FOR THE DOCTOR! THE baby is coming!" Charles stood wild-eyed in the doorway and screamed at Mariah, who was already flying down the stairs in search of Ezra. She heard the moaning and the sobs of her mistress Eliza and was terrified at the urgency marking the desperate moment. The baby was not due for almost two months!

Eliza cried out to Charles. "Our baby is coming. Squeeze my hand, Charles. Oooh, please help me!"

"Be brave, my love. The doctor is on his way," soothed her husband, as he glimpsed Mariah returning with boiling water and a "sick room" helper. Her eyes indicated Ezra had left to fetch Dr. Paul.

Charles and Mariah stayed at her side, assisting her as best they could. The doctor, running up the stairway, was greeted by the feeble cries of the newborn child. After careful examination, he assured the parents that their baby son was fine. Then he congratulated them for the excellent work they had done in birthing him.

Charles' face was wreathed in smiles of relief as he held his son. "Beloved Eliza, you have given birth to your father's namesake: George Lucas Pinckney. And darling, he looks just like his brother Charles looked at birth. Isn't he handsome?"

Eliza nodded, exhausted and barely able to respond. She allowed the doctor to take her baby away and tend to his needs. After she fell asleep, her physician instructed the others in the baby's care. Charles listened to every word, knowing that he would be responsible for their baby's supervision until Eliza recovered.

"Doctor, please be honest with me. Is my son defective in any way, born as early as he was?" Charles, hesitant and frightened, carefully studied the doctor's face.

"Colonel Pinckney, it is too soon for me to tell. His colour is pale, but his vital signs seem good. However, we must keep him warm and nourished 'round the clock. Can you employ a wet nurse in the event that your wife will not be able to feed him?"

"Naturally. Please find one straightaway. And may we expect to see you again in the morning? Eliza is very much tuckered out and I would request that you return soon. Thank you for your visit."

Charles slept on the sofa next to his wife. Mariah slept in little Charles's room and took charge of his needs. The baby divided his days between the two rooms, depending on his feeding schedule.

Eliza recovered slowly, fighting periods of hopelessness and melancholy that had accompanied the end of this pregnancy. Charles attributed this to her frailty and lack of milk. She was devastated that she could not feed her baby, and even more distraught that her father would never hold his tiny namesake.

"Oh Charles, I'm so downcast that I'm not able to feed little George. His colour looks bad to me; I fear for his health."

"Eliza, please do not speak like that. We are doing the best we can with him and he seems to be growing a wee bit each day. Can you not see that?" he asked her.

She blinked rapidly and turned her head, offering no response. After staring fixedly at him for an instant, she reached for his hand. "My love, I want so badly to take my sons to the West Indies and present them to my family. I want my mother to know that my father's name will be carried on through our son. 'Tis my greatest desire."

"Then gather up your strength and we shall do that very thing. Just as soon as you are able to travel."

"What about our plantations?" she questioned.

"We will leave them to our capable workers. Your family comes first," he replied, dropping kisses onto her parched lips.

"Please baptize the baby before the end of the month. I will only rest knowing he's in the Lord's hands."

⟡⟐⟡

George Lucas Pinckney died two weeks after his birth—five days after his baptism. When Charles broke the devastating news to Eliza, she demanded the tiny body be brought to her. Clutching him to her chest, she sank weeping to the floor—her heart gouged with pain.

"'Tis too much for me to endure. The weight of my grief is crushing me," she wailed.

As the afternoon shadows faded into the night, Charles and Eliza mourned their baby, connected by a cord of devastation and grief.

For days Eliza lay in bed, lacking the will to carry on. She could not throw off her sorrow over the loss of her father and now her son; she wanted to crawl out of her skin and walk away from it all. She found no joy in living; not even her husband and toddler could arouse her and she refused to see them for days.

One afternoon she permitted Charles to enter her room. His face was drawn and pale. Suddenly, she felt compelled to reach out to him and assist him in his anguish. But she found she could not.

"My husband, I want to help you, but I am thrashing about in a horrid storm. I've been dumped in the ocean and feel tossed by the water and battered against the rocks. I am fighting daily to keep afloat. Most of me doesn't want to keep my head above water. Apart from leaving you and our son Charles, I would stop fighting and just sink away."

Tears coursed down Charles's face as he listened to her words. "NO, ELIZA! Do not speak to me of that! You must fight these wicked demons and return to us. We need you, my darling," he sobbed.

Eliza prayed.

Oh God, Thou hast never forsaken me in the past. I believe in Your will and I understand I must accept it and meet disappointment and sorrow with an inner strength. Through Your word, I learned how You suffered the loss of Your son for my sins. Now I have lost mine, and I am shattered. Although I do not wish to, I now must absorb the most intense pain without abandoning my sense of hope. Allow me to succumb to Your control. 'Twas wrong of me to hurt my family through my grief. Show me how to be strong and loving.

Her recovery was slow, but eventually her strong constitution defeated the physical challenge, and she was able to claim victory over the depression.

Several days after her emotional dialogue with Charles, she asked him to return to her bedside.

"Charles, thank you for still being here with me. 'Twas a terrifying and difficult battle, yet one I had to fight alone." Her tears were dried up; a tentative smile lightened her weary face. "My grief will not disappear, yet I shall learn to live with it. I have fought my demons and won. Forgive me for giving you so much pain." She leaned into his chest and wrapped her thin arms around him. "Now, please help me to my feet, and take me down to the water once again."

Charles exhaled an enormous sigh of relief. Turning his face to conceal his emotions, he reached for her delicate hand and helped her dress warmly for their walk through the marshes. *Lord, I thank You. You knew she would make it, and now I am able to believe it as well.*

chapter thirty-six

ELIZA HAD SUFFERED TWO MAJOR LOSSES IN A MATTER
of weeks. Throwing herself into her work to recover, she
turned to the experimental interest she had long carried in her
heart—cultivating silkworms. She dedicated herself to this
project, making certain the caterpillars would be hatched in
a clean shed, regularly disinfected with lime wash. Her well-
trained housemaids did the cleaning while a man she trusted
oversaw the whitewashing. The plantation workers' children
brought in mulberry leaves and fed them to the caterpillars.

The process of feeding them took about forty-two days. It
amazed the children that caterpillars could eat twenty times
their weight in ripe leaves each day. They learned how a cat-
erpillar spun its cocoon with the front part of its body raised,
waving slowly from side to side. The motion was part of the
spinning.

Charles and Eliza approached the working women as they
laid out the cocoons in the sun.

"Look Charles. The women will dry them and then boil the
cocoons to soften the gum. This will break down the filaments
that hold them together."

He looked perplexed. "What happens after that?"

"We'll work together, reeling and winding the raw silk thread they produce." She looked up at him and smiled. "In several days I'll bring you back and you can watch us work."

Fortunately the mulberry trees thrived in the low country. The production of silk, her newest business venture, did little to interfere with the other crops due to its short time frame. The entire process was completed in less than three months. And the shipping expense to England was minimal, because the bulk and weight were so small.

"Eliza, do you know that Lord Bacon considers silk one of the most profitable products a plantation can export?" Charles asked enthusiastically.

"Mr. Deveaux tells me ours is 'equal to the best Lyons silk.' Let us see what the merchants in England decide," she responded cautiously.

When Eliza realized she was once again pregnant, she asked Charles to take her and little Charles back to Wappoo Plantation for an extended visit. He agreed at once, knowing she would find peace back on her father's land.

Eliza felt better once she was at Wappoo. The wind had freshened and was blowing from the east. She and Charles, with their small son, stood on the high bank of Wappoo Creek, breathing in the deep cool air. Eagles called and the tall sea grasses swayed softly with the breeze, slightly parting as two blue herons lifted their wings to soar over the marshy inlet. Eliza closed her eyes and allowed the bay winds to caress her face.

She thought of her mother with deep longing. *Was she finally recovered from all the ailments that had plagued her over time? How she would adore little Charles! They must find a way to go back to Antigua; perhaps before next summer, when her baby was due.*

"You miss them, don't you my love?" Charles asked softly, encircling her and the toddler with his strong arms.

"Oh yes Charles. It's been much too long since we've seen them. And Polly must be a young lady by now," she said sadly. "I've missed watching her grow up." Tears pooled in her eyes.

"We can only pray that peace will come soon. Then we shall go to Antigua, or find a way to bring them all here to us. Would you like that?" he offered, wiping her cheeks with his long fingertips.

Eliza nodded. After a long pause, she shook her head forcefully. "Peace came too late for my Papa. He died fighting to preserve it, but Papa never saw the end of the fighting."

"'Twas not in vain, beloved. Our children will honour him for what he did for England. Pray remember that."

◈

Eliza sat alone in the library, contemplating British philosopher John Locke's method of early education. His "tabula rasa" theory subscribed that a person's mind at birth is like a blank slate upon which personal experiences create impressions. This could be applied to early education in the form of play, and both she and Charles agreed to follow his technique. Charles made their son a set of blocks to teach him his letters, and at just under two years of age, baby Charles knew them all.

"You are a very clever lad, my son. Just listen to your prattle! Soon you'll be joining in on our conversations!" She watched with tender eyes as her son glanced up lovingly and giggled with her.

Every year as her birthday approached Eliza reviewed and added to a scroll of papers she had labeled *Belonging To Myself Only*. These were her private thoughts and resolutions that she had never shared with anyone. Reading her private thoughts brought her joy and at times sorrow, yet she always finished this ritual by lifting up prayers and praising God.

Her resolutions included: to govern her passions, to endeavor to subdue vice, to improve virtue, to avoid giving any show of pride, haughtiness, ambition, ostentation, or contempt of others. She asked for divine guidance and strength to be a good wife. She prayed for Charles, her husband—to guard his health and to watch over his interests and reputation. And she resolved to be a good mother.

Oh God, may you show me how to set a good example to my child and children to come; to give them good and pure advice, to watch over their bodies and souls. Instill in them piety, virtue and religion. And use me to correct them in error, no matter the pain it might cause me.

Regarding the servants, she asked that she always treat them with humanity and good will by providing sufficient and comfortable clothing and adequate food. *Care for them in sickness and make their lives as comfortable as possible.*

Eliza massaged her eyes as she lifted herself up from her knees. She sat down in the frayed leather chair at her father's desk and instantly became aware of his presence. Her skin tingled with the sensation that he was there, embracing her.

Oh Papa, I miss you so very much. At times I physically ache, knowing I'll not see you again on this earth. Are you holding my baby, the one I named for you? Cuddle him, Papa; cuddle him heaps for me. Look after Mama when she joins you. Will I ever see her again? Oh, I am feeling such pity for myself when I should count my blessings. She wiped at her eyes with the back of her hand.

Esteemed Papa, let me share my blessings, so you will know that I resolve to be grateful. Here I am, almost twenty-six years old now. Do you remember when we arrived at Wappoo? Only ten years ago and soon after we settled in, you beseeched me to look after Mama, Polly and the three plantations. Together—you from Antigua and me from here—we successfully developed the rice field and finally—indigo. God was with us as well, and we did it! And now I'm married to a man who you knew and respected. I know you smile down on us now as we hold our Charles and await his sibling. I hope this one is a little girl. Hah! You already know that, don't you Papa? I should be delighted to spend just a few moments with you in Heaven to share my joys.

To her surprise, Eliza felt much better. Her eyes twinkled as a slight smile broke over her face.

Now then, please visit me more often. This has been so good for me and our son Charles. See him playing across the floor, Papa? Isn't he a handsome lad? He resembles you, even though he's named for Charles. I shall return to Wappoo often, as it calms me and brings me closer to you. But you are invited to visit me in Belmont or The Mansion as well. Please Papa, just come 'round now and again.

Eliza picked up her smiling boy and walked out to her garden. The clouds had scattered and the eastern horizon glowed golden pink. Gauzy clouds, carried by a wind strong enough to bend treetops and toss branches, gave the horizon a pastoral feeling.

It was at that moment, holding little Charles in her arms, that Eliza finally comprehended the depth of her husband's love for her. He had given her all of himself—unselfishly, unreservedly. When she simply got herself out of the way, she was able to clearly see what love meant.

She smiled broadly, her face soft with compassion, as understanding washed over her. *Thank you, Papa, for this moment of grace. I shall never forget it.*

chapter thirty-seven

GREAT BRITAIN'S WAR WITH SPAIN AND FRANCE ENDED and the peace treaty was signed at Aix-la-Chapelle on October 18, 1748. Eliza, Charles, their son and their two-month old daughter celebrated it as a family. Harriott Pinckney had been born on August 28, 1748. Her arrival brought great joy to Eliza and Charles.

"Charles dear, I am so happy with our sweet little family. If only Mama and my brothers and sister were here with us, it would be perfect. Don't you agree?"

Little Charles dashed through the house in high spirits. A happy child, he was easy to teach and delightful to be around. With blond curly hair and huge hazel eyes, Charles was a beautiful boy. Fortunately, he was quite fond of little Harriott, and enjoyed chattering to her in "grown-up" words.

His sweet disposition was a blessing and a pleasure to his parents, giving Eliza the peace of mind she needed as mistress of Belmont and their city home. She enjoyed her social obligations as the wife of the leading lawyer of South Carolina, and felt extremely proud of her husband.

Their family continued to grow. On October 23, 1750, they welcomed another son, Thomas Pinckney, named after

Charles's father and Eliza's brother. Letters from Antigua confirmed that Ann, George, Thomas and Polly were all well.

Polly had been studying in a London finishing school, as Eliza had done, and was living with the Boddicotts. She would soon return to the West Indies. Ann wrote that she had finally overcome the various ailments that had plagued her over the years. Eliza was grateful to learn that her mother was active and living peacefully in Antigua, surrounded by her children and friends.

❦

One evening Charles returned home in the late afternoon from a two-day visit to Charles Town, sweaty and worn out from the ride, but with enthusiasm shining in his sparkling eyes. He waited patiently until the children were put to bed before sharing his excitement with his probing wife.

"What is it, my love? You have such a keyed-up look on your face," she inquired impatiently.

"Oh Eliza. This is very big news. It's huge. I think you will be enchanted with these tidings."

"Do tell, Charles. How much longer must I wait?" She frowned slightly, causing him to laugh.

"Not a minute more, dear one." He paused slightly for effect. "You are sitting next to the newly appointed Chief Justice of South Carolina."

Her hands flew to her face as her eyes widened in astonishment. "Charles, has Royal Governor Glen bestowed that honour on you?" Eliza called out, overwhelmed by the news.

"'Tis a fact. He has. I just learned of it this morning. I shall have to direct the Carolinians now, as this is an office with great responsibility. I understand it is the second highest office in the colony. Do you think we shall be comfortable with so much responsibility?"

Eliza laughed giddily. "You shall, that's for certain. And I will support your decisions, darling. But don't you remember how we used to complain that England saved the top positions in our colony for the Englishmen? You've just proven otherwise."

Draping his arm around her shoulder, Charles nodded. "I begin my duties in a fortnight. And King George II must confirm it, but you and I already know about patience, do we not? That could take a year, so I've been told to commence without waiting for his confirmation." They laughed as he held her close with a long kiss.

⌈⌈⌈⌉

Less than six months later Charles received official word that an English gentleman was arriving with the Royal Commission to take over the position of Chief Justice of South Carolina. This announcement took the citizens of Charles Town by total surprise, and was received as a severe insult to their colony. Only later did they learn that Peter Leigh had been removed as High Bailiff of Westminster due to political shifts in England. The ministers of the British government were obligated to find a place for their ousted adherent, and since the King had not yet confirmed Charles Pinckney, the post was conveniently open for Peter Leigh.

Eliza ached for her husband and the offended citizens. Charles counseled moderation to them all.

"The Crown has spoken. Mother England did what she needed to do. Besides, I was never officially the Chief Justice. We must assist this gentleman and I intend to give him my full support."

Eliza's eyes beamed with respect and admiration for her husband. "Charles, you are so noble—just another of your numerous outstanding qualities." She pressed her face against the top of his head, inhaling his familiar smell. "I am certain our people will consider you their Chief Justice, no matter who holds the title."

As it turned out, the colonists were so outraged by this slight that they offered Charles a new position and title. In a unanimous vote, he was tendered the position of "Commissioner of the Colony in London." He would handle the business of the Royal Governor of South Carolina, the Council and the Commons House of Assembly with the Lords of Trade and of Plantations, as well as with other official boards in London. Naturally, he and his family would reside in London and his salary would be less than what he had received in South Carolina.

"Eliza, what shall we do?" he asked, genuinely bewildered. "Your friends are all here now. Even Polly has returned to Antigua. Yet it is a great opportunity for our boys' education. What do you say? I seek your opinion."

Eliza thought of her mother's words of so many years ago. *Daughters are infused with a soft and delicate nature, necessary to maintain peace and harmony with their husbands.* She smiled tenderly, her hand reaching up to the nape of his neck. "You will know what the correct decision is. For me, it shall be a winning option either way. As long as we are together as a family, we will have a lovely life."

"What a gift I have in you, dearest Eliza," whispered Charles, gazing into her deep emerald eyes. "You have already made me completely happy in this life."

London, England

1753-1758

chapter thirty-eight

"OH CHARLES, I TRUST WE ARE PUTTING THE RIGHT items into our luggage. I do know for certain that this raw silk will produce such lovely gowns for the Queen Mother of England and the Lady of Lord Chesterfield. After all her husband has done for the American colonies, we simply must gift her a silk gown as an example of our colonial industry."

Charles laughed, his eyes dancing as he watched Eliza bustling about in preparation for their extended stay in England. "So you are carrying in your luggage raw silk produced at Belmont to be woven into gowns once we reach England? Do you know the shapes and sizes of these women you'll be gifting them to?"

Eliza tossed back her chestnut hair and shot him a sharp look. "Now Charles, naturally I shall divine that once we arrive. And I do know my size for the gold brocade gown I shall have cut for myself."

Charles could not help asking, yet tried hard to conceal his insolent grin. "And darling, please tell me exactly why we are carrying singing birds in cages to London?"

Her eyes blazed briefly, then softened as vivid memories

overwhelmed her. "For gifts dear, as these particular birds are quite unknown in England. I've selected some of our Polly's favourites. You do remember how she loved all the birds, and imitated them so well when she lived here, do you not?"

Charles leased out their Mansion to Royal Governor James Glen. He knew their absence would be for several years and wanted the house to be lived in and attended. During the hurricane of September, 1752, he had been forced to remove his family by boat as water poured into the Mansion. A pilot boat had battered the flight of stone steps leading to the first floor, causing a breach in the corner of their house; at least four feet of sea water soon collected in the basement. The house was repaired and Governor Glen felt fortunate to be able to reside in it during the Pinckneys's time in Europe.

"I've turned over the affairs of our plantations to my brother William, who I am confident will do well with our crops. Naturally all the servants will stay in their homes and help him out." Charles was comfortable with his decision, knowing it was the best solution for their prosperous indigo and silk production.

The Pinckney family set sail at the end of March of 1753. The sea waters soon became very rough and they experienced extreme seasickness, especially Eliza and young Harriott. It was the first time any of them had experienced a rough sea crossing. The shrieking wind, muscular waves and dark skies took on the tempestuous character of a wild man, challenging Eliza to carry on without cowering before him.

They hid below deck for most of the voyage. Eliza forced herself to sit at her small table every day and write to her mother and Polly.

Charles reports to me that the passage is fine and we are making good time. I only feel that never a poor wretch suffered more who can possibly escape with life than I. Even Harriott and the boys are faring better than I, and Charles seems not to even notice the rolling and swaying of the ocean waves.

On April 29, 1753, they arrived in Portsmouth, England. Eliza was dismayed when Charles finally came below to break the bad news to his family.

"The port has closed for disembarkation due to a severe epidemic of smallpox. I've been advised that we will sail up the Thames to Richmond with the others onboard, and take up residence in one of the houses for a series of inoculations."

"Egads Charles! Are you saying that we must subject our small children to the pustules of diseased people? What would our doctors recommend?" Eliza would take no chances with her children's health, and felt dismayed about exposing them to the disease through the variolation or inoculation process. Through her reading she understood the risks.

"I'm reporting to you what the doctor aboard our ship has suggested. Eliza, pray remember that they have been practicing this method in England since 1721, when Lady Mary Wortley Montagu used it with good results on her own family." Charles tried to appear calm and confident, although he too had reservations.

Their month of inoculation passed quickly at the Richmond facility. The Pinckney family befriended many others also waiting out their time and was finally allowed to leave the facility. They reached London and were met by the Boddicotts, as well as several school friends of Charles. Eliza had not seen the Boddicotts for more than fifteen years, and was overcome with emotion.

"How wonderful to embrace you once again, dear friends," she exclaimed warmly. "And to know that you've seen my sister Polly recently. Pray tell me she has done well in her studies."

"All you Lucas children have made us so proud," replied Mr. Boddicott. "And just look at you now, Eliza. A beautiful young woman with children of your own. You are certainly welcome to stay with us for as long as you need. We've compiled a short list of recommendations for houses you may wish to lease, whenever you feel ready to do so."

The home they eventually found to lease was on Craven

Street. It was a new house, having been built in the last decade, with a great room featuring a fetching coved and coffered ceiling in gold, green and white. Eliza and the children were amazed at the house's sophistication and ornate touches.

Despite the extravagance, it was considerably less expensive than most of the rental homes in London, yet large enough to entertain comfortably, as Charles knew they would. Renewing past friendships was enjoyable to both Eliza and Charles, and while they appreciated their friends' list of suggestions for the boys' future education, they were content to first settle in and begin unpacking.

✦

One of their first invitations was from the widowed Princess of Wales, who lived privately with her nine children at Richmond Lodge in Kew. Eliza considered Princess Augusta a woman of very high standing in the Royalty of England, and was greatly pleased to receive the invitation. Earlier she had told her husband she was not keen to meet King George II, *who was reputed to have held a disreputable court that included many scandalous women.* Charles visited King George II alone, on his official visit as agent of the royal province of South Carolina. But when the Princess of Wales's invitation arrived, Eliza was thrilled.

"Oh Charles, isn't it brilliant that our children are invited as well? I can hardly believe that they will be in the company of the royal children. Oh, I do hope they are mindful and watch their manners."

Charles' dark eyes crinkled at the corners as he laughed out loud. "Have you not considered that all small children have the same characteristics, my dear? Pray do not fret over minor details."

"Oh my goodness; now I am quite pleased that I brought the birds from the Carolinas! We could have Harriott present them to the Princess of Wales. I shall write up the note straightaway." A note was written and sent without delay.

Miss Harriott Pinckney, daughter of Charles Pinckney Esq. of His Majesty's Council of South Carolina, pays her duty to her Highness and humbly begs leave to present her with an Indigo bird, a Nonpareil, and a yellow bird, which she has brought from Carolina for her Highness.

The day after the note was delivered, the Pinckney family was invited for a one o'clock audience with Princess Augusta. They arrived in formal dress and were led through several grand rooms in the Princess's apartment until they reached the dressing room, where Princess Augusta personally met them at the door. Despite the finery and ornate coiffure, and her charming German accent, the Dowager Princess had a very friendly, straightforward manner that quickly put the family at ease.

"I'm extremely delighted to meet you, lovely family from America," she beamed, grasping Harriott's small hand and kissing her on the cheek. "Tell me: how do you like England, my dear child?"

"Quite well, Your Highness, but not nearly as well as I like South Carolina," answered the six-year-old candidly and simply.

"How charming!" laughed Princess Augusta. "It is only natural for such a little woman as yourself to love your own country best. And thank you ever so much for these lovely birds. I believe one of them will quickly become a favourite of mine. Come now, all of you. I should be quite pleased for you to meet some of my children."

The Pinckney family followed her to another room where her children—Princess Augusta, Princess Elizabeth, Prince William and Prince Henry were quietly playing on the wooden floor. They stood up at the arrival of the guests and received them with smiles, giving them no time to consider how to introduce themselves or worry about protocol.

When Charles glanced over at his wife, he could see that she felt quite at home.

chapter thirty-nine

"YOUR HIGHNESS, YOU HAVE MADE US EXTREMELY happy by bestowing on us the incomparable honour of this audience with you," murmured Charles Pinckney, when Princess Augusta turned to him.

"In answer to your question, we arrived in London a little over a month ago. We are still in the process of unpacking our belongings and finding our way around the city. It has been a long time since Eliza and I have set foot on English soil."

"And how are you finding life here at this time?" she asked him with genuine interest.

"Indeed as lovely as I remembered it from days past," he responded with a smile. "And may I compliment you on your splendid gardens and considerable horticultural activity. We were amazed as we entered the Kew garden precincts and viewed the lake, the bell temples and the Orangery and Pagoda. What an outstanding architect you have in Sir William Chambers."

Princess Augusta beamed her pleasure. Colonel Charles Pinckney was certainly knowledgeable about her home and landscaping, and undoubtedly had heard of her pride in her gardens.

The Pinckneys had been standing for nearly an hour while the Princess of Wales interviewed them, thoroughly engrossed in their news from the New World. She asked both Eliza and Charles about the governor of the Carolinas, admitting that she had forgotten his name.

Charles noticed the children were getting restless, especially Harriott, who turned to him with arms in the air, whimpering with fatigue.

"Princess Augusta, we have intruded long enough and should now retire and leave you to rest," he suggested, lifting his child in his arms.

"Oh, please no! You've just arrived. Come here, little Harriott. Pray sit on my lap and rest a bit. You must be very weary by now," she coaxed. "I want you to meet the Prince of Wales, and I shall send straightaway for him and Prince Edward, who live in a house just opposite mine."

Harriott, now seated comfortably on Princess Augusta's lap, quickly settled down. She leaned forward to chat with the three youngest princesses sitting in front of her on the carpet covering the dark wooden floor. The boys were seated next to the young princes on the other side of the room, conversing animatedly about schools in London and Carolina.

As the warm family atmosphere embraced them, Eliza smiled inwardly at how astute her husband had been in counseling her to avoid thinking that the Royal family would be a breed apart.

Little Princess Caroline, only four years old, jumped up to embrace and kiss Harriott on the cheek. "Mama, this is my new dear friend," she announced to the Princess of Wales, generating giggles from Harriott, who returned her hug. Three-year-old Prince Frederick drew closer to Harriott for his hug as well. Eliza asked the Princess if she too could kiss the little ones.

"Most certainly," exclaimed Princess Augusta. "My children have been educated to mingle with the public and encouraged to ask questions."

Eliza realized that the attending servants had disappeared and they were completely alone with Princess Augusta and her children. Over the next hour and a half, the Princess was called from the room several times to resolve household issues. During her absence Eliza surveyed the high-ceilinged room, sparkling with gilt and bright scenes of idyllic life in the country. There were many fine china pieces in her cabinets, and a carefully displayed collection of exquisite dazzling crystal goblets.

After a while the royal children were called to dinner and left the room. Princess Augusta invited Harriott to sit in one of their chairs.

"Oh, thank you kindly Your Highness, but we must not sit in your presence. Not even the children," Eliza cried out.

"Nonsense. I know nothing of that," retorted the Princess with a hearty chuckle. "I am only sorry I have no pretty trinkets for little Harriott here, but when I go into London I shall find something lovely and send it to her."

Prince Edward and the Prince of Wales, George III, took Charles Pinckney aside and queried him about South Carolina, the slaves, and his plans for his sons' education. Glancing over at his boys, Charles replied, "I believe Charles might have the capacity and inclination for the bar, but my younger son Thomas is too young to make any determination."

"Will you send your sons to Westminster, Colonel?" asked the Prince, evidently curious about their future.

"One day I shall, but first I will enroll them in suitable primary schools in London."

Eliza and Princess Augusta conversed like close friends.

"Have you suckled all your children?" the Princess asked abruptly.

Eliza was flabbergasted at the candid question and felt her cheeks redden. "Umm, I attempted it but my constitution would not bear it."

"Pray do not be distressed. It is best not to if the mother is anxious. The doctors here say that could be harmful to the child. I put out my nine children to nurse."

"Were they not living with you?" asked an incredulous Eliza.

"Well yes, they were under our roof, but in separate living quarters until they stopped suckling."

"Oh, my. I cannot imagine not having my child in my own room. Is that not unnatural for a mother? We have black wet nurses living in our homes who often bond so closely they become nannies to our babies," murmured Eliza, deeply disturbed by what she had heard.

The Princess stroked Harriott's pale cheek. "I see that the 'suckling black women' made no difference in this one's complexion."

Princess Augusta continued the conversation for nearly an hour, seated in a comfortable chair next to Harriott Pinckney. Charles and his older son moved into another room with the Prince of Wales. Both conversations turned to a discussion of the government of the Carolinas, whether the New World had earthquakes and hurricanes, the colours and manners of the Indians, how their houses were built, and whether the French were corrupting the Indians.

Eliza and Charles answered their royal hosts in the most straightforward manner, feeling like unofficial diplomats from the New World.

Before the Pinckneys took their leave, they were able to meet and speak with all nine children. After nearly three hours, they kissed her Royal Highness's hand and withdrew regretfully. Princess Augusta ordered Prince Edward to escort them to the door.

As they returned to their new home by carriage, Eliza snuggled close to Charles. "Darling, I have never seen or heard of such an account of a semi-royal audience before. I especially enjoyed meeting Princess Augusta, the eldest daughter, whom I believe will do her mother proud."

"You are so correct, Eliza," he murmured. "The Prince of Wales is intelligent and also, an avid listener. How unusual for royalty!" He smiled at her, squeezing her hand. "And did our children make you proud?"

"Indeed they did, Charles. And for the first time, I felt quite honoured to be referred to as an *American*. Did you hear the Princess call us that?"

"I did, Eliza. And that is exactly what we are. We own land in and loyalty to America, yet we remain British subjects. I wonder if that will ever become problematic." Turning to glance at her expression, he discovered that his fatigued wife had fallen asleep on his shoulder.

chapter forty

Dearest Mama, Polly and blessed brothers,

I must impart the saddest piece of news to each of you who knew him so well and loved him as I did. My heart breaks as I write this; I cannot stop the tears from flowing. Our most kind and generous friend, Mr. Boddicott, has succumbed to apoplexy just the week past. At least Charles, the children and I were able to spend a few moments with him and Mrs. Boddicott before he passed, and we thanked him for everything he had done for our family. I feel in my heart that it was not enough. He told me he would have treasured seeing each of your faces once more. Now all that is left for us is to know that he will continue to love us from the Heavenlies.

Eliza grieved the death of their dear family friend. He had been a father figure to her when she was a young girl studying in London. Her children were frightened to see her mourning so deeply. Charles knew how much the Boddicotts meant to Eliza and to the Lucas family.

For the sake of Charles and her young ones, Eliza pushed herself to move on. She renewed old friendships and met with her female friends to play cards—a British social activity she did not enjoy. She and Charles attended the theatre, enjoying all productions that David Garrick starred in or produced. He was always the subject of conversation at any female gathering.

"Is he not the most dashing King Lear?" gushed Lady Carew, one of Eliza's dearest friends from her school days in London. She was now married to Sir Nicholas, a gentleman of power and means.

"I find his talent far more attractive than his looks," replied Eliza. "And I believe I preferred his role in *Richard III*. Have you met him?"

"Not yet, but we shall find a way. Give me a few days, and I'll arrange it," she laughed.

Eliza and Lady Carew often frequented the Bath spa resort. They journeyed together by rail to bathe and rejuvenate in the health-giving qualities of the Roman-era hot mineral springs. Sometimes their husbands accompanied them. Eliza enjoyed the fact that Bath had a wonderful daily market.

As their old friendship blossomed into a more mature one, Charles discovered just how important Lady Carew's friendship had become to his wife.

"Eliza, I'm thinking of selling some property in the Carolinas so we can buy a home in Surrey. That would put us much closer to Lady Carew's Beddington home. Would you like that?"

Eliza's face lit up. "That would be wonderful, Charles. I would very much like that!"

He found them a furnished house in the center of London for the very reasonable price of 120 pounds a year. It was a perfect home for their family. Although not as finely furnished as their previous house, it was so comfortable and accommodating that Eliza sometimes caught herself looking out the spacious front windows in search of the golden marsh sunsets of South Carolina.

Over the next two years Charles, Eliza and their children traveled extensively, visiting Wiltshire, Stonehenge, and appreciating Old Sarum at sunset. They toured majestic Salisbury

Cathedral, Pembroke at Wilton, and Bristol. Eliza and Harriott agreed that Stonehenge had been their second favourite excursion, only eclipsed by Bath.

"What do you most like about Stonehenge, Harriott dear?" Charles asked his pretty blond daughter.

"The history and the mystery of the old days," she quickly responded.

"Very well said, Harriott," concurred Eliza. "I particularly like its symbols of power and endurance—the fact that it was a temple made for the worship of ancient earth deities."

Charles Cotesworth, the avid reader, voiced his opinion. "I like that it is an astronomical observatory where they marked significant events on the prehistoric calendar."

"Others claim Stonehenge was a sacred site for the burial of high-ranking citizens from the societies of long ago," added Charles with a nod. "It certainly impressed the lot of you, and rightly so."

Their youngest son Thomas caught a severe fever from standing too long in the damp outdoors. Eliza watched him closely and noticed that his cheek was swollen. They bundled him up and took him into London, where the doctor prescribed rest and kept him under observation. Seven days later, they were able to return to Ripley. Thomas continued with a light fever and Eliza stayed by his side until he recovered, keeping occupied by writing countless letters to friends and family.

Lady Carew, I know you too have been indisposed, off and on for two years now. You write me that your daughter is also ill. How do you manage to keep your wits about you? It matters little to me what ailments plague me or dear Charles, but when it affects our children, I find it so difficult to manage. Pray mend quickly and warm our hearts with your visit in November.

The three young children's schooling was closely supervised by Eliza. She and Charles had chosen grammar schools close to their home since Eliza insisted that the children live with them.

How fortunate we are in this regard, Eliza mused, *compared to the Princess Dowager, who lives apart from her lovely offspring.*

Charles worked constantly to gain fairer treatment of the American colonies. His correspondence with Lord Pitt, the enlightened British statesman who recognized that England should avoid coercion when handling the "settlers" in the New World, supported Charles's goal.

They received news that yet another war had erupted in the Carolinas. The French, with the help of the Native American Indians, were trying to wrest land from the English settlers, and the Pinckney's properties were in danger.

"Eliza, the governors of all the Provinces have met to discuss common protection against the French and Indians. Benjamin Franklin has declared that the English Colonies would never know peace as long as the French were masters of Canada. The intelligent thing for us to do at this point would be to return to South Carolina and sell most of our estates. We could then invest the money in a more secure though less improvable part of the world."

Eliza searched his eyes, saying nothing. She seemed so vulnerable, tender; he wanted nothing more than to protect her from the difficulties in the colonies.

More bad news arrived from abroad. In India, the British had lost Calcutta. On the continent, Frederick the Great had been defeated by the Austrians and the French. The Duke of Cumberland surrendered his English army to the French.

"Charles, whatever is happening to the British military?" asked his apprehensive wife.

"I fear the French will gain control of all North America west of the Alleghenies. We are becoming aware of the alarming strides the French are making 'on the backs of the English Colonies.' I believe it is imperative that we return to the New World."

Eliza turned to face him, surprise flickering on her face.

"Oh, Charles. Not now, please. We have finally made arrangements to meet the Carews in Bath in a fortnight!"

"Darling, if there is trouble looming over the colonies, I must dispose of the greatest part of the properties we own. We must see for ourselves what threat this poses on us."

"And the children? What shall we do with them if there may be upcoming danger?"

He went to her, folding her into his arms. "They should stay here where they are safe."

She shook her head passionately. "No, Charles. I shan't leave my children. How can you even suggest leaving the dear creatures for whose advantage we are content to undergo all inconveniences?" Her deep green eyes flashed dangerously.

"I will look into more permanent schooling for them at once. Let us give this some thought and then make our decision carefully," he replied calmly as she gradually relaxed in his arms.

chapter forty-one

"ENGLAND IS SIMPLY NOT DOING ENOUGH TO PROTECT the Carolinas! I am appalled at how little attention and assistance the Crown is giving the colonies!" snapped Eliza, cutting him off in mid-sentence. Her face was flushed, her eyes smoky and alive with ripe emotions.

"Perhaps we are not aware of what is being done for them," suggested her husband. "After all, we are only receiving second-hand information."

"Four years ago we left a flourishing colony in profound peace—a colony so valuable to this nation that it would have been called absurd to leave it unprotected and uncared for in case of a war. Granted, war then seemed a very distant contingency. And indeed, we ourselves looked upon an estate there as being as secure as in England, and in some ways, even more valuable. Now we hear that war is erupting in various locations—and where is the assistance from the Mother country?"

"Darling, your fury is understandable. You struggled so long to produce crops that supported England and brought her profits. I beg of you: do not condemn her until we can see for ourselves. We must return to Carolina and evaluate the situation as quickly as possible." He lifted her face between his hands, his tone warmly reassuring.

Eliza studied his expression for a long moment. "What is it, Charles? What are you not telling me?"

Charles cradled her head against his chest. "'Tis true. There is more. My brother William has suffered a paralyzing stroke. He is incapacitated and can no longer oversee our plantations."

Eliza gasped. Reaching for his hand, she led him to a chair. "Oh Charles, I'm so sorry for you," she murmured. "Yes, it is time to return for a year or two—long enough for us to put our affairs in order." Bending over him, she spoke gently. "Is there anything else? I feel a heavy weight of despondency has overcome you."

A small smile spread across his face. "How perceptive you are, dear Eliza. Yes, there is something else. My temporary position has ended. I will no longer be paid as the trade commissioner for Carolina." He searched her face. "I believe the good Lord is sending us home."

Eliza's eyes abruptly filled with tears. "And our children?" Her voice broke. "Charles, I cannot bear to leave them behind. What if we never see them again?" She covered her eyes, collapsing into a rawhide chair, her body limp.

"Dearest, they are safer here than on the high seas. Remember the long sea voyage over? If we are captured, they would be in the enemy's hands, and you can merely imagine how they might suffer."

Eliza shuddered, recalling her father's capture by the French and his ensuing death at their hands. She sat very still, tears streaming from her eyes. Finally, her gaze riveted on him. "We will leave the boys behind. Harriott must come with us. I fear for her sweet disposition if she is made to stay here without us."

Charles nodded. "Very well, Eliza. It will be as you say."

"Where will the boys live? Where will they study?" She tried to swallow but her throat ached. Impatiently, she flicked the tears from her lashes.

"I've arranged for them to stay at Camberville, the school here in Surrey. They can stay with dear Mrs. Evance and her family. You know and respect them. The headmaster, Mr. Gerard, has given me his word that they will be well-attended during our absence."

Eliza nodded, her mind in a whirl. So much to prepare for—their departure and the arrangements to leave her sons comfortably in London.

Once again she heard her mother's voice in her head: *Learn to please the men around you and ensure a harmonious, stable family.* Eliza smiled at this unsolicited, loving remembrance of her far-off mother.

"Oh Charles, can we find time to visit my family in Antigua while we are in South Carolina?" She looked up at him, her glistening eyes varnished with tears.

"Indeed, my love. Just as soon as we rest up from the long journey."

"Oh bless you, dearest. It will mean so much to them and to me."

In March of 1758, Charles, Eliza and ten-year-old Harriott Pinckney boarded an English man of war vessel and headed home to Carolina. The boys—spirited twelve-year-old Charles Cotesworth and his introverted eight-year-old brother Thomas—watched them sail away with courage beyond their years.

"Oh my darlings, two years will fly by quickly and I'll be embracing you warmly once again," wept Eliza, clutching them to her breast. "Mind your manners and write us often. We shall pray for you every day." A sob burst from within her with such force that her sons felt the rush of their own tears.

Eliza could never have dreamed that fourteen years would pass before she held both of her sons again.

Charles Town,

SOUTH CAROLINA
1758-1793

chapter forty-two

T HE VESSEL SAILED UP THE COOPER RIVER ON MAY 19, 1758, after a long and trying ten weeks at sea. Charles, Eliza and Harriott stood on the deck to breathe in the sweet low country air. Through the fringe of masts they could see their own handsome mansion appear on the horizon as they neared the Charles Town waterfront.

"Oh Papa, is that our Mansion? It is so lovely! I can barely remember it." Harriott's words tumbled from her mouth in childlike enthusiasm as her eyes sparkled with joy.

The Mansion was still occupied by Royal Governor Glen so the Pinckney family leased a smaller, more modest home on Ellory Street.

Soon after their arrival Charles turned his attention to the plantation records, quickly realizing that his brother William had been correct in his assessment of their condition. His affairs were in a dreadful state—badly neglected and run-down. He would need to visit each plantation for a physical assessment. Eliza and Harriott accompanied him to Belmont and decided to stay there to begin work on the restorations. Both were dismayed to see how it had "gone back to woods again" in their absence.

Sitting together in Charles's office, Charles and Eliza compiled lists of essentials necessary for the restoration.

"Go at your own pace on these restorations, my love. I shall return shortly and work with you and the others. It will not be too long before it will look as good as when we left it," he pledged, sending her an optimistic grin. Charles took his leave from them and set out to inspect his holdings.

Only a few days into his journey, Charles was seized with fever and became violently ill. Returning straightaway to Belmont, he was examined by the physician. The diagnosis was a severe attack of malaria.

"Oh darling, perhaps you've been away so long from the Carolina swamps and the mosquitoes that you've lost your immunity," soothed Eliza, wiping his burning brow with cold compresses.

"Eliza, you remember summer in the countryside is dangerous. 'Tis the reason so many of the planters move into Charles Town to escape the fever," he murmured.

They agreed to move Charles to the salubrious fresh sea breezes of nearby Mount Pleasant. Their old friend Jacob Motte offered them his plantation for Charles's recovery. Eliza was certain the curative air of the ocean would be the miracle her husband needed.

The malaria stormed through Charles's weakening body. Eliza sat with him during his waking moments, doing everything she could to make him comfortable. She assured her terrified and tenderhearted daughter that her father was a fighter, and would soon be up to join them on their walks to the river. She found a harpsichord and sang one of Charles's favourite hymns, written by Joseph Addison.

> *When all Thy mercies, O my God,*
> *My rising soul surveys,*
> *Transported with the view, I'm lost*
> *In wonder, love, and praise*

Their Charles Town friends visited them at Mount Pleasant and offered Eliza support. All plans for restoration were postponed until Charles could recover.

❧◉❧

Eliza remained at Charles's bedside, declining food and rest. Inwardly she raged at her inability to heal him—outwardly she remained calm, regaling him with her soothing voice as she read him his favourite verses.

"My darling, you are like the proud bow of my boat, leaving quiet lovely ripples in your wake," he remarked.

She turned slightly, hiding the rush of tears gathering in her eyes.

"You have struck your arrow deeply into my heart," he continued in a quiet voice. Taking hold of her trembling fingers, he said, "Thank you for loving me so."

"Oh Charles, you are my life. Pray remember that always. I shall depart for a few moments so that you can sleep, and return later with your supper." Eliza closed the door softly, blinking through a blur of tears.

Charles reached out to her around midnight on July 12. "My little visionary, it is time. I am ready."

"NOOO, Charles!" she screeched in terror. "Do not speak that way! We need you with us!"

He smiled compassionately as he unsteadily linked her slim fingers through his. Tenderly, devotedly, he lifted them to his lips.

"Dear Eliza, let me die the death of the righteous. Let my end be like His."

"Oooh, my Lord. Please hear him not! Spare him, sweet Jesus. Heal him," she choked, hot corrosive tears marring her speech and stinging her eyes as she prayed over his quiet body.

A storm of thoughts crashed through her mind, like angry waves beating against jagged rocks. *My darling, my beloved, I entreat thee not to leave me; for whither thou goest I shall follow.*

Eliza became aware of a terrible noise inside her head as tears streamed down her face.

The sensation of Harriott's small hand on her shoulder cracked open the slight hold she had on herself. The dreadful roaring noise gushed forth from deep inside her. It was a living siren; an unearthly keening. Cruelly, it pushed through Eliza's skin and radiated heat through her daughter's outstretched fingers as Harriott struggled to stop her mother's piercing howling of anguish.

Eliza's pupils were dilated as if she were in physical pain; it was like all the air had been kicked out of her. Still struggling to make sense of it over the noise in her head, Eliza reached out to her daughter, clasping her tightly, defensively. Harriott had dropped to her knees, gray-faced and wailing through her own burning tears.

"He wanted it to be finished," Eliza whispered, her face crumbling. "Now he is at peace."

Unbridled tears poured from Harriott's eyes, racing down her face as she brought her lips to her father's still cheek. Her tender heart was shred with pain.

They rose up together, numbed by grief that turned the room dark and the air as thick as oil. Silently, clinging to each other, they stumbled through the ruined garden down to the water. The crickets were busy in their nocturnal concert; the bullfrogs just warming up. A light breeze stirred the leathery leaves on the live oak trees, and triggered their drooping branches to bend and sway, flinging their shadows in a melancholic dance across the ground.

"I must reach the water," mumbled Eliza. "My hope and our connection."

"Connection, Mama?" asked her trembling daughter, holding fast to her hand.

"Our souls' bond, Harriott. Charles understands the power of water to our love. It is the link that will unite us forever."

They heard the discordant clicking of a fiddler crab as they approached the water. The feel of the salt air, so heavy it felt like raiment against their skin, soothed their hot tear-stained faces. The distant swish of the surf breaking on the beach softened their pain.

"He gave my life beautiful colours. Now I must drink of the cup it pleased God to hand to me."

chapter forty-three

THE SKY GROANED AND CRACKED. COLD, SHRILL needles of rain covered the ground. Lightning sang and hissed through the library window where Eliza sat writing at Charles's mahogany desk. Trees danced and roared as if on fire in the drenching rain. Thunder bellowed. The substance of grief is not imaginary, she thought. It is as real as storms; as real as the absence of air.

My dear Mrs. Lucas—my Mama,

With a bleeding heart I inform you that since you heard from me the greatest of human evils has befallen. Oh! My Dear Mother, dear, dear Mr. Pinckney, the best of husbands and men, is no more!

You were but a short time witness of my happiness. I was for fourteen years the happiest mortal upon earth! Heaven had blessed me beyond the lot of mortals and left me nothing to wish for. The Almighty had given every blessing in that dear, that worthy, that valuable man, whose life was one continued course of active virtue. I do not know of a virtue he did not possess.

I had not a desire beyond him, nor had I a petition to make to Heaven but for a continuance of the blessings I enjoyed, for I was truly blessed. Think then what I now suffer for myself and for my dear fatherless children! Poor babes; how deplorable is their loss.

Their Example, the protector and guide of their youth, the best and tenderest of parents has been taken from them. God alone, who has promised to be the Father of the fatherless, can take up this dreadful loss with them. I trust He will keep them under His Almighty protection and fulfill all their pious Father's prayers upon their heads and will enable this helpless distressed parent they have left to do them well.

Grant God that I may spend my future life in their service and show my affection and gratitude to their dear Father by my care of those precious remains of him, the pledges of the sincerest and tenderest affection that ever was upon earth.

My sons know not of their Father's passing as yet. The news will pierce their tender, infant hearts. Know that my Charles parted this life with less pain than the parting with his sons. Resignation to the Will of the Deity made him happy and cheerful through life, and made all about him so, for his was true religion. In his sickness and death the good Christian man shined forth in an uncommon resolution and patience, humility and resignation to the Divine Will.

Little Harriott was at my side when Mr. Pinckney took his last breath from the dreadful malaria. She suffers quietly; we grieve together and seek consolation in Christian resignation and with faith and hope in Eternity in the next world, where there is a union of virtuous souls...no more death, no more separation.

*The memory of what he was soothes and comforts me for a time.
This pleases me while it pains and may be called the "Luxury of
Grief." Earth has no more charms for me, for I have indeed had
a large share of blessings. How undeserving was I; how unexpected such a treasure, and yet Bounteous Heaven gave him
to me. Yet if Heaven had spared him to see his dear children
brought up and let us go to the grave hand in hand together, what
a Heaven would I have enjoyed upon Earth.*

*I was informed by the good Colonel Talbott that my brother
has sailed to England. Had it been a year ago, it would have
given us great pleasure and comfort to meet with him. Now
I pray he will be there with my boys before the melancholy
tidings reach them.*

*Your dutiful and affectionate tho' greatly afflicted Daughter,
E. Pinckney*

c✦✦ɔ

Eliza was executrix of Charles's will. He left her his slaves and
rings, except two morning rings that he left to Harriott and
Thomas. A third diamond ring would remain hers for her
lifetime and be given to Charles Cotesworth upon her death.
He bequeathed to her the use of the plantations, the houses
and the land in Charles Town. His will left instructions to his
children to live a godly life. He wanted Charles Cotesworth to
be an attorney. He did not choose a profession for Thomas, but
stated he had some hope and expectation he would chose the
same as his brother.

Finally Eliza could put off writing to her sons no longer.
This was the hardest letter she had ever written, and in it she
did her best to make them understand her acceptance of God's
will.

To my dear children Charles and Thomas Pinckney,

My children, you have met with the greatest loss that you could ever meet with upon earth! Your dear, dear father, the best and most valuable of parents, is no more! May God Almighty enable you to put your whole trust and confidence in Him, to rely on him that He will be your father, your comfort and support.

Let it be a comfort to you both that you had such a father who set you a great example! His affection for you was as great as ever was upon earth! And you were good children and deserved it. He left you in the care and protection of the Great and Good God, who had been his merciful Father and Guide through life. Know that your father did not forsake his love of the Lord when he stood in most need of support: in the hour of Death! He met the king of terrors without the least terror, without agony, and went like a lamb into Eternity, into a blessed Eternity—where I have not the least doubt he will reap immortal joy forever and ever.

My children, we have met with the greatest of human Evils, but we must drink of the cup it has pleased God to give us—a bitter cup indeed. Yet we still have reason to thank the hand from whence it comes for all his mercies to him, through life and death, and to us for having given us this inestimable blessing: having spared him so long to us, for all the graces and virtues he endowed him with, for the goodness of his understanding, for one of the best hearts that ever informed the human body.

The joyous hope that we shall meet in Glory, never more to be separated, is the comfort of my life, a life which I endeavour to preserve as a duty due from me to the remains of your dear dear father, to you and your dear sister. May my future life *be spent in showing you how much, how truly I loved and honoured your dear father by my affection and care of you.*

Adieu, my beloved children! God Almighty bless, guide and protect you! Make you his own children, and worthy such a father as yours was, and comfort you in this great affliction is the fervent and constant prayer of your ever affectionate tho' greatly afflicted Mother,

Eliza Pinckney

❧❦❧

The next letter she wrote was private, and it was to Charles. This letter would never be seen by anyone but her, Charles and her all-seeing Heavenly Father.

Beloved husband, I love you with every ounce of strength I possess. Relinquishing you into His hands was agony. You must go on believing that I will love you beyond the temporary pause at the grave. You need not fear the distance between us again. There is only light ahead that darkness cannot extinguish. My love for you shall have no end.

Eliza smiled softly as she rose up from the gnarled oak stump by the river, feeling her heart take off lightly like a butterfly. Dark clouds alternated with sunshine, causing the colours of the marsh grasses to change from slightly purple in the shadows to a soft yellow in the sunlight. Across the tidal pools, herons and egrets glanced up, startled, as she passed them on her walk home.

She understood that a part of Charles had survived in her. No longer did she have to run from the pain. Perhaps she could finally embrace it and find some consolation there.

chapter forty-four

ELIZA AND HARRIOTT GRIEVED FOR FOURTEEN MONTHS, remaining in their small home on Ellory Street. Eliza was devastated by her loss and lived quietly, receiving only close friends. She had the companionship of Lady Amelia MacKenzie, a dear friend who had moved in after Charles's death, caring for Eliza during the long weeks of her mysterious illness. Eliza came close to losing her life twice from extreme fever, intensified by her lethargic state of mind and lack of desire to live.

Near the end of the grieving period, and during an extremely dangerous stage of illness, her beloved mother Ann passed away in Antigua. Polly and her brothers knew about Eliza's fevers and depression and chose not to tell her about Ann's death for several months. They wrote her the news when they were certain she had recovered. Although she would have preferred to have seen her mother one last time, she knew through personal experience that they had done the right thing. She still held hope that her family could be reunited in the near future.

After their grieving, Eliza and Harriott returned to Belmont and worked on the planting of crops and restoration of their plantation. With renewed energy they cleared the woods and planted groves of trees, including the native magnolia and palmetto royal. Eliza loved the magnolias, calling them the *loveliest of all trees*. She sent magnolia seeds to the King family in England. She dubbed the palmetto royal the "pennento royal" and wrote to the Kings that *the palmetto bears the noblest bunch of flowers I have ever seen. The main stem of the bunch is two meters long with hundreds of white flowers hanging pendant upon it.*

Eliza wrote to Mr. Morley, her agent in London, describing the drought that had dried up the crops. She told him about her dishonest overseers, explaining that she was seeking a new man—*a good man to direct and inspect the overseers, comfortable in his circumstances to work with women and children not able to do for themselves.* Her nephew Charles Pinckney, whom Charles had educated for law in England, tried to help her but knew little about managing a plantation. Her husband's brother William also assisted where he could, yet remained incapacitated by his stroke. Eliza Pinckney, now thirty-six years old, found herself managing several plantations with only the help of her young daughter.

In her letter to Mr. Morley, she wrote of her hard work.

'Tis precisely what I need to heal. Perhaps better for me...had there not been a necessity for it, I might have sunk to the grave in that lethargy of stupidity that seized me. I do hope it pleases God to send us good seasons so I can clear the estates of debt. It is a difficult thing to manage property in Carolina.

She was now responsible for more than three hundred people, a task she took quite seriously. She set up a rhythm to her days. Arising early, she walked through the gardens to the water where she wrote in her journal, and then returned to meet with the caregiver of the sick, giving advice and issuing medicine. The health of the servants was of great importance to Eliza. She visited the sick at that time and again in the afternoon.

Eliza returned to eat her breakfast and met with the men and maid servants to assign their daily tasks. She visited the fields, encouraging her workers and resolving any problems that might have arisen. Over time she was able to increase indigo production and cultivated more of the other crops. Her holdings were extensive, but money was hard to collect. And her residence at Belmont still resembled a wild jungle. Lady Amelia MacKenzie helped her in the struggle to reclaim it.

Eliza had always been genuinely interested in her coloured workers and was endowed with an extraordinary ability to teach them to read. She enjoyed training them for the varied duties on the plantations and in the city home. She read the Bible to them on Sundays, and encouraged them with instruction in morality and industry, much as she had taught her own children.

A great deal of writing needed to be done, especially since more than one plantation required written directions. Orders had to be sent to the respective overseers: records of the plantings—the results, profits and losses; the credits and the debts—and then the cost of each slave. Eliza handled all these tasks herself, including the recording of the financial accounts of each plantation.

She taught the handmaidens to weave and spin, to cut and to make clothes for everyone on the plantation, as well as the livery worn by the house servants, the gowns for the family and the suits for the men. Meat had to be cured, soap made, candles molded, sheep shorn and wool carded. The dairy had to furnish butter and cream and the garden vegetables and fruit.

She and Harriott also worked on school lessons during the late morning and early afternoon. Eliza educated her as she had once taught Polly, preparing her to become a planter's wife. She brought music teachers into the home and was delighted to discover that her daughter shared her love of singing and musical instruments. Harriott learned French with the help of a tutor, and could soon read French and English classics equally well.

"Darling, I am thrilled with your interest in music," Eliza

said warmly after listening to her daughter's practice. "I would have thought you would learn the harpsichord, as I did, but your skill with the flute is astonishing." She smiled softly, remembering the days when her dear friend Cameron wooed her with harmonious flute melodies.

In 1760 a violent smallpox epidemic broke out in the community. The physicians claimed it was carried to them by Governor William Henry Littleton's troops, after their time spent in the Indian country. Harriott had been inoculated as a child in England and Eliza was immune, but a large part of the black population succumbed to the disease, even after inoculation.

Eliza stayed at Belmont to help the victims. Three hundred whites and three hundred-fifty blacks died within several days in the outlying areas. She opened her sick house as a smallpox hospital and supervised its operations, working many hours every day.

A short time later a violent epidemic of typhus reached Charles Town, and once again Eliza Pinckney opened her sick house as a hospital to the ill. This time she lost only eight people to the disease. She wrote a recipe book that included medicines she had compounded in her kitchen, with ingredients such as mugwort, red poppy flowers, hickory ashes and Madeira wine.

One day Eliza received a letter from her best friend in England regarding the "rumour" that she was about to remarry. Eliza laughed as she read it and quickly penned her response.

My dear friend, Mrs. King,

I must satisfy your curiosity about my suitor. I told him gently that I appreciated his interest in me, but that I had no intention of leaving my plantations or sharing my life with any man. To you I will confess that I do not have the financial need to marry. Also, I did not love the gentleman. I have loved only one man, my Charles, and to this day and forever I will love only him.

Allow me to share with you my intense desire to return to England—so forceful I've set aside some money to do so in a year or two. I've written Dr. Kirkpatrick about the boys' education, asking him to constantly counsel and advise them as how to conduct themselves. Judging from my dear sons' missives, he seems to be doing a superb piece of work with them.

A year later she transferred the boys to another school, because the air at Camberville did not agree with Thomas. Charles Cotesworth, now fifteen years old, wrote that he wanted to attend Warrington, where his friend Tommy Evance studied. If that were not possible, he would like to attend Harrow. With a loving but determined heart, Eliza wrote him that his father's wishes were for him to attend Westminster.

Charles dearest, it is the father who gives his sons identity as well as demanding filial duty. Your dear father was explicit in his will about the direction your lives should take. Now the supervision of your education falls upon my shoulders. I definitely do not want you to acquire corrupt principles, which would be fatal to you. Warrington prepares young men for the ministry, and you are not to be brought up to the church as a vocation. However, your father did insist that you be brought up virtuously and make the glory of God your principal aim and study. Pray respect your father's wishes.

In 1762, the St. Cecilia Society of Charles Town, originally a musical club of amateur gentlemen who presented concerts on November 22, St. Cecilia's Day, began to sponsor elegant balls. The music was excellent; often as many as two hundred-fifty ladies were present at the dances. Their headdresses were not as high as those of the ladies up north but the richness of their gowns surpassed them. The gentlemen dressed with lavish elegance, many with swords, which had become uncommon in the north. These balls evolved into the venue for the aristocratic daughters of Charles Town to effect their debut.

Eliza prepared Harriott for these formal affairs, acknowledging that her daughter required cultivation in both musical and social graces. For that reason she accepted many social invitations, taking Harriott under her wing as Charles and Elizabeth Pinckney had done for her years before. She accepted invitations to dinners and dances of her neighbours and good friends, enjoying herself while keeping close watch over Harriott. Discouraging any male attention to herself, she scrutinized all possible suitors for her daughter. Not a day passed that her husband's memories were not fixed in her thoughts— her *guiding light*, as she dubbed her bond with Charles.

The colonists were becoming more troubled as they learned about England's change of attitude toward them. Even the Pinckney boys, studying and living in England, found their patience wearing thin when Parliament passed the Stamp Act in 1765. This law imposed a tax on books, newspapers, playing cards, legal documents and almanacs arriving from the American colonies. This Stamp Act became a symbol of the *absentee-landlord* standing of the Crown over the colonies. Many of the colonists began to earnestly question their allegiance to the mother country.

chapter forty-five

1765

WORKING QUIETLY ON HER NEEDLEPOINT IN THE SUN-drenched parlour, Harriott observed her mother from beneath her eyelids, watching the movements of her slender fingers as she wrote to her brother, Charles Cotesworth, now in his fourth year at Westminster. Harriott thought her mother looked beautiful—serene, feminine, healthy and contented. At forty-three, Eliza was a stunning woman.

"Mama, please tell me about Papa," she blurted out, suddenly aching for information on her father.

Eliza set down her pen and studied Harriott's face, so like her husband's features except for the dark green eyes. Her blond hair was silky and straight, her body long and lithe. She was tall like her father, with high pronounced cheekbones that gave her face an ethereal elegant quality far beyond her years. Her face was a feminine portrait of Charles.

A warm smile crossed Eliza's face. "He was full of life. Excitement hung around him like a garment. It shone through his eyes and awakened his every feature." Her exquisite eyes sparkled. "Especially when we were together," she added quietly.

"How did you meet?"

"At a mutual friend's home in Charles Town. I was with my father. How well I remember the first time I saw him. His eyes locked on mine for just a second longer than necessary. For that one moment, it was as if he'd taken all the vitality he'd brought into the room, tucked it into a bouquet and offered it to me as a secret gift."

"Did you know from the beginning that it was love?" asked Harriott, eyes wide in wonder.

Eliza gave her a sober nod. "That is quite possible. I saw the love and warmth reflected in his eyes on the occasions he came by to visit me, shortly after we had met. Of course he was married, so I didn't determine that until much later, but it was plainly there. The warmth and tenderness in those dark eyes let me know he was attracted to me, as I was to him. Yet the time was not right. Later our cordial friendship grew into deep respect and eventually, an intensely loving relationship."

Eliza sighed deeply. "Your father was without a doubt the most appealing man I've ever met. Also, he was warm, loving, intelligent and kind. "

Mother and daughter sat silently for a moment, as if respecting an honoured family member passing through the room.

"My goodness, Mama, how beautifully you speak of him! Even listening to your words, 'tis nothing compared to what he used to say about you in praise behind your back." A smile broke slowly across her face. It was so similar to Charles's smile it made Eliza's heart ache.

"My darling, you were only ten when he passed. How is it possible that you remember such comments?" Her voice broke gently.

"Oh Mama, but I can. One of my favourite remembrances was Papa's remarks on your loving kindness. He told us your enthusiastic admiration for the achievements of others delighted him. He prayed that we would attain that level of generosity."

Eliza's eyes filled unexpectedly with tears. Harriott watched as sorrow rushed over her face, and then disappeared as quickly as it had appeared.

"And he loved your self-confidence and composure, your strength of character. He told us you were a true original."

Eliza's eyes crinkled at the corners as she smiled.

"Mama, do you remember your first kiss with my Papa?"

Eliza's face brightened. She laughed. "I believe so. It was at a ball in Charles Town. We had been dancing all evening and his arms were circling my back and my waist and I felt so deliriously happy. Before I knew it, I stood on tiptoe and touched my lips to his. He was surprised but, without missing a beat of the waltz, scooped me closer and cradled me against his chest."

"Oh, Mama, how glorious! He was so gone on you!"

"And I on him, Harriott. We had almost fifteen delightful years together. I shall always be thankful for those years, and for you and your brothers: the proof of our love."

Harriott leaned over and squeezed her mother's hand. "Thank you Mama. I pray that one day I shall find a man who loves me as Papa loved you," she said, her voice a whisper.

Eliza fixed her eyes on her daughter, sending her a soft look. "You shall, my love. Your Papa will make sure of that from up there, and I will insist on it."

❧∞❧

Eliza followed the enormous growth of the indigo trade with great interest and delighted in the wealth it was bringing to her colony. Unlike large heavy barrels of rice, small cubes of indigo could be transported on a few well-protected ships. She was secretly proud to have been the initiator of this godsend, sustained by her loving father's faith and later supported by her devoted Charles. She helped arrange the visit of Moses Lindo from England, who stayed at Belmont and taught all the local planters how to sort and grade the dye.

Eliza spent a great deal of time with botanist-physician Dr.

Alexander Garden, Commissary of the Bishop of London in Charles Town. The plant "gardenia" was named for him by Swedish plant classifier Carl Linnaeus, to whom Dr. Garden sent samples of numerous types of flora from the Carolinian lowlands. Dr. Garden spent many years in Charles Town sharing his vast knowledge of botany and zoology, and especially enjoyed sharing his findings with Eliza because of her love of all things botanical.

Eliza yearned to join her sons in England for a lengthy visit. Something constantly prevented her from booking the journey, usually the financial means. Both boys had completed their studies at Westminster School and Christ Church. They were matriculated in law studies in the Middle Temple, London, and the school was tremendously costly for Eliza.

They were also taking military science at the Royal Military Academy at Caen, France because of the possibility of war with the mother country. Whatever the cost, her boys would be trained to assume some responsibility in America's future. Although her heart ached over the long separation from them, she knew she was working toward her goal: the complete and proper education Charles had planned for his sons.

chapter forty-six

"MISS ELIZA, I WOULD BE HONOURED TO RECEIVE YOUR blessing to marry your daughter."

Eliza nodded, tears spiking her lashes, and hugged them fervently.

Harriott and Daniel Huger Horry approached Eliza together to request her permission and blessing for their marriage. Although Harriott was only nineteen years old, Eliza realized she had blossomed into a mature, well-rounded and kind woman. She rejoiced that her daughter had fallen in love with a good and decent man, who would love her and offer her the same type of happiness that Charles had given to her.

Harriott was quite popular and had enjoyed many suitors, among them the wealthy French Huguenot widower, Daniel Huger Horry of Hampton Plantation. He was tall and good-looking, with an olive complexion and dark serious eyes. Unlike most of her other suitors, he was quiet and persistent and quickly won her heart.

Daniel was the third generation of Horrys to live on the Santee River, a popular settling area for French Huguenots. It was the delta of the Santee River that General Lafayette paid his first visit to the brave little New Republic, when he was only twenty years old. And it was one of these brave Huguenot gentlemen, Colonel Francis Kinloch Huger, who years later risked his life to rescue General Lafayette from the Austrian dungeons—this he did in gratitude for what General Lafayette had done for Carolina.

At the time Daniel proposed to Harriott there were seventy families of Huguenot background living on the Santee—a temperate, thrifty and industrious group who planted rice on the delta and indigo on the highlands.

Daniel's first wife was Miss Judith Serré, who died of malaria in 1766, along with her two small children. They lived in the family plantation which began as a modest six-room farmhouse. Built in the 1740's, they named it Hampton Plantation, and that is where Daniel took his new bride. She and Daniel would later add a few more rooms, and finally, Eliza and Harriott would re-model once again, turning the farmhouse into a mansion.

Daniel and Harriott were married on February 13, 1768 by the Reverend Robert Smith, Rector of the St. Philip's Parish of Charles Town. He was thirty-five and she was nineteen. The gala event was commemorated by their many friends, since it was the first celebratory gala for Eliza Pinckney and her family in ten years. Eliza's happiness was a bit tarnished by the absence of her sons and siblings, but she refused to feel sorry for herself. Harriott, glowing with youthful elegance, radiated joy as she floated down the aisle to unite her life with Daniel's.

The Santee Plantations were quite inaccessible. It was a long water trip from Charles Town to the mouth of the Santee River. After the Cooper River was crossed by sail or rowed ferry, there still remained forty miles over deep sandy roads before reaching the plantations, by horseback or horse-drawn vehicles.

Mail delivery to the area was almost impossible, unless an obliging neighbour happened to make the difficult journey to the city and agreed to carry letters between Eliza and Harriott. Fortunately, both women loved to write, and when Harriott became pregnant, it was even more important to keep up their correspondence. During the hot "fever season" both Eliza and the Horrys moved into Charles Town to escape the heat, arriving in mid-June and often remaining there until October. Eliza continued to rent out the Mansion house to the Governor and stayed in a smaller town house nearby. Harriott and Daniel resided in his family's town house near the center of the city.

Eliza learned that her sons were signing petitions and working diligently to enlighten the British of the injustices committed against the colonies. They kept their mother informed of their visits to Parliament to listen to the debates, in order to understand what options were available to them and the colonists.

It saddened Eliza that George III failed to speak out against these injustices, remembering him as a kind young lad of fifteen during their pleasant visit with him in Kew. Surely that kind boy, so interested in her son Charles's stories about Carolina, would now want to stop the prejudices against the New World.

∽✿∾

"Harriott and Daniel, I sincerely support the actions of my little dissenters, do you not? I am proud of their courage in standing up to the British, even as they finish their studies in England." It was summertime and they were gathered at the Horry town house in Charles Town.

"Miss Eliza, do you believe that the King's attitude has been inflamed by a tax-hungry Parliament?" asked her son-in-law Daniel.

"Indeed I do. Those are the views my sons express as well. Oh dear, how I wish they would return. And I long for the Crown to stop their tyrannical treatment of our colonies."

"Mama, look at this! Charles writes that Tom has become so vocal in his arguments for liberty that in Oxford he is known as the 'Little Rebel!'"

Eliza laughed gleefully. "I knew it! I had already given them both that appellation. It suits them well."

A few weeks later they received the long-awaited news that Charles would be returning to Charles Town. He had graduated *cum laude* from Oxford, studied law at the Inner Temple and been admitted to the Bar. He had even "ridden on Circuit to observe the English practice." After ten years of arduous studies, he was finally ready to come home. Eliza was beyond joyful, counting down the hours until she could embrace him again.

The rumblings of a possible Revolution were growing louder, yet many were not paying heed. Their colony was too prosperous for them to think about war. The Peace of Paris in 1763 had given freedom and safety to their commerce. Rice and indigo paid off magnificently in international trade, giving all the planters in Carolina's low country a well-deserved and long-lasting windfall. Indigo had become the fifth largest export item from the colonies by the eve of the Revolution. It was so valuable it was even used as a form of payment.

Charles Cotesworth's sailing vessel finally landed in Charles Town. Harriott was surprised at how long her mother had been able to stand on tiptoe as his ship maneuvered its way slowly to the dock. The horizon seemed to become only the width of the narrow gangplank as the line of bedraggled passengers stumbled ashore. Then her Charles, her young hero, was steadily advancing straight into Eliza's ecstatic embrace.

Back at the house, Eliza found herself unable to keep her eyes off him. "Charles, I see you grown up and, blessed be God that you have become the man your father and I hoped for." Tears gathered in the corners of her eyes as she held him tightly.

"You are as lovely as I remember you, Mama. You must have many suitors, yet you spend your time running plantations and assisting the less fortunate." A huge smile spread across his handsome face as he slipped his arm around her waist and led her into the garden.

"I am living the life the Lord has granted me. I have been blessed abundantly. Now when Thomas is in my arms once again, our family will be complete."

"'Tis my assurance he will return soon. He is finishing up his studies and preparing for the Bar. Then he has promised to come home."

Charles returned to Charles Town fired up with enthusiasm for the American cause. He felt resentful of having been treated as a "Colonial," or a member of the second class in England. Yet he soon discovered that in Charles Town, he was considered an aristocrat. His father had been Speaker of the House of the Assembly, a member of the King's Council and Chief Justice of the Colony. His sister Harriott had been presented at the St. Cecilia Society Ball. He quickly found work as an attorney in Charles Town, and in short order was elected to a seat in the Colonial legislature.

Near the end of 1769, Harriott and Daniel presented Eliza her first grandchild—baby Harriott Horry.

"My daughter, we are so very blessed to hold your beautiful child in our arms. Another generation has begun in our family. May the Lord bless little Harriott always."

After years of separation from her sons, the loss of her husband and mother, and fear of an impending war, Eliza cuddled the tiny baby and felt she had been made whole.

chapter forty-seven

ELIZA STRUGGLED FOR WEEKS OVER RENOUNCING HER loyalty to the Crown. After all, her beloved father was a British army officer and Lieutenant Governor of Antigua. This allegiance had been instilled throughout her schooling in England and while living with her family in London for nearly five years. She had enjoyed the friendship of many interesting people during her time spent in England, and learned to deeply appreciate the character and traditions of British society. And many of her fellow colonists were still loyal to the Crown.

Yet no mother stood more proudly behind her son when he was among the first to volunteer to bear arms in the Colonist's War for Independence. Charles Cotesworth Pinckney knew his father's will called for his sons to "employ all future abilities in the service of God and their country." Eliza supported her son on the importance of every citizen's freedom. Liberty had been a cornerstone of British democracy, and could not be so easily laid aside because the Crown had demanded it.

To Eliza's great delight, Thomas Pinckney finally returned to Charles Town in 1773 and was admitted to the Bar the following year. He arrived just as the province was preparing for war.

On an official day of prayer and fasting, the churches were crowded. Bishop Smith's patriotic sermon ended with "Lord, defend us in our difficult great struggle in the cause of liberty." The women shed tears, the men were animated, but all still hoped His Majesty would overrule his oppressive counselors in London. The First Continental Congress met that same year to coordinate relations with Britain and the thirteen self-governing provinces. They also petitioned King George III to intervene with Parliament.

Events moved quickly when King George III failed to intervene. The colonists felt betrayed by the Parliament of Great Britain. In support of their fellow colonists to the north, Carolinians staged a "Tea Party" and dumped crates of taxed tea into the Cooper River.

Their pleas to the Crown were once again ignored and British soldiers were billeted in Boston. By 1775 the Provincial Congresses formed the Second Continental Congress and authorized a Continental Army. Both of Eliza's sons volunteered as full-time regular officers, receiving captain commissions as General George Washington began to organize his Continental Army.

Eliza was staying at Hampton Plantation with her daughter and two grandchildren while the men were away for their military training. She began collecting, packing, and dispatching necessaries to her sons. In late April of 1775, Harriott received a letter from a friend in Boston.

"Oh Mama, the British have taken action. They have moved into Lexington and taken shots at the colonists!" Harriott's eyes widened in shock and then grew fearful.

Eliza's eyes roamed quickly over the letter. "Look Harriott! They were alerted. Mr. Paul Revere and his cohorts warned the American soldiers of the Redcoats' advance so they were prepared for them."

"It seems the northerners are no longer in support of the Crown. Could we now be at war?" Harriott's face trembled. She was on the edge of sobbing.

The early battles in Massachusetts were for liberty from

British oppression rather than for independence from British rule. The next battle, known as the Battle of Bunker Hill, resulted in a small British victory, but a major demonstration of the colonists' willingness to fight the Mother Country.

Congress was still reluctant to completely separate from England, and sent King George III a petition calling for greater liberties yet disavowing independence. In response, the King promptly declared war against America.

Eliza, working her indigo plantation at Belmont, grew increasingly concerned about the war's impact. The southern colonies were producing 1,122,220 pounds of indigo a year for export to England. She wondered what would become of her valuable crops.

By June of 1776 John Adams was working with Thomas Jefferson, Robert Livingston, Benjamin Franklin and Roger Sherman to draft a declaration of independence. The final version was approved on July 4 and read from the balcony of the State House in Boston to throngs of people gathered below.

Eliza and her daughter followed the events of the fledgling nation as closely as they could. As they diligently sewed clothing and mended uniforms with the other women in their sewing circle, one of them mentioned that she heard the authors of the newly written *Declaration of Independence* were now in hiding.

"Why would they be in hiding?" Harriott asked.

"Fear of the British, I'm certain. Surely they have a price on their heads for disloyalty, don't you think?" answered one of the seamstresses.

"That's it, of course! Many have been enlisted to help! Why, they even asked a woman to print out the *Declaration*. Her name is Mary Katherine Goddard, and she's the publisher of the *Maryland Journal*. They say she's signed the *Declaration* as well, on the bottom corner of the document. Now there's a brave woman," added Eliza with an authentic smile.

As captain of his regiment, Charles Cotesworth Pinckney raised and led the elite Grenadiers of the First South Carolina

Regiment. He had successfully defended Charles Town in the Battle of Sullivan's Island in June of 1776, when the British forces under General Sir Henry Clinton staged an amphibious attack on the state capital.

Yet he felt constant concern for his wife, Sarah Middleton, whom he had married in 1773. She was the daughter of the Honorable Henry Middleton. Eliza, still living at Belmont Plantation, spent time with her as well as with her other children's families. In 1776, Charles Cotesworth took command of his regiment and was promoted to the rank of Colonel—a position he retained throughout the war.

Thomas Pinckney, also a captain in the First South Carolina Regiment, saw a great deal of action in 1779, after becoming an aide-de-camp to General Horatio Gates. He had inherited the Auckland Plantation at Ashepoo, considered the safest of all the plantations. All the Pinckney valuables were stored there. The family was incredulous when it was plundered and burned to the ground by marauding British regiments.

Eliza's home in Belmont was left intact, but the contents were destroyed and her servants were taken or encouraged to run away. Just as she had stood up to Nicholas Cromwell and the defeats of her early years, she fearlessly faced the British. When she learned they also plundered and destroyed her Mansion House, she furiously endeavored to reason with the officers during a hastily called meeting in their bivouac.

"I sincerely believe in the rights of humanity," she told the row of Redcoats. "That is the reason for this struggle between America and England. I am a peace-loving woman and throughout my lifetime have sought to carve out for myself some calm in this wild new land. But there comes a time when the peace must be broken, and the time is now. If need be, I am willing to fight again."

The officers watched her intently, expressions of bewilderment expanding their features.

In times of distress Eliza looked to nature for comfort. She found her spot in the forest and nestled her body into the womb of her special trees, blending into the earth and settling her bare feet into the moss and spiced pine needles, peat and mud. The rich dark syrup of Mother Earth oozed between her toes and through her pores. Eliza gulped in huge salt breaths from the forest-filtered air, bowing to the sturdy great oak and slim cedar pine.

When she reached the water, she lifted her skirt and squirmed down into it, waiting for the incoming tide to loosen the earth under her. Mud reached her calves and she felt calm and secure. Raising her arms, she let them sway like weightless boughs. Then, completely at peace, she received her reward, chillingly beautiful in the purest of melodies. The crystalline note of the hermit thrush stilled the earth and became her spirit song.

chapter forty-eight

ELIZA CONTINUED TO TAKE REFUGE IN HER JOURNAL writing.

The plantations have been—some quite, some nearly, ruined—all with very few exceptions. They have suffered the loss of crops, livestock, boats, carts—all gone, either taken or destroyed. The crops grown this year will yield only a small amount because of the desertion of the Negroes. The country must be greatly impoverished by the death of many slaves from the smallpox that ravaged the British camps. When the British soldiers moved into Belmont, they were disruptive of my property and paid no rent. I was forced to leave my home and move forty miles away to Hampton Plantation, on the South Santee River, to live with my daughter and her children.

Eliza Lucas Pinckney saw her sons rise from junior officers to become close confidants of the Commander-In-Chief George Washington. When the war shifted back to the home territory, Charles Cotesworth joined his brother in an unsuccessful campaign to thwart the British attacks coming from Florida. After Savannah fell, the British established a firm foothold in the south and rampaged through South Carolina during 1779. In the late summer Eliza received a highly anticipated letter from Charles Cotesworth. She read it out loud to her family that same evening.

My dearest and most honoured Mama,

It has been a difficult yet edifying experience to serve as protectors of our home and precious shores. It seems our colony is experiencing the majority of the battles and playing an important role in ending the dreaded colonial conflict.

The years spent in our beloved Charles Town and also in our military training in England could never have prepared me for the physical and social challenges that we find ourselves facing each day. My fellow soldiers are of the highest caliber, yet many suffer from a lack of adequate schooling and knowledge of the world beyond their fields and publican houses.

It strikes me truly that as a new nation, we must do everything possible to advance the cause of superior education and cultural pursuits. Only a nation of scholars may call itself fully prepared to meet its responsibilities and potential.

Thomas, not surprisingly, has fixed his gaze on the far horizon. I frequently find him deep in debate with a group of fellow officers regarding the most salubrious diplomatic and political activities that our future leaders may take as they establish worthy relationships with our European allies, while studying the Western regions with a worthy goal of expansion and renewing our resources.

As to my health, pray let not your heart be troubled. I am as fit as a fiddle and twice as spry!

Both Thomas and I look forward to hearing the best of news from you most quickly about hearth and home, and will endeavor to keep you well apprised of our progress and fortune in return.

With all best wishes for a calm and prosperous planting season I remain,

Your most devoted and respectful son,
Charles Cotesworth Pinckney

Eliza was living through the horrors of invasion and great personal impoverishment yet remained confident that the American cause would be triumphant in the end. She had been widowed for twenty years now and had managed on her own since she was seventeen years old. When Thomas's plantation was destroyed, Charles Cotesworth offered to divide his property with his mother and brother. They declined, unwilling to take it from his young family.

Several families of women and children moved into Hampton Plantation with Harriott and her family, seeking safety while their husbands and sons desperately attempted to save Charles Town. But the British finally captured Charles Town, the south's paramount city, in May of 1780. Major General Benjamin Lincoln surrendered his five thousand men to the British on May 12, 1780. From Charles Town, the British now controlled most of Georgia and South Carolina.

Charles Cotesworth Pinckney was taken prisoner and held at Snee Farm across the Cooper River. His family was turned out of their home and sought refuge with Harriott's family at Hampton Plantation. From his prison, Charles tirelessly maintained the defeated troops' loyalty to the Patriots' cause. His letters to them inspired unwavering dedication to their sense of destiny.

If I had a vein that did not beat with the love of my country, I myself would open it, he wrote. *If I had a drop of blood that could flow dishonourably, I myself would let it out.*

Belmont was plundered, and the British soldiers commandeered her home and forced her out. She walked away with her head held high. Her cattle were used to feed the soldiers. As she left, she commented to Colonel James Moncrieff that her son Charles had planted many of the oak trees and they meant a great deal to the family.

"Ah, and where is your son now?" asked the Colonel.

"He is a prisoner at Snee," she replied, leveling her eyes on his.

"Then tell him his trees will make excellent firewood. He can depend on the trees being burned for my men." Eliza was shaken by his ignoble audacity.

Charles was kept in close confinement until his release in 1782, when he was named Major General by General Washington. Thomas had escorted the governor from the city when it fell under siege, thereby escaping capture for a time. The British evicted women from their homes in the city, or kept them on to grace their British balls. The women who engaged in this whirl of social events were marked for life by others who refused the invitation. Some felt it was safer than to join the women living on the plantations.

A South Carolina warrior named Francis Marion, the "Swamp Fox," led a regiment of irregular troops, who fought without pay, using weapons and horses captured from the British. He urged the women to remain on their properties, make provisions, and send information to the American soldiers. He arrived at Hampton one afternoon, searching for conversation with the Pinckney women as well as a good meal.

Despite the desperate conditions under which they were forced to live, Marion and his men were polite and appreciated the offer of a hot meal to be enjoyed after some well-deserved rest.

But as they slept into the late afternoon, the British troops rode up to Hampton.

"They're approaching now, Mama. I can hear the horses!" exclaimed Harriott.

"We must make haste and warn them now," answered her mother. "You go and awaken Francis Marion and his men, and I shall meet the soldiers at the door."

"Mr. Marion, wake up!" Harriott entered the area where the men were sleeping. "The Redcoats are nearing the plantation. You must escape posthaste."

The Swamp Fox and his soldiers scurried to their feet, gathering their meager belongings as they stumbled out the door. There was no time to give them food. Harriott ran before them, showing them the fastest route to the creek.

"Go quickly; swim across to the nearby island!" she pleaded. "You will be safe there."

In the meantime, Eliza invited around two dozen British soldiers into the Horry's home.

"May I be of assistance to you, gentlemen?" she smiled.

"Good evening, Ma'am. We've been riding all day looking for the 'Swamp Fox.' Word has it he and his men alighted here this morning."

Eliza gasped. "The Swamp Fox here? Oh my. Please come forward and have a look."

After searching the house and grounds, the troops realized their mistake and apologized.

"Gentlemen, now that you are here, we have a simple but ample supper cooking, and would welcome your company. Please, consider joining us," offered Harriott, Mistress of Hampton Plantation.

The soldiers accepted gratefully and enjoyed dinner and conversation with the Pinckney women. After several hours, they left in a jolly mood.

"But Mama, after all we did for them, I could hardly contain my indignation when General Tarleton confiscated one of your favourite leather volumes of Milton."

Eliza shook her head slowly. "Indeed, and it was bound in crimson and gold."

On their next visit to Hampton Plantation, the British soldiers were searching for Daniel Horry and Thomas Pinckney. Thomas escaped but Daniel was captured, prompting Harriott to write to a friend: *We have lately been well-plundered by the enemy.* Thomas was eventually returned to his unit, injured in battle, captured by the British forces and imprisoned in Camden, South Carolina. His wife Elizabeth, pregnant and frightened, returned to the home of her mother Rebecca Motte, where she stayed with family members until the birth of her first child.

Eliza received news of Thomas's imprisonment. He had been severely wounded; one of his legs was brutally shattered. She wrote to him immediately.

How readily I would part with life, dear Thomas, could it save your distress. I suffer more from my anxiety and gloomy apprehensions than if I were near you. I have not yet seen your baby son, but my friend has and pronounces him as a fine lad—hearty and healthy. Gracious God, I entreat You to support me in this hour of distress.

Thomas was extremely fortunate to have been discovered among the wounded by an old school friend from England. That British soldier persuaded his senior officer to send for a physician, whose ministrations to Thomas saved his injured limb and most likely his life.

His impromptu "hospital" was the residence of Mrs. Clay in Charles Town, a woman whom Eliza had met during her early days of attending social outings. Eliza sent comfort packages and paid small fees to the British officers in Charles Town to assure their delivery. She enlisted a servant to go and help care for her son. She also wrote Mrs. Clay many letters, thanking her profusely for her *"truly maternal care for my son,"* and including words like *"my heart overflows with gratitude."*

Lieutenant General Cornwallis allowed Thomas to return to his in-laws' home under house arrest shortly after the birth of his son. He was to remain there indefinitely, until a prisoner-exchange program was drawn up. Eliza constantly worried that the care of her son and her grandson would wear young Elizabeth out. Her anxiety was well-placed, as the fatigued young mother almost died nurturing her gravely wounded husband back to health.

Both Charles Cotesworth and Thomas Pinckney were on parole under house arrest until an exchange could be coordinated. They were wooed by their loyalist friends but never wavered from their patriot beliefs. Eventually, they were shipped to Philadelphia for the complicated prisoner swap. Then they went together to visit their friend and leader, General George Washington, and requested to serve under him for the rest of the war.

After Thomas Pinckney left the Motte property, the British took it over and established a garrison, forcing the women and children to live in a farmhouse nearby. A few days later, a troop of American soldiers, led by Francis Marion and Henry Lee, surrounded the British encampment on the estate and demanded their surrender. The British soldiers refused to give up, believing reinforcements would soon come to their aid.

The American leaders felt they had no option but to destroy the Motte Mansion in order to deprive the British troops of their stronghold. Yet neither Lee nor Marion could bear to raze the house. Rebecca Motte had cared for their sick and wounded and her son-in-law was a Continental Army hero.

They went to her for advice, and together they devised a plan. She had some East Indian arrows that burst into flame when they struck their target. She provided the arrows and they set the roof on fire. At this point the British realized they could not win and surrendered. Most of the mansion was saved through the quick thinking of Rebecca Motte. Afterward, she served up a meal to the officers of both armies. The casing for the arrows became the scabbard for her knitting needles.

Eliza Pinckney, now fatigued and disillusioned, eventually came to the realization she could no longer pay her bills. She described her desperate situation in a letter to her longtime friend, Dr. Alexander Garden, who supported the British.

I find myself robbed by the British and deserted by my slaves; my property pulled to pieces, burned and destroyed, my money of no value, and my children sick—now prisoners of war. It may seem strange that a single woman, accused of no crime, who had a fortune sufficient to live in any part of the world.. should be so entirely deprived of it as not to be able to pay a debt under sixty pound sterling. Yet this is my case, dear friend I have been left destitute.

These words were penned by the same woman who years ago had planted the oak trees with the hope they would one day supply an American shipping business. Those trees were all gone, cut down as spoils and plunder in the War for Independence.

chapter forty-nine

ELIZA'S FORTUNE WAS DESTROYED, BUT HER SPIRIT WAS not. She still had her house in town, yet the British kept the rent. Her new money-making plan was the sale of wood, from which she would pay off her bills. If that were unsuccessful, she would have to rent out her few remaining slaves.

Her grandson, thirteen-year-old Daniel Horry, was sent to England to study, in the footsteps of Eliza and her sons. He was extremely unhappy and Eliza wrote him loving and strong letters of encouragement. *This country will need abilities and improved talents of the rising generation to aid her Second Infancy,* she wrote. Later she shared the disastrous news that her house in town had been hit by a cannonball. *I no longer have in country or town a place to lay my head*

In September of 1783, Eliza wrote her grandson a joyful letter. *Blessed be God! The effusion of human blood is stopped The Paris Peace Treaty has been signed War has ended! The British troops left Charles Town last December.*

After Yorktown signaled the end of the war and independence was at long last won, Eliza left the city to live with Harriott and her family. She did this in part because her daughter had written her several tormented letters about her husband Daniel's health.

> *Mama dearest, Daniel is seriously ill. He is as yellow as the darkest orange. His bile is mixed with blood and he has had the hiccoughs for two days. His speech is very thick and he seems terribly confused. The tongue is crusted and he complains of a great oppression in his stomach. And then he cries out that he is too warm.*

Daniel Huger Horry died on November 8, 1785 of the "Country Fever." Shortly after his burial Eliza moved into Hampton Plantation to spend the rest of her life with Harriott and her granddaughter. Daniel had deeded Hampton Plantation to his son in his will, with the understanding that his wife Harriott would stay there as long as she wished. Harriott and Eliza worked together to manage the plantation.

Harriott's son Daniel never returned to America to live. He changed his name to Charles Lucas Pinckney Horry and spent the remainder of his life in Europe, marrying the niece of General Lafayette, Eleonore de Fay la Tour Maubourg.

With Eliza at the helm, Hampton Plantation once again flourished as a rice plantation.

Eliza's American patriotism slowly evolved over the years, and she frequently took stock of all that it meant to her. She prayed to be able to forget the cruelties of war. She taught her grandchildren to forgive and prayed that the joy and gratitude for their great deliverance would equal and then surpass the former anguish. She taught her family that even grieving can one day be transformed into grace.

Charles's wife Sarah died in 1784 and he moved with his three daughters to Hampton Plantation. Eliza, who had lived through so much pain and loss, could now enjoy her extended family in this time of peace. She helped Harriott and Charles raise their children, advising them on plantation management and also on matters of the heart. She encouraged her son Charles to find another woman to marry, even though she steadfastly avoided any romantic associations herself. In 1786, Charles Cotesworth Pinckney married Mary Stead.

Eliza's delicate beauty and thoroughbred elegance was still very apparent as she reached her late sixties. Her daughter's hair had darkened with time and the two women were often mistaken for one another. Eliza continued her walks to the water, where she contemplated nature and wrote in her journal. Her family could find her standing in front of the river, hands shading her eyes, following the flight of a flock of white herons winging over the marshes toward the bay. The attraction of their freedom continued to amaze her.

Eliza's son Charles represented South Carolina at the Federal Constitutional Convention in Philadelphia in 1787. His friend General George Washington presided over the Convention and led the others in writing the Constitution. Charles advocated the idea that slaves be counted as a basis of representation. The capital of South Carolina was moved to Columbia, a more central location that mollified the up-country population. That year, the spelling of Charles Town was officially changed to Charleston.

Charles and his brother Thomas played prominent roles in the ratification of the Federal Constitution at the South Carolina Convention of 1788. Two years later, Charles Cotesworth helped frame the South Carolina Constitution at the Convention of 1790.

Eliza followed these events closely and discussed them at length with her sons and daughter.

"General Washington has a vision of a great and powerful nation that would be built on republican lines using federal power," she told them. "I feel certain this is just the right man to lead our new nation. Do you agree with me?"

Her sons were proud of their friend General Washington's success.

In the meanwhile, Thomas Pinckney had been elected the Governor of South Carolina for the two years prior to the adoption of the U.S. Constitution, 1787-1789. In 1791, he served in the Carolina House of Representatives.

On April 6, 1789, the two newly-formed houses of Congress met to count the ballots of the Electoral College. General George Washington, by a unanimous vote of the electors, became the nation's first president. On Inauguration Day, April 30, President Washington put pageantry aside and appeared in a plain American-made brown suit to take his simple oath. In his own manner, he signaled that the pomp of European courts would not be practiced in the New Republic.

The country, although still torn and bleeding, was free—no longer a group of provinces—now known as the United States of America.

ⲥⲟⲟⲋⲟ

Thomas and Charles Pinckney returned to working their plantations. Charles had inherited Pinckney Island from his father's estate and became an early planter of the highly valued Sea Island cotton. Thomas hired a Dutch engineer, Mr. Van Hassel, to devise a system of embankment that made salt marshes along the Santee River profitable for rice planting. He shared his scientific farming expertise with fellow planters, following his mother's example with the indigo seeds some fifty years before.

Eliza's sons continued to be active in political affairs. Thomas served in the Carolina House of Representatives. Charles, now Major General, became head of the forces for the protection of the American shores. When the men were away from the plantations, Eliza and Harriott, with the help of their grandchildren, managed them efficiently.

It was a time of cherished peace at Hampton Plantation. Eliza, after having lived through so much, was finally enjoying the gay company of her grandchildren and the pleasure of living close to her children. She thought often about her siblings, wondering how they looked now, and continued to exchange letters with them. How different their lives were from her own, yet she believed each had found contentment.

Eliza entered the library and found Charles seated at the large mahogany desk in front of the window, poring over a letter.

He rose slowly and went to her, letter in hand. "Mama, the President has asked me to become a Cabinet member. I have been given the choice of the position of Secretary of State or Secretary of War."

She stared at him: intense and searching. Her legs were shaking. "My goodness, son. What an honour he has bestowed upon you!"

He nodded absently, head still bent over the letter. "He also offered me a position on the Supreme Court of the United States." Glancing up at her shocked expression, Charles realized that he too was stunned by the news.

"Son! That is even a greater privilege, is it not? Dear Charles, whatever will you choose?"

He led her to the sofa, enclosing her hand tenderly inside his large one. Through the window glass he watched the sun's rays shine through her almost translucent white hair, giving her a brilliant radiance. Tears glistened in her eyes as she felt his warmth.

Charles's eyes were quiet on her face. "What is it, Mama? Is there something the matter?" he asked gently.

Her gaze met his. "For a moment I thought I was holding your father's hand." Her voice softened. "Your hands feel so much like his."

Charles put his arms around her thin shoulders and drew her into a loving embrace. After a long moment, he asked. "Does it bring you pain to think of him, Mama?"

Eliza considered his question for several moments. "Sometimes there's a raw ache—still present after all these years. Pain is an unlikely companion; it doesn't go away. Yet I believe life void of heartbreak is self-centered and loveless." Smiling at her son, she fixed those smoky green eyes on his. "My sorrow keeps me humble and grounded. But mostly it brings me peace; especially these days." She licked a tear from the corner of her lips. A strange calmness settled over her, like a soft transparent veil.

She offered him a small but loving smile. "Charles, you haven't told me which appointment you will choose," she said.

He searched her still vivacious face. "You must already know, Mama. My duties lie here in South Carolina, with my family."

Eliza's smile broke through, lighting up her face. She laughed delicately.

"Yes, son, I *did* know, and I am so proud of you." Tears spiked her lashes. "You have gone beyond fulfilling your father's wishes. He must be overjoyed."

chapter fifty

ELIZA STOOD BESIDE HER DAUGHTER ON HAMPTON Plantation's newly-built portico to receive the first President of the United States. President Washington had embarked on a grand tour of the southern states and requested a stop at Hampton Plantation. Thomas Pinckney accompanied him to his sister's home. The President sent word he would share breakfast with the Horrys and Eliza Pinckney.

As the two women waited on the portico to meet their esteemed visitor, Eliza closed her eyes and imagined herself as a teenager at Wappoo Plantation looking out over her beloved marshes and fields. She could barely recapture those feelings of dread and inadequacy that had filled her heart those many years before. Now she breathed in the peace and tranquility that this remarkable moment of her life was offering her.

President Washington was greeted by the lady of the house and her mother. The women and the young girls sported headbands and sashes for the occasion that displayed words of welcome. The plantation house had been freshly painted and had been given important new additions—a ballroom, two more bedrooms and the colossal portico—reflecting the profits that

Harriott and Eliza had realized from the rice crop. Thomas introduced them and then stepped aside.

President George Washington spoke in his dignified manner.

"Madam Pinckney, Madam Horry, I have long looked forward to this meeting with the mother and sister of my esteemed friends, Charles and Thomas Pinckney. Your sons and brothers truly reflect your love of principle. Their country will soon call them to an ever greater service. Madam Eliza, mothers like you light fires that are never extinguished. Madam Harriott, as their sister you have earned my most sincere respect and that of your brothers. And as lady planters, let me congratulate you both on your early work with indigo, then silk, and then cotton. You are patriots and distinguished lady planters. With women like you, this Republic has nothing to fear."

His complimentary words deeply touched them. Eliza had always respected him; she now knew she liked him as well.

President Washington enjoyed his opulent breakfast, and after a walk about the plantation was easily persuaded to stay for dinner too. Harriott Horry was an excellent cook, known throughout the lowlands for her fine table.

As they passed by the kitchen to enter the elegant ballroom, President Washington commented on the exquisite dining table, with its heavy damask cloth, silver candlesticks, sparkling crystal and old-fashioned arrangements of roses and ferns.

"My soul, I am surrounded by the most delicious mixture of mouthwatering smells…an apple pie, loaves of bread baking, an Irish stew simmering in a huge pot—emitting fragrant wafts of steam."

The women laughed with pleasure. In addition to the other delicacies, Harriott served him her signature dish—calf-head soup, prepared with her own ingredients that she shared only with her mother.

As he was taking his leave from Hampton Plantation, President Washington commented on a young oak near the front portico. Because it obstructed the view, Harriott's daughter mentioned that it would probably be cut down.

"But my dear, only God can make the oak. Who will replace it? Pray spare that one, and think of me each time you notice it obstructing the view."

So the "Washington Oak" continued to obstruct the view, and the Horry and Pinckney family smiled fondly whenever they thought about their president's request.

Charles Cotesworth Pinckney joined the presidential party as it traveled into Charleston. He escorted his friend George Washington in a twelve-oared barge, rowed by twelve American captains of ships—each elegantly dressed and happy to be exerting such unusual effort in honour of their passenger.

∽☙◉☙∾

Eliza saw President Washington's prediction come true when he appointed Thomas Pinckney as Minister of Great Britain the following year. Eliza, now seventy years old, learned that she had breast cancer. After being treated by the best physicians available in Charleston, her sons insisted she travel to Philadelphia to see the top doctors in that field of expertise: Dr. William Shippen and Dr. William Tate.

Before leaving to consult these eminent physicians, Eliza took stock of her situation and wrote to an old friend, George Keater, a poet and artist. He had sent her an elegantly bound edition of his poetry to read during her sea voyage to the north. First, she thanked him for the personal inscription.

> *Your kindness to your old friend warms my soul. Your works are exceptionally enjoyable when I consider the virtues they inculcate as being all your own, originating in your benevolent heart. I am honoured to read your convictions and sentiments through your outstanding poetry.*

Her daughter Harriott and three granddaughters (two of them also named Harriott) accompanied the fearless Eliza on her voyage. Their rough ten-day sea passage through the

Gulf Stream exhausted her. She was very ill when they finally reached Philadelphia on April 20, 1793 and was carried in a chair from the ship to a small boat. Mrs. Izard's coach was on shore to drive them to their lodging. They took rooms in a house on Spruce and Third Street, opposite Mr. Bingham's glorious garden.

In addition to the physicians, all of Philadelphia came to call on Eliza. President Washington, Betsey Hamilton, Anne Bingham, Eliza Powel, Lucy Knox, and their husbands and family were frequent visitors. In one week alone, Harriott counted twenty-one guests in their house.

President Washington, despite the urgent issues he needed to deal with, came to pay homage to Eliza. She was pleased with all this attention, but modestly attributed it to respect being shown to her sons.

Harriott, who began journaling as a child with her mother, wrote the following.

President Washington was extremely kind. Because Mrs. Washington was sick, he offered in her name as well as his own everything in their power to serve us and requested we use no ceremony with him.

Harriott dedicated her time and nurturing abilities to her mother, but found a few opportunities to be social as well. She visited Mrs. Washington on May 9, the same day she accepted the doctor's invitation to accompany him as he visited other cancerous patients who had been cured. She asked them questions about their pains and sufferings, and was encouraged about her mother's prospects as she learned more about breast cancer treatment.

On May 2 Eliza began Dr. Tate's medicinal treatment: one pill each night for the next four nights, then one each night and another the following morning. On May 10 Eliza complained of a bad stomach ache. Dr. Tate explained to them that the medicines were killing the cancer.

Eliza knew she was dying, yet no one else would accept it. Sadly, both her sons were absent in her last hours. Charles was in Carolina, never suspecting that his mother was nearing the end. Thomas was in England serving as the United States Ambassador to England and Minister to the Court of St. James. Still Eliza was surrounded by an outpouring of love and honour, gently supported by many loving hands.

"How are you feeling, Mama?" asked her daughter as she carried in another bouquet of flowers.

"I was thinking of your dear father, Harriott," she said with a sweet smile. "Remembering the many happy and pleasurable hours we passed together. And I feel quite happy contemplating his virtues once again—those virtues I truly revere. I find myself in the company of the memory of the man I tenderly love and whose uncommon affection I shall gratefully remember to my last hour."

Her last hour came as a blessing.

Dear Mother continued to suffer extremely with the sick stomach and the vomiting and for several hours was in great agony. At last, it pleased Almighty God to take her to Himself.

Eliza Lucas Pinckney passed away in Philadelphia on May 26, 1793. Her funeral took place the following day at St. Peter's Church. President Washington, at his own request, served as one of the pallbearers. She was buried in the St. Peter's Churchyard, far from the low country she had cultivated and cherished.

To the very end of her life, she displayed a lively spirit and a questing mind. Harriott Horry Ravenal, her great-great-granddaughter, wrote about Eliza in her account of her ancestors' lives. She concluded her writing with the following annotation.

The women of all the colonies had committed to them a great, unsuspected charge: to fit themselves and their sons to meet the coming change in law and soberness; not in riot and anarchy as did the unhappy women of the French Revolution.

Eliza Lucas Pinckney's obituary appeared in the *Charleston City Gazette* on July 17, 1793.

Her manners had been so refined by a long and intimate acquaintance with the polite world. Her countenance was so dignified by serious contemplation and devout reflection, and so replete with all that mildness and complacency which are the natural results of a regular uninterrupted habit and practice of virtue and benevolence. It was impossible to behold her without emotions of the highest veneration and respect. Her understanding, aided by an uncommon strength of memory, had been so highly cultivated and improved by travel and extensive reading, so richly furnished with scientific and practical knowledge, that her talent for conservation was unrivalled. Her religion was rational, liberal and pure. The source of it was seated in the judgment and the heart, and from thence issued a regular and uniform life.

afterword

Eliza Lucas Pinckney was one of the eighteenth century's most distinguished women whose story has long been known in South Carolina. It has been my privilege to portray her story in novel form so many more people will come to know and understand her invaluable contributions to colonial society.

President George Washington once told Eliza, "Your country will soon call your sons to great service." How accurate he was in his assessment!

After Eliza's death, Charles Cotesworth Pinckney became the Federalist candidate for the vice-presidency of the United States in the 1800 election, running with incumbent President John Adams. They were defeated by Thomas Jefferson and Aaron Burr, the Democratic/Republican candidates.

In 1804, Charles ran for president against Thomas Jefferson and lost again. His final attempt was in 1808, running as the Federalist candidate for president and losing to James Madison. He was not only active politically at the state and national levels, but also played a major role in advancing educational and cultural institutions within South Carolina.

He died on August 16, 1825, and is buried in St. Michael's Churchyard in Charleston, South Carolina. Charles Cotesworth Pinckney's tombstone reads:

One of the founders of the American Republic. In war he was a companion in arms and a friend of Washington. In peace he enjoyed his unchanging confidence.

His brother Thomas Pinckney was appointed by President Washington to be United States Ambassador to Great Britain in 1792, and was serving in England when his mother Eliza died. During his time abroad, he also served as Envoy Extraordinaire to Spain. He arranged the *Treaty of San Ildefonso (Pinckney Treaty)* with Spain in 1795. This treaty gave the United States free usage of the Mississippi River—a favorite boundary settlement in the southwest where American lands were adjacent to Spanish territory.

The Federalist Party made Thomas Pinckney a candidate for president in the 1796 election and he finished third, after John Adams and Thomas Jefferson. He was elected to the United States House of Representatives from South Carolina, where he served from November 1797 to March 1801. He then served as major general in the United States Army during the War of 1812. His last public role, before his death in Charleston on November 2, 1828, was as President General of the Society of the Cincinnati from 1825-1828. He is buried in St. Philip's Churchyard in Charleston, South Carolina.

Harriott Pinckney Horry lived to eighty years of age and remained happy and beloved. She died in 1830, leaving Hampton Plantation to her daughter Harriott Horry Rutledge, who had married Frederick Rutledge in 1797.

All three of Eliza and Charles Pinckney's children were devoted to their families, friends and fellow citizens. They were kind and benevolent by nature, and through their inherited love of agricultural experimentation, helped develop critical resources of their new nation.

Many scholars have maintained that plantation women of the eighteenth century (and early nineteenth century) felt caught between great numbers of children and slaves. This does not apply to Eliza Lucas Pinckney. Her life reflected contentment and harmony. Although her destiny was somewhat determined by factors she could not control, she used her intelligence to direct those areas where she could. Eliza never saw a need to separate intelligence and domesticity.

In 1989, almost two hundred years after her death, Eliza Lucas Pinckney was inducted into the South Carolina Business Hall of Fame, honored for her tremendous contributions to South Carolina's agricultural production.

acknowledgments

Betty Smith, my delightful friend who weaves for fun, introduced me to Eliza Lucas Pinckney. She came to my house during my "rest period" after a hectic period of marketing my last book, *Splendid Isolation*.

"I know who your next subject should be," she told me with a mischievous grin. I groaned and stuck my fingers in my ears.

"I'm not interested. I'm resting for awhile."

"Her name is Eliza Lucas Pinckney," she continued, prying the fingers from my ears. "She was the first colonist to successfully cultivate indigo in the New World, and she did this at age seventeen."

I nodded, slightly interested now.

"And her sons were good friends of President Washington, serving under him during the Revolutionary War. Oh, and did I mention that President George Washington insisted on being a pall-bearer at her funeral?"

Now I was hooked. I left the following week to spend ten days at The South Carolina Historical Society in Charleston, S.C. to research this amazing woman's life. Thank you Betty Smith for bringing Eliza into my life!

I often feel a sense of amazement that I get to write for a living. A writer becomes a host—readers come to you for food and drink and company. When you write, you get out of yourself and become a conduit for someone else. It's a sense of connection for both reader and writer, and the giving is the reward.

A writer cannot create a published book without the assistance of many team members. My team is talented and exceptional, and heartfelt thanks go out to them: Pam Pollack, my New York editor and esteemed friend; Patty Osborne, my patient and accomplished "bookmaker" who started this process with us twelve years ago; Ray Hignell, my print broker and visionary with the patience of Job, whose wisdom has guided me through the printing of nine books; Sharon Castlen, whose outstanding marketing skills have resulted in reviews and great sales; and Trip Giudici, fellow author, editor and longtime friend, who graciously turns each first draft into enhanced manuscripts.

Hats off to Buddy Sullivan, Coastal Georgia historian, fellow author, editor and manager of the Sapelo Island National Estuarine Research Reserve! You spent endless hours reading my manuscript and offering your academic advice. Please accept my deep appreciation for that enormous favor!

Profound thanks go to Mary Jo Fairchild and Karen Stokes for volunteering to read and make suggestions to the manuscript. You two were so helpful throughout my days of research at The South Carolina Historical Society. Your enthusiasm and encouragement, plus your knowledge of Eliza Lucas Pinckney, were invaluable and made the work much more fun.

Gini Steele, your beautiful artwork once again enhanced the cover art. It is always a special honor to work with you.

Cathy McLain, in addition to being my good friend, your proofreading skills are beyond awesome! Thank you for being so meticulous!

Thank you, Ms. Johnie Rivers, for assisting me in finding the photos for the book and answering my many questions. I truly enjoyed learning from your extensive knowledge of the colonial times.

I am deeply indebted to The South Carolina Historical Society for their caring staff and easily accessible resource materials. Thank you for many of the photos included in the book. Most especially, thank you for your kindness.

I also wish to thank the authors and editors of the numerous sources I used in my research, who have been acknowledged and credited in the following *Resource Pages*.

Lastly, I am deeply indebted to my beloved husband Michael. I place great value on your solid and unbiased criticism of my writing. You are my encourager, my light and my fellow collaborator in this fascinating adventure we call life—so much more enjoyable experiencing it with you.

book group discussion questions

1. Upon reading the *Prologue*, what effect did the scene of chaos and sabotage have on your interest in the story that follows?

2. How did you react to the enormous amount of responsibility placed on young Eliza when her father told her she would be in charge of the family?

3. What do you think motivated Eliza as a young girl and later, as a grown woman? In what ways do you identify with her? How are you different?

4. Eliza and her family must deal with Ann's constant illnesses. How does Eliza's forced "Mistress of the Plantations" status influence her character as she grows into womanhood?

5. What kind of a relationship does Eliza have with her mother? Does it evolve or change? Do you think Eliza sees her mother as manipulative?

6. Were Eliza's attitudes toward slavery in tune with the times? How about her ideas about the woman's place in society?

7. How did Eliza deal with the dichotomy of being self-sufficient and relying on God? Do you feel she made wise choices? Was she a victim of circumstances?

8. How do the dynamics of Eliza's and George's father/daughter relationship compare with your own or your loved ones? How might their relationship be perceived differently today?

9. Discuss Charles's character. What are his strengths? His values? His fears? Does he change in any fundamental way by the end of the story?

10. Explore the role of nature in the story, particularly the use of plants, birds and water. How did the author employ them in symbolism, plot development and the revelation of the theme?

11. Eliza weathers major life upheavals with strength and resolution. What attitudes does she adopt and behaviors does she engage in to help her get through them all?

12. How do you think American readers may approach the story differently from British or Spanish readers? What are some different perspectives? What about the fight for independence is universal?

Resources

Primary Sources

Bowers, Jeannette Frances, *How Uncommon Life I Have Mett With: Life of Eliza Lucas Pinckney*, thesis presented to the faculty of South Dakota State University, 1990

Ravenel, Harriott Horry, *Women of Colonial and Revolutionary Times: Eliza Pinckney*, South Carolina Heritage Series No. 10, New York: Charles Scribner's Sons, 1896

Roberts, Cokie, *Founding Mothers: The Women Who Raised Our Nation*, Harpers Collins Publishers Inc. New York, 2004

Secondary Sources:

Alford, Robbie L., *Eliza Lucas Pinckney:1780*, edited by Dennis T. Lawson, Historic Georgetown County Leaflet Number 6, The Georgetown Times, Georgetown, South Carolina

Amrhine, Karen, *Pinckney Painting Joins London's Ambassador Row*, Trends, The News and Courier, June 22, 1974 2-B

Bonta, Marcia, *Eliza Lucas Pinckney: Colonial Gardener*, The American Horticulturist, October 1985

Coon, David L., *Eliza Lucas Pinckney and the Reintroduction of Indigo Culture in South Carolina,* The Journal of Southern History 42, February 1976

Egan, Timothy, *The Big Burn,* Houghton Mifflin Harcourt, New York, 2009

Eastman Rivers, Margaret Middleton, *Hidden History of Old Charleston*, History Press, Charleston, South Carolina, 2010

Eliza Lucas Pinckney, "People," Charleston Magazine 1976

Fryer, Darcy R., *The Mind of Eliza Lucas Pinckney: An Eighteenth-Century Woman's Construction of Herself,* South Carolina Historical Magazine 99, July 1998

Gibson, Iris Hallman, "Persistence and Hard Work Paid Off for Elizabeth Lucas of Wappoo Plantation," May 1963

Ide, Arthur Frederick, *Women in the Colonial South,* Mesquite: Ide House, 1983

Keber, Martha L., *Seas of Gold, Seas of Cotton: Christophe Poulain DuBignon of Jekyll Island*, The University of Georgia Press, Athens, GA

McNulty, Nancy G., *Eliza Lucas Pinckney: Lady Planter and Founding Citizen*, November *1976*

Price, Eugenia, *Don Juan McQueen*, Berkley Books, New York, *1974*

Ramagosa, Carol Walter, "Eliza Lucas Pinckney's Family in Antigua, 1668-1747," *The South Carolina Historical Magazine*, July 1998, Vol. 99, No. 3

Risjord, Norman K., "Eliza Lucas Pinckney," *Representative Americans—The Colonists*, Rowan & Littlefield, 2001

Sass, Herbert Ravel, *Love and Miss Lucas*, The Georgia Review, Vol. X-Number 3, The University of Georgia Press, 1956

Spruill, Julia Cherry, *Women's Life and Work in the Southern Colonies*, University of North Carolina Press, 1972

The Letterbook of Eliza Lucas Pinckney: 1739-1762, edited by Marvin R. Zahnister, University of South Carolina Press, 1972

Voices of the Old South, edited by Alan Gallay, The University of Georgia Press, Athens, GA 1994

Webber, Deborah, *Eliza Lucas Pinckney*, South Carolina Historical Magazine, January 1938

Williams, Frances Leigh, *Plantation Patriot: A Biography of Eliza Lucas Pinckney*, Harcourt, Brace and World Inc., New York, 1967

Internet Websites:

"At Table: High Style in the 18th Century", www.carnegiemuseums. org/cmag/bk_issue/1996

"Charles Cotesworth Pinckney", en.wikipedia.org/wiki/Charles_ Coesworth_Pinckney

"Distinguished Women of Past and Present: Eliza Lucas Pinckney 1722-793", Danuita Bois, www.distinguishedwomen.com/ biographies/pinckney, 1998

"Eliza Lucas Pinckney Chapter-Daughters of the American Revolution", www.rootsweb.ancestry.com

"Elizabeth Pinckney", Encyclopedia Britannica, www.britannica.com, 2010

"Eliza Lucas Pinckney", Enterprising Women Exhibit, www. enterprisingwomenexhibit.org/farm/pinckney, 2005

"Eliza Lucas Pinckney", en.wikipedia.org/wiki/Eliza_Lucas

"Eliza Lucas Pinckney", National Humanities Center, www.
nationalhumanitiescenter.org, 2008

"Eliza Lucas Pinckney: Production and Consumption in the Atlantic
World", Eliza L. Martin, www.worldhistoryconnected.press.
illinois.edu/6.1/martin, 2010

"Eliza Lucas Pinckney", www.greatfemaleinventors.com, 2009

"Eliza Lucas Pinckney", www.infoplease.com/ipa/A090018, 2007

"Eliza Lucas Pinckney", www.nwhm.org

"History: French, Spanish, English Colonization", www.infoplease.
com/ceb/us/A0861203

"Indigo-plant profile", www.plantcultures.org/plants/indigo_plant_
profile

"The Time Page: 13 Originals", www.timepage.org/spl/13 colony

"Thomas Pinckney", en.wikipedia.org/wiki/Thomas_Pinckney

About the Artist

Combining her mutual love of photography and history, Gini Steele and her husband Richard have created an extensive collection of photographic images of times long gone by. Through their work with historical societies, archivists and researchers, they realized that there was a need to restore and reproduce these historic images and make them available before they are lost forever.

Staying true to the genre, Ms. Steele used traditional photographic processes to restore and reproduce the collection of old glass plates, negatives and photographs. She enjoys the challenge of interpreting the old negatives in her darkroom and prints the silver gelatin photographs by hand one at a time.

Inspired by the architecture and the natural beauty of the coastal southeast, Gini likes to create her own original photographs. She is currently working on a series of miniature black and white photographs that she tints by hand.

Gini Steele resides in Beaufort, South Carolina with her husband Richard and her two cats Bailey and Penelope Butterbeans.